Nancy Kilpatrick has published seven novels and a collaboration with Don Bassingthwaite, *As One Dead*. Her short stories have appeared in numerous magazines and anthologies, including *Razor's Edge*, *The Time of the Vampires* and *Northern Frights*. *Sex & the Single Vampire* is her collection of short stories, she has edited four erotic horror anthologies, and has written a series of comic books for Vamperotica. She has twice been a finalist for the Bram Stoker Award and the Aurora Award, and won the Arthur Ellis Award for best mystery story. She lives in Toronto, Canada.

CHILD
OF THE
NIGHT

Nancy Kilpatrick

Raven Books
London

Robinson Publishing Ltd
7 Kensington Church Court
London W8 4SP

First published in the UK by Raven Books, an imprint of Robinson
Publishing Ltd, 1996

A copy of the British Library Cataloguing in Publication data is available
from the British Library.

ISBN 1-85487-446-2

Typeset, printed and bound in the UK

10 9 8 7 6 5 4 3 2 1

ACKNOWLEDGEMENTS

Thanks to Claire Lang and Elizabeth Noton for help with the mystical. To the stalwarts who read and re-read the first drafts of this manuscript: Mike Kilpatrick, H.L. Lightbown, Peter Reid, Karl Schroeder and Caro Soles. To Marc Cormier, Philippe Laguerre, Darren Price and Michael Radulesco for details about Bordeaux, and particularly Jean Lalet, for the pictures as well as other information on that city. To Ivan Kilpatrick for information on Canada. To Benoit Bisson and Caro Soles for enduring my fractious French.

I'm eternally grateful to the people who have given me love and support over the years, and who believe in me and my work: Naomi Bennett, Benoit Bisson, Bob Hadji, Don Hutchison, Vera Jacyk, Eric Kauppinen, Mike Kilpatrick, Ricia Mainhardt, Elizabeth Noton, Michael Rowe, Mandy Slater, Caro Soles, Fran Turner, John Went, and especially Steve Jones.

'If this life be not a real fight, in which something is eternally gained for the universe by success, it is no better than a game of private theatricals from which one may withdraw at will. But it *feels* like a real fight.'

– William James

Part I

_____

'. . . it is not the blood-letting that calls
down power. It is the consenting.'
                              – Mary Renault

ONE

Carol crossed her legs and rolled the stem of the wine glass slowly between the thumb and fingers of her right hand, too aware that this was her third dry white since dinner. Let's not overdo it, she warned herself, but then took another sip. She sighed. Better turn her attention from the local grape drink to something less toxic.

By the light from the café's quaint oil lamps Carol went back to reading *The Philadelphia Inquirer*, barely able to make out the print. Not that it mattered; she'd read the week-old newspaper already, just after boarding the plane to Paris, and again on the flight to Bordeaux. Still, it was something from home. But feelings of comfort and pain cancelled each other out; the paper couldn't hold her interest. She drank more wine, trying to wash away the disappointment she'd also brought across the ocean.

The small outdoor café on Les Allées de Tourny, one of Bordeaux's main downtown streets, faced *Le Grand Théâtre*. She studied the details of the building's classical façade. Her guide book had mentioned this theatre as the model for the old Paris Opera House. The immense colonnaded portico, topped by twelve statues of muses and graces, each representing a month of the year, was breathtaking, even magical, especially illuminated against the impenetrable black of the night sky. At least there's still some beauty and magic left in the world, she thought, if not in *my* world.

She wondered if an opera or a play was being staged and decided to check it out tomorrow. Maybe *La Traviata*. Right! she thought, the one where the woman is rejected and dies of consumption! She swallowed the rest of the wine.

'*Pardon, Mademoiselle. Vous permettez?*'

She looked up. A smartly dressed man stood at her table.

'*Je ne parle pas français.*' She stumbled through the only complete French sentence she could manage.

'I asked if I can share your table.' His English was flawless, his tone confident, his face haughty enough to be irritating.

Carol felt annoyed. The whole reason she had come to an off-the-beaten-track place like Bordeaux was to avoid encounters like this one. 'I'd like to be alone. Sorry.'

'Understandable,' he said, but continued standing, watching her.

She felt uncomfortable and went back to reading.

'The café's full. There are no other seats.'

She peered over the top of *The Inquirer*. Every chair was occupied except the one at her table. She looked back up at him.

He was handsome, well-heeled Rob would have said. Except for streaks of silver at the temples, his hair matched his fashionable leather clothing – midnight black. His skin was pale. For a moment, probably because of the darkness behind him, she had a peculiar visual image, a weird blend of two dimensional on three dimensional, like the cardboard effigies tourists stick their faces and hands through for a photograph. His most outstanding characteristic was his grey eyes. They were like smoke, a disturbing colour, intense, even in the faint light. A year ago she probably would have found his features an interesting combination.

She shrugged. 'Have a seat.'

'*Merci*. You're too kind.'

She tried to go back to reading but having another person in her space felt like an invasion. But Carol didn't want to talk either so she turned away, folded the paper onto her lap and gazed out at the typical French scene before her. As in the downtown of any insular city, everyone seemed to have a nodding acquaintance with everybody else. Mopeds and motorcycles swerved between small, gas-conscious cars. Many drivers were young, dressed in denim or leather clothing, shouting to their friends. The sidewalks quivered with life – people carrying brown paper parcels with baguettes or vegetables sticking out the top; men and women lugging thick briefcases or plastic lunch pails; chicly dressed couples out for the evening. It was interesting, if only because everything here was fresh to her. But already she'd heard other tourists substituting the word 'boredom' for 'Bordeaux'. She'd arrived bored. She suspected she wouldn't be staying here very long.

'You're from the United States. The accent gives you away.'

She turned to her unwelcome companion. He was staring, his expression casual but fixed. 'Yes, I'm an American.'

'Midwest, east coast or both?'

'Recently, Philadelphia.'

'But you weren't born there.'

The waiter deposited a large glass of red wine in front of her table mate. The man handed over a ten franc note. He picked up the glass, sniffed the contents, then put the glass back down on the table.

'An interesting country. I know it and the language well,' he said, pocketing the change. 'Not as old in history or tradition as France, of course, but what you lack in depth I'm sure you make up for in innovation.'

'Probably,' Carol said, turning away again.

'My name's André. And yours?'

She turned back. He was tilting the glass, rolling the contents around. The wine coated the glass briefly before it slid down the sides. His face reflected a fine blend of jaded disinterest and idle curiosity plus a hint of condescension.

'Look, I'm not in the mood for conversation. I really want to be alone.'

'As you like.' She knew he felt insulted but that was his problem.

Carol started to turn away again, but immediately he said, 'Not many females travel alone to Bordeaux at this time of year, especially beautiful women. I've always loved the look – slim hips, large breasts, firm ass, chestnut hair, sapphire eyes, as clear as a summer's sky . . .'

With a disgusted sigh, Carol picked up her bag, turned her back on him and hurried away.

It was April but already warm enough for just a light jacket at night. She decided to walk along the river before going to sleep. She wasn't tired, and she wanted to think.

The water of the Garonne was murky, the result, she'd been told on a tour of the city, of being tainted by a winter's accumulation of snow and mud as it flowed down the mountains from the northwest towards the Atlantic. She strolled along the wide stone road on the left bank. During the day, pedestrians and vehicles filled the waterfront with a cacophony of energetic sounds. But at night the docks belonged to the darkness. The squeak of thick ropes rubbing the bollards, imprisoning cargo ships, lulled her. Overhead the black sky was accentuated by the thinnest sliver of a new moon. It was quiet here, peaceful, with no one to interrupt her thoughts.

The whole thing had been like something out of a melo-drama. Now, looking backwards, she realized she should have known right from the start Rob was unfaithful. All the embarrassing signs had flashed like the lights when intermission ends; everyone else saw the end of the play coming. Like they say, always the last to know, she thought, aware again of just how saturated with bitterness she had become.

She heard a sound and turned. The path was empty.

'Great nerves,' she told herself. This is what happens when you're used to being part of a couple – you're afraid to be alone. But she knew that wasn't it. More, she wanted to be alone now. Even after a year she was still afraid to get involved. That's why she'd left home. Why she was in a country where she didn't speak the language. And as agonizing as the divorce had been, the aching loneliness had been even worse. But she'd endured it, day and night, until it became a sort of friend; now she refused to part with a feeling she considered an ally.

Again, that sound, like a pebble kicked.

Carol stopped and turned. The path was empty and the waterfront still quiet. Ahead, a tunnel led under the Pont de Pierre, the four-lane arched stone bridge in the middle of the city, built during the Napoleonic era, that prohibited large vessels from travelling further south. It was unlit there.

She thought about heading back to the main street – it was within sight – but didn't want to face the real world yet. There's no one here, she told herself. The tunnel's empty. You can see through to the other end. It's probably just a cat.

The path sloped down into hollow darkness. Sound waves from river water flowing over rocks and slapping wooden barriers bounced around the walls accompanied by the echo of her heels clacking on moist stones. Traffic noise from the bridge overhead dimmed.

Suddenly she heard a rustling. 'Who's there?' she called out in a high voice, realizing that if anyone was there they probably didn't understand English. She turned. The immediate darkness engulfed her and, beyond, the white light of the moonlit path.

She was halfway through, as close to where she would exit as to where she had entered. She hesitated but finally took a step forward. It sounded like there was a step behind. Then silence.

The thud of her heart filled her ears. Her lungs felt compressed and she realized her back and neck muscles were tight, the skin slick with perspiration.

Carol took another step forward but again heard a step in unison with her own. When she stopped, a split second later it stopped. She moved faster, running towards the far end of the tunnel, all the while looking behind.

Wham! She hit a solid object and screamed. She turned her head and stared up into the face of the man from the café.

'You!' she said, equally frightened and angry, stepping back and away from him.

He said nothing but only watched her. His face seemed thinner than before; he looked a little starved. He was a lot taller and larger than Carol remembered.

She regained her equilibrium quickly. 'Who the hell do you think you are, following me? I should report you to the police.'

His lips curled into a humourless grin but he still said nothing.

Carol, furious, tried to elbow past but he caught her arm. 'Let me go or I'll scream!' she warned.

'Go ahead, if you like sound effects. I do. But don't fool yourself anyone will hear. And if they hear you they won't help.'

She swung out with her shoulder bag and, at the same time, tried to knee him in the groin. He grinned, eyes glowing with amusement, obviously enjoying her help-lessness and fear. His mouth opened briefly, long enough for her subconscious to record seeing something strange. A warning flooded her body as a wave of fear broke over her.

'Qu'y a-t-il?' The male voice was close by.

'Help! Help me!' she cried.

Suddenly her assailant shoved her away from him. She tripped and twisted, landing face down on the path.

She held her breath, expecting to be attacked. But instead she heard struggling and, when she turned, saw an older man, at least sixty, trying to fight off her molester.

She jumped up, screaming, waving frantically, hoping to attract attention from the bumper-to-bumper traffic on the bridge above. But the harbour was too poorly lit to be seen, and the noise from the vehicles drowned out her cries.

The older man was no match for the younger, taller one. She had to help him. She pounded on the back of the attacker and bludgeoned him over the head with her shoulder bag. As the three struggled, she heard the old man cry out once then watched him go limp.

Carol froze. She backed away a few steps. In the chilling silence, the man who had identified himself as André positioned the old man so that his head was bent and his throat exposed. André's face, pale, intense, seemed to emerge from the darkness. When he opened his mouth, a flash of light glinted off sharp-looking incisors.

Suddenly his lips met the exposed flesh in a kiss that seemed almost erotic. At the same moment, his eyes locked onto Carol's. It was as if a laser beam connected them. She couldn't look away.

Instinctively she squeezed her eyes shut, but she was mesmerized by the sucking sounds and so horrified that she still couldn't move. A survival instinct must have surfaced because she was aware of edging back. The further she got, the less hooked she felt.

When she was far enough away to feel relatively safe, she turned and ran screaming towards the street.

'Mademoiselle Robins, describe your attacker again, if you please,' Inspector LePage asked, flipping to a clean sheet of paper with a well-practised movement. In the two hours since the murder, lights had been set up, the body examined and photographed from all possible angles, the area flooded with policemen, reporters and curious onlookers and Carol had answered this question ten times. She had vacillated between fear and sadness before slipping into depression. Finally emotional numbness settled in.

'Look, I've already told you what he looked like. And I've told you what happened. Can't I go back to my hotel? I'm exhausted.'

'Once more, Mademoiselle.'

Carol sighed. Her nerves were frazzled. It wasn't just her own brush with death that bothered her. The old man was dead and she was still living *because* he had died. She sensed that guilt would lock onto the image of the grizzly murder and stay imbedded in her mind for a long time to come. But now she just wanted to get back to her room to be alone.

'He was tall – five ten or eleven, kind of an athletic build. Black hair, white at the temples, grey eyes. Pale skin. Large teeth. He was wearing a dark jacket and pants – leather. And a dark shirt and shoes – expensive. You know, one of those trendy mismatched outfits. He looked about ten years older than me, maybe thirty-five, thirty-seven, and spoke both French and good English. He told me his name was André.'

'Distinguishing facial features?'

'I've already said I wasn't paying much attention to him.'

'But you sat with him for fifteen minutes in a café?'

'More like five minutes. And I told you, I was reading. I only let him sit there because there weren't any other seats.'

The short stocky detective in the rumpled brown jacket continued taking notes and chain-smoking. Carol had a sense that he was totally uninterested, routinely jotting down the information because he was expected to fill his notebook. She also got the uneasy feeling he wasn't taking her seriously.

'And why were you out walking alone so late?'

'I couldn't sleep. It was a nice night.'

'Do you often walk alone at night?'

'Sometimes.'

'Along dangerous harbours?'

'I didn't know it was dangerous. This is supposed to be a safe city. That's what the tour guide said.'

LePage snorted. 'Tell me, Mademoiselle Robins, why are you in Bordeaux?'

Carol shifted. She had no intention of exposing her life story to this man. 'I'm on vacation.'

'At this time of year? Most tourists visit in the summer, when the weather is pleasant, or the autumn, when the grapes ripen.'

'I'm not crazy about new wine.'

LePage sighed. 'So, you saw this man named André assault the carpenter.'

'Yes. I told you all this before. He leaned over the old man, bent him backwards a little, and maybe broke his back or his neck and then . . .'

'You realize, Mademoiselle, the amount of strength it would take to break a man's spine with the bare hands.'

'I realize. It was dark. I'm just telling you what I remember.'

'Go on.'

'And then the man, the carpenter as you call him, was quiet.'

'He was vocal until just prior to being bent backwards?'

'No. I'm not sure. It all happened so fast. I think he was already dead.'

'And if I told you that the carpenter, his neck and spine, they are not broken?'

Carol stared at him blankly for the space of two heartbeats, then said, 'I didn't say they were. I said maybe.'

The policeman sighed and ran a hand through his greying hair as she continued. 'Then the murderer opened his mouth and bit the carpenter's neck, like an animal, watching me the whole time.' She shivered involuntarily at the memory.

The detective lowered his notebook. 'Tell me, Mademoiselle, have you recently been to the cinéma?'

'What are you getting at, Inspector?'

'I am only wondering if lately you have viewed any films. *Cinéma Fantastique*, for example.'

'Look, I know this sounds like *Dracula*, but it's what I saw. I can't pretend it was something else. I saw him bite the old man. That I'm sure of. I don't know if he took his blood or what, I just know what I'm telling you.'

Inspector LePage sighed again, slipped his notes inside his jacket pocket then lit a fresh cigarette before dropping his butt and crushing it underfoot. Almost wearily he took her by the arm. 'Very well, Mademoiselle. One of my officers will accompany you to your hotel. You will, of course, not leave the city just yet. You will need to come to headquarters to sign your statement. And I may have further questions.'

He led her across the pavement to a police car and opened the rear door. As she got in he said, 'A warning. Since the assailant knows your appearance, you may be in danger. A man will be stationed nearby.'

'You mean you're going to keep me under surveillance.'

'For your protection. And, please, Mademoiselle, do not go for any more walks alone at night.'

He slammed the door shut and the driver sped off.

TWO

The following day the police questioned Carol again at her hotel both in person and several times on the phone to clarify details. Inspector LePage, in particular, seemed more and more sceptical as though the sooner time passed, the faster he could forget this case. He was keeping her in the dark, asking most of the questions, answering few. All he admitted was that the autopsy report was incomplete and there were no suspects in custody. Other than the police, she talked with no one.

The murder had left her shaken. Carol dreamed of a large wolf with the face of her attacker, ready to pounce, blood dripping from its gaping, fanged mouth. She jolted awake, body coated with sweat, heart banging hard in her chest. It wasn't until nearly ten o'clock at night that she had the nerve to even venture out of the hotel.

'I need a taxi,' she told the Royal Medoc's doorman. While waiting, she glanced around. A short man smoking a cigar stood halfway down the street leaning against an ornate street lamp. He looked in her direction yet tried to appear as though he did not notice her. Obviously he's the police guard, she thought, and a lousy one at that.

Once inside the cab she instructed the driver, with considerable language difficulties, to take her to the St James, a small restaurant across the Garonne in nearby Bouliac. She had eaten there her first night in Bordeaux. The food was good, expensive but *prix fixe*, and the place charming. And she felt the need to get away from the hotel, if only for a meal. Going by taxi seemed safe enough. And she'd take one back, too, so there shouldn't be any problems.

A waiter seated Carol near the fireplace, in front of a window. Only two other tables were occupied, both with couples. The suburban restaurant at the top of a low hill looked out over the flat city. Lights twinkled from the houses spread out before her, as did strings of red and amber lights along the main arteries through downtown. Inside, quiet incandescent bulbs enriched the walnut furniture and violet linen. The flickering fire gave off a comforting glow and warmed her a little – overnight the weather had turned unexpectedly cold.

She ate slowly, savouring the food and the chance to be in different surroundings. But her thoughts were troubled, drifting back first to the horrible murder and then further back in time until, oddly, she began remembering how she and Rob had met.

I was so different then, she thought. Younger, although it was just a few years ago, but definitely more naive. Rob had been the kind of guy she had always been attracted to – blond, boyish good looks, brilliant smile, suntanned, athletic, successful career. She remembered thinking, he looks like he just stepped off the pages of *GQ*.

Both of them came from a middle-class, middle-America background. They'd met at the opening night party of an amateur theatre in Philadelphia when he was a senior editor with a slick city magazine and she was struggling to finish law school at the University of Pennsylvania. He was so easy to fall in love with, she thought. Too easy.

The waiter stopped to refill her water glass. He smiled at her and she looked down at her *coq au vin*.

The wedding was three months later. They bought a townhouse in the City of Brotherly Love, the fashionable Society Hill area downtown. Carol managed to find a position as a law clerk in a small legal firm until she could take the bar exams. Rob's position and expense account allowed them to share an enviable lifestyle. They travelled out of the country often on vacations, were busy many nights with friends at parties or cultural events. Rob bought a Mac and devoted his spare time to writing 'the great American screenplay,' as he liked to joke. Carol continued doing costumes and props and generally helping out at the theatre and took a series of acting classes – it was the first time since college that she could get back to doing what she loved best – acting. Things had seemed perfect, until she found the letter.

She knew he'd hidden it but there was always the suspicion that maybe, subconsciously, he'd wanted her to find it. The letter was addressed to Phillip, Rob's best friend, her oldest friend in the city. Rob had told her he'd been bisexual, before their marriage. She could accept that. He was different now. But the way he'd written about his feelings, it was obvious that not only had the affair with Phillip been going on since long before he'd met Carol, but also, throughout the marriage, there had been endless other men, and women. Rob swore to Phillip he was being faithful now – to him. He asked Phillip to be patient, he was trying to tell Carol he wanted a divorce. He was looking for the least hurtful way.

And then the accusations, the tears, the arguments, her recriminations, his apologies, mutual pleadings and hurtful rejections. And finally the horrifying truth – Rob had contracted the HIV virus from a woman who wrote for the magazine, one of his many affairs. He'd passed it to Phillip. Phillip tested positive for the virus three times; both were carriers. He'd only found out recently.

Carol had been devastated. In a stupor, she forced herself to go for a test. It was negative. Then a second test. Negative. But those results felt like some divine come-on. She was terrified to take the test a third time. What's the use? she thought. Eventually I'll show up positive. The clinic had assured her that was not a given conclusion. She might not have been infected. But she was good at research and read up on the virus; Rob likely infected everybody he had sex with more than once; the hopeful words of the staff at the hospital did not put her mind at ease. It wasn't in her make-up to face a positive result; she knew she wouldn't be able to live with that kind of knowledge.

Even though the divorce had been simple, it was still an ordeal. A lawyer from her firm handled the suit, getting her out of the marriage quickly. And she had wanted out fast. Torn by a spectrum of emotions, she longed for the misery to end.

Her plate was cleared away. She decided against dessert but had coffee and a liqueur. Only one other table was occupied now.

For a year she had lived alone in their townhouse, eating frozen gourmet meals, watching a lot of TV, working as an office temp and doing nothing else. She failed the bar exam – twice. She kept missing the acting classes and eased out of the theatre. Her friends drifted away and she let them. She quickly got used to being alone, even preferred it. And the few times people had tried to play matchmaker, she always made excuses.

The pain had dulled, replaced by a fragile layer of welcomed numbness that eventually solidified. She had no intention of disturbing that palliative.

As she sipped the liqueur, the waiter brought the cheque. Carefully she counted out the correct number of francs. Unsure if the bill had a tip already included, she added one on.

It was on the spur of the moment, really, that she had quit her job. Rob settled more than reasonably. She sold the house, her car and everything else and decided to travel. The money would hold out for three years, if she was careful. She had no idea what she would do after that, but it didn't really matter. She just wanted to go far away and see if she could recover some reason for living, something that inspired her, because she now knew that it wasn't just the divorce and his betrayal. She had betrayed herself. The marriage, in retrospect, was an illusion. They had both played their parts well, but not well enough, not from the heart, and now she was living with the consequences. And that made her question everything. It's funny, she thought, I've always tried to be fair and honest, do things the right way. So why does it feel as though my life's been wasted?

She had read that even if she did test positive – which so far she hadn't – being a carrier didn't necessarily mean the virus would ever activate. But the percentages were continually increasing. She had no symptoms still, there was always that chance. And just before leaving Philly Rob called – he was diagnosed with Kaposi's sarcoma. She had been terrified by the news, furious, depressed and filled with grief for herself, for Phillip, for all the people that connected to this terrible chain with Rob as the central link. This was a living nightmare without end. She felt no regrets that her old life had ended, but there was no new life to replace it with. And in her mind there didn't seem to be much in the way of possibilities.

The meal was finished and the bill paid. She emptied the glass of Cointreau. She was the last customer left in the restaurant. There was no reason to linger.

Outside a cold wind blew around her legs. Carol pulled her beige spring coat closer. This street had few cars and none of them were taxis. She thought about going back inside and phoning for one, but then the lights of the restaurant went out and when she peered through the lace curtains she couldn't see anyone inside.

A main street's only a block away and, no doubt, my police protection is still lurking, she assured herself.

She turned into the wind, heading down the low hill towards the brighter lights. Even before reaching the corner, she heard a car behind. It was a taxi. She waved and the driver slowed.

'The Royal Medoc,' she told him, closing the door.

He pulled away immediately.

A little drunk from most of a litre of wine and the liqueur, Carol rested her head against the back of the seat and closed her eyes. Instantly a vision of the attacker appeared on her eyelids. She opened her eyes briefly but then closed them again.

The police had not taken her seriously, at least the part where she'd seen him bite the old man. She didn't even believe it herself. It was like something out of a horror movie. It didn't make sense and if somebody had told her they'd seen a man murdered like that, she would think they were either joking or crazy.

The strong odour of cigar smoke interrupted her thoughts. She stared at the back of the driver's head wondering if he was the police guard.

The streets she saw out the taxi window looked unfamiliar. He was taking a different route, less direct, to the hotel. She checked the meter. Already it read sixteen francs and the whole ride had only cost eighteen on the way over. Obviously he was going the long way around to get more money out of her.

'*Pardon*,' she said. The driver ignored her. 'Look, I want

you to go right to the hotel. By the Pont de Pierre, *s'il vous plaît.*'

Still there was no response and she wondered if he spoke English. He didn't change direction. In fact, he sped up.

Carol turned around. Out the rear window she watched the bright lights of the downtown on the other side of the river recede. She decided to jump out at the next stop sign.

The car raced along the right bank, the road dim with intermittent lighting. It had rained here and the streets and sidewalks were slick, the smell of ozone saturating the air.

Carol saw no other vehicles on the desolate streets, and no pedestrians.

'Stop the car, now! Let me out,' she yelled, but the driver paid no attention.

She opened the door. They were driving so fast if she leaped out she knew she would be hurt. He began to slow. She glanced up. Ahead, a long silver limousine was parked by the water. A tall man stood beside it.

Although she couldn't see him clearly, instinctively she knew he was the murderer.

Carol hurled herself from the cab. She fell onto the street with a sickening thud and a groan, scraping both knees and bruising her left hip. But she wasn't worrying about the injuries.

Instantly she clambered to her feet. The driver was out from behind the wheel and running towards her, as was the murderer. She kicked off her high heels and raced back the way the cab had come.

The cobblestones were slick, making her slide, so she went along the rougher pavement. 'Help! Someone help me!' she yelled.

Behind she heard one pair of feet.

She could either go along the waterfront or back behind the loading docks to the narrow buildings that looked like warehouses. She made a quick decision. The waterfront road was too long, she didn't have the stamina to make it back to a more residential area. Better to go between the buildings where she could hide or maybe find some help.

She ran up a small street, turned down another, rounded a corner, trying to throw him off her trail. She paused to catch her breath and listen. The footsteps had either stopped too or she had lost him. She didn't want to risk making a mistake.

Silently she edged along the wall of a stone building. A cat hissed nearby and she gasped.

An alley lay just ahead. There was a chance she could find a place to hide there.

She inched along, glancing ahead and behind. Just before she turned the corner she checked both directions and exhaled slowly and silently, her breath clouding the air. She peered around the corner. The murderer was in the alley, coming towards her.

Carol retreated. She ran back the way she had come but at the last block before the waterfront turned left instead of right so she wouldn't end up at the car.

Every street looked the same now, a maze of grey slickness, minimally illuminated, boxed in by buildings centuries old. She was out of breath, panting loudly, and in an effort to cover all directions tripped over a rotting two-by-four, gashing her foot on a nail, and almost collided with a metal trash bin.

She couldn't hear him but had an image of a shadow, a mist, blending with the darkness. Yet at the same time he was solid, as stealthy as a jungle cat hunting prey, and could probably pick up her scent. He's playing with me, she thought, and the idea scared her.

Carol tried to think clearly. She knew her only hope was to work her way out of this confusing area and back to a part of the city where there was life.

She turned down a street that led into a wide courtyard.

Off to the side she noticed another street and headed up it. But when she reached the next turn off she was shocked – it was only an indentation between buildings, bricked in, not a street at all. She had trapped herself in a cul de sac.

Carol started back out but he was already coming towards her. Desperately she looked around. There were no walls low enough to scale, no street-level windows that weren't boarded up or grated over, no way out. She noticed a fire escape hanging against a building but felt it was too high to reach. She tried anyway, jumping up and falling short of the bottom rung by a foot. No rescuer was going to show up this time. She scanned the ground for weapons.

A few small rocks lay within reach and she scooped them up, pitching them at him overhand, like a baseball. He twisted out of the way and caught the last one in his fist.

But now he was too near and she inched back, up against the sooty wall. She gasped for air, shaking; he wasn't even breathing hard.

She side-stepped to a corner. He moved at an angle, his body blocking what light there was. Every direction of escape was cut off. And then he came towards her, his face thin, haggard, hungry-looking.

Carol felt she wouldn't make it but tried to pass him anyway. He slammed her back against the bricks, still advancing.

Instinct took over. She attacked, using moves she had practised in a university Wendo class until they were automatic. She kicked at his groin. His reaction was faster than she expected. He blocked her leg with his, knocking her off balance. She made a fist, knuckles up, then corkscrewed them down as she aimed for his solar plexus. He didn't even flinch. Before she knew what had happened, he caught both her wrists, pinning them behind her back. His hands were icy. He pressed his body into hers until she was locked into the corner unable to move.

'We meet again.' His voice was smooth, confident, as though her maximum efforts had a minimum effect on him. 'You wouldn't tell me your name, but it's Carol, isn't it? Carol Robins. Like the bird.'

'How do you know that?' She heard her voice quiver and knew he heard it too.

'The police. I assume it's true, unless you're a liar.'

'Why would they tell you?' she asked, as much to delay what seemed inevitable as out of curiosity.

'I asked. Let's just say I have connections.'

He leaned in close and whispered in her ear, 'Your blood should have been mine already, Carol.' He held her wrists with one hand and stroked her hair back with his other. She jerked her head away to the extent she could and glared at him.

'Don't play games with me,' she said angrily, and he looked surprised. 'I know what you're capable of. If you're going to kill me, get it over with.'

He must have perceived a courage she didn't feel because he hesitated. 'I'm used to my victims begging for their lives. If you're going to plead, now's the time.'

'I'm not going to plead. I doubt it would do any good.'

'Perceptive.' He grabbed the back of her neck. Even through her thick hair his hand still felt unbelievably cold, sending a chill through her.

As he looked in her eyes, she thought she saw traces of a grudging admiration. 'There's something about you . . .,' he said slowly. 'You're brave.'

He scanned her face and she could almost hear him weighing the possibilities in his mind. 'It's been a long time since I've taken a woman. I've been bored. But you . . .'

Fear took a back seat to other emotions. She felt angry, and bitter. She'd had it with misfortune dragging itself out, pounding her down, crushing her spirit. If this is the end of my life, let's make it quick, she thought. I'm not interested in more suffering. She felt ferocious.

She snapped her head around and clamped her teeth onto his wrist. He jerked away from her in horror. A look of total surprise crossed his face that instantly dissipated to black fury. Carol didn't waste time studying it. She started running. But before she could get very far he tackled her. She hit the rough pavement face down, so hard she wondered if her jaw was broken.

Her head was spinning, her ears ringing. She heard him say, 'If anybody does any biting here, it is going to be me!'

Suddenly he snatched her up by the arm and dragged her out of the cul de sac and along the streets, moving too fast for her to fight back. The rough concrete littered with glass and other debris scraped and tore her feet.

Finally they reached the limousine. He opened the door, shoved her inside, then slammed the door closed. Through the tinted rear window she watched him walk away quickly.

Immediately she tried one handle then the other. Both doors were locked. She pounded on the opaque partition, desperate to get the driver's attention. But if he was in there, he didn't respond. She picked up the phone and pushed the buttons, including 0, 911 and 999; it was dead.

Eventually she calmed down enough that she began to feel the scrapes and wounds on her legs and feet, her bruised hip and the swelling at her jaw. She sucked in her lower lip and tasted blood.

Her shoes, and shoulder bag which contained most of what would identify her except for her passport stored in the hotel safe, had been lost. In her coat pocket she found a couple of tissues. Hands shaking, she rolled her pantyhose off; her feet were a mess. She used saliva to clean up as much as was possible. And when the surface wounds had been looked after, Carol sat back waiting, trying to deal with the emotional damage and weighing her options.

Eventually her thoughts turned to a role she had played once in acting class. That performance had been brief – only a scene – but she'd received a standing ovation. With a little improvising, it was a part she thought she could pull off again.

THREE

Carol heard a click. The rear door on her right opened and André climbed in. She slid across the seat to get as far away from him as possible. He glanced at her briefly; in the dim interior light his smoky eyes seemed to glow and that threw her off balance for a second.

The beam of a street lamp caught his hand just before he closed the door; his fingers were tapered, the movements precise, his nails long and well manicured. She heard the front door open and close. He picked up the phone, punched in three numbers then spoke in French. As soon as he hung up, they pulled away from the curb.

He relaxed against the plush upholstery, leisurely stretching his legs out and his left arm over the back of the seat, then turned towards her. In a movement too fast for Carol to react to, André reached out and grabbed her arm, yanking her close to him.

If he was going to kill me, he would have done it back in the cul de sac, she told herself. That leaves rape. She'd read that the best defences against a rapist are to flee, fight or, if everything else fails, cooperate to avoid injury and wait for a chance to escape and get help. She didn't see how she could get out of the car. He seemed amazingly strong; if she fought him physically she would probably end up hurt far worse than she was already. Carol tried to stay calm.

He took a fistful of her hair and pulled her head back. As they drove under the street lights, a quick continuous pattern was created, light-dark, light-dark. Whenever the light flickered through the rear window she glimpsed his features. He looked fuller now, not so starved and haunted.

He untied the hand-painted scarf around her neck and slowly unbuttoned her coat and the top of her dress, baring her throat. Her heartbeat quickened in fear. His hand, now as warm as it had been chilly, slid down inside her bra. His fingers rubbed her left nipple until it firmed.

'How long's it been?' she asked quietly. 'Since you've had a woman?'

He paused to answer. 'A long time. Maybe too long.' He looked at her strangely.

'What are you going to do to me?'

His lips curled into a nasty smile. 'Whatever I like, Carol. Whatever I like.'

His mouth came down hard onto hers, pinning her back against the velvety seat. She felt stifled but he held her so tightly she couldn't escape him now. She focused on keeping calm, remembering how she had to play this. It was the only way.

She reached up and touched his cheek with her fingertips only. His skin felt hot, smooth and waxy. She pushed his face away gently, sensing that any aggression would be countered immediately and crushed. Maybe because the pressure was so light he pulled back.

'I have a deal for you,' she said, breathless.

He threw back his head and laughed. A car headlight streaked through the side window. Light glinted off his teeth. It was only a second but she was startled by how pointed the incisors were, and long.

'Where did you get the idea you have anything to bargain with?' he asked, still obviously amused by the idea.

'How about my body? You want it, I can give it.'

'I'll take it whether you give it or not.'

'I know that,' she said softly.

He eased up on her hair but continued staring. The street lights showed his face as inquisitive so she took advantage of it. 'I don't think you remember how to make love to a woman.' Carol kept her voice soft and level, her eyes holding his. She had played this scene before, or one similar enough that she could improvise her lines.

For a brief second he looked stern, angry. But suddenly he laughed again. 'You've got guts, I'll say that. It's going to be a pleasure breaking you.'

'I know you're trying to scare me, but you don't have to. You can have me freely. I'll give my permission.'

He pulled her hair, forcing her head back again. 'If you think I need your permission, you've got a serious problem with reality.'

Carol instructed herself to remain calm and to keep eye contact. This was no time to panic. She knew if she could save her life, and there was no certainty about that, she had to stay in control, play this carefully, not let the terror take hold. He'll use my terror against me, she warned herself. He's a master at intimidation.

'All I'm saying is I think I can give you what you want. We both know you can take it, but it might be more interesting if I give it.'

He continued holding her head back, his face over hers. He looked tight, controlled, impossible. She knew she was inches away from catastrophe. After what seemed an eternity he said, 'Let's hear this "deal".'

Carol touched his cheek again. His skin was almost too

smooth. She would have found the texture and contours of his face fascinating if the situation wasn't so dangerous. She ran her hand through his stylishly cut hair. He looked confused.

'I can give myself to you,' she said seductively. 'I can be warm and wet and open. Wouldn't you like that?'

He caught her hand. His face was stern again. 'And?'

'Let me go.'

'Now the pleading!'

'I'm not pleading.' Her voice was firm, a little annoyed, the fear disguised. 'This is a contract. We both know you're a blood fetishist. But you can get blood from anybody, can't you? I'm offering you something better. My blood's not special, is it?'

'No one's blood is special, but it's all important.'

'Are you saying you have a hard time finding it?'

'Not at all.'

'Well, then, mine isn't a great loss.'

He hesitated and Carol felt she had gained a slight edge. 'Tell me something? The police. When you say you have contacts, what's that mean?'

He let her hair go again and faced front. 'I say exactly what I mean.'

She decided to humour him, stalling for time. 'The town haemophile, right? Everyone knows and fears you. You're wealthy enough that they let you have whoever you want, don't they, just so you'll leave them alone.'

'Of course. Normally I take what I need from people passing through the city. The man by the river was unfortunate, but he shouldn't have interfered. The death was accidental; he died of a sudden cardiac arrest. The autopsy shows the only wound on his body is a small cut on the neck. The police believe it happened when he fell. He suffered some loss of blood, not a significant amount – at the moment of death.' His look challenged her to contradict him. 'Besides, the material witness seems to have vanished.'

She didn't believe him about the old man but found herself shuddering. No one will be looking for me, she realized. I'm really in his power. It took all her willpower to keep from showing the fear she felt.

They had left the harbour road, crossed over the Pont de Cubzac and were now travelling along a two-lane highway. A sign ahead read: *Soulac-sur-Mer, 90 kilometres.* Traffic was almost non-existent.

'Here's my offer,' she said finally. 'We spend the night together, just you and me. At my hotel.'

He laughed sarcastically. 'Guess again.'

'Your place, then.' She tried humour. 'Or do you sleep in a crypt?'

He looked contemptuous. 'Let's hear the rest of this.'

'Well, we'll go wherever you like. We'll be together as much or as little as your schedule allows. I'll do anything you want me to, willingly, eagerly. Tomorrow morning you let me go, without taking my blood. I'll leave Bordeaux immediately, I won't tell anybody and you'll never hear from me again, I promise.'

He tilted his head, looking at her as though she had just said there were cyborgs standing on the side of the road trying to hitch a ride. Finally he said, 'I can take some blood. It's like giving to the blood bank. You won't be affected, unless I let you drink mine, and there's no chance of that. Membership in this club is exclusive – by invitation only.'

Carol thought about scaring him off by telling him she probably carried the virus. But that would destroy her only bargaining chip. And she found it shameful to admit. The fact that he imagined he was some kind of vampire was unnerving enough so she said nothing but kept eye contact.

He folded his arms across his chest. A few seconds later he said, 'There are two flaws in your plan.'

'What?'

'You think you'll do whatever I want willingly. You can say that now but there are things you won't be so eager to do.'

'I'll do them, whatever they are. I promise.'

He sneered, disbelieving.

'And the second problem?' she asked.

'The second is that one night isn't much of a trade-off.'

'What's a fair exchange?'

'There is no fair exchange, only what I want. That's all that matters here!'

He was getting testy and Carol knew she had to tread cautiously or everything was lost.

She turned towards him, letting her right breast brush against his arm. Her lips moved close to his ear and her hand to his pants. Through the light wool fabric she could feel that he was firm. She stroked the material gently. 'Two nights? The weekend?' She breathed. She unzipped him and touched his penis lightly with the tip of her index finger. It was warm and solid, the skin a little waxy.

Carol forced herself to kiss his cheek, working towards his lips. She kissed them too but his mouth didn't respond. But she felt his fingers intertwine with the strands of her hair. She ran the tip of her tongue across his upper lip, outlining it, and then back along the middle of his lower lip slowly, being as sensuous as she could. Still there was no reaction. But beneath her hand he was growing firmer and she felt encouraged that her tactics were working.

Suddenly he yanked her head back. He looked furious. 'What are you, a professional whore?'

She felt stunned. The consequences of rejection could be deadly. 'N-no,' she said softly, frightened, about to cry in frustration.

There was a pause and then he said, 'All right. I'm intrigued.' While he fixed his clothes he said, 'Two weeks.'

The thought of spending such a long time with him made her ill. But what else could she do but carry on this charade until she found a way to escape?

'You stay at my place and give yourself to me. The key word here, Carol, is "willingly". Fourteen nights from now I drop you back in the city and you leave. Immediately. I can hypnotize you, but I won't; no challenge. Besides, these will probably be the most exciting memories of your uninspired little life. I'd hate to cheat you of them. But don't entertain any illusions. If you try to escape, and later, if you tell anyone about me, who or what I am, I will hunt you down. The rest I'll leave to whatever shreds of imagination you possess.'

Carol nodded. 'And you won't take my blood?'

'Agreed!'

Thirty kilometres from the resort town of Soulac-sur-Mer the car left the highway for a gravel road. They headed towards the ocean and a large stone house. All the downstairs lights were on and it seemed bright, cheerful and inviting.

Just before the car stopped, André looked at her. 'I told you I can drink without harming you. Why are you so eager to keep me from your blood?'

She turned away without answering.

FOUR

'Well, look what the bat dragged in!' A slim girl dressed in black and white in her early twenties with coppery hair and eyes the colour of mocha truffles came over to Carol as soon as she and André entered the house.

'For me?' The girl reached out a pale hand towards Carol; a large matte-black plastic ring on her index finger was shaped like a painter's pallet with little splashes of primary colours around the edge. Carol pulled back. 'Gee, kiddo, you shouldn't have!'

André stepped between them. 'Gerlinde, butt out. Karl!'

The man he called came into the hallway. He was of medium build, also in his twenties. Both his hair and eyes were the colour of silt, his clothing shades of brown. He looked serious, intellectual, his cheekbones prominent in a Germanic way. His eyes travelled to Carol's bleeding foot.

'Call her off!' André said, annoyed.

Karl dragged his attention away from Carol's wound to look at the girl named Gerlinde whose generous lips curled into a mock pout. The redhead stepped over to him, intertwined her arm with his then kissed him on the cheek, making sure to rub her body against his the way a cat would. 'I was only teasing,' she purred. 'He's so uncool.' She winked and Karl laughed.

Something told Carol she would not be getting any help from these two. Still, she was about to demand, or at least beg that they let her go when an older woman came through another door.

Her long loose snowy hair framed an oval face, setting off the pale blue caftan she wore. Her eyes were almond shaped and inquisitive, the colour of lapis lazuli. She and André spoke to one another in French. They looked a little bit alike, the shape of their foreheads and jaws, the wide-set, intelligent eyes.

Carol glanced around the hallway. It was an old house. In here the upper half of the walls were papered in subdued blue flowers, forget-me-nots, and the lower half wainscotted in varnished wood. The floor and stairs leading to the second floor were carpeted in light grey, accented by a polished oak banister. A small chandelier hung above them and three little bronze lamps with amber glass globes were affixed to the walls. Four doors led off the hallway, all of them closed. She wondered which one led to the back door.

The older woman approached her, and Carol sensed something odd about her, about all four of them. Their skin was a little too bright, almost reflective, and they each had the same mesmerizingly, nearly inhumanly attractive quality as André; four perfect life-like mannikins. Each exuded confidence, even haughtiness, but André was the most extreme.

The older woman looked Carol over, from head to toe, then smiled and said to André, '*Elle est belle. Ne perds pas de temps à la baiser.*' The others, including André, laughed.

'What did you say?' Carol demanded. She wasn't going to let them play with her.

The woman turned to face her. She gazed deeply into Carol's eyes and Carol felt herself being drawn into those liquid blue pools. The woman smiled again and the action animated her features, breaking the spell.

'I said you're lovely. I also suggested that he bed you quickly, because you're so ripe.'

Carol felt her face redden. Gerlinde giggled, revealing two incisors as long and pointed as André's, shocking Carol to silence.

'Ummm!' The redhead licked her lips. 'Nothing like a vampire in the sack,' she said when she could catch her breath. 'Ohhh, when those long, thick fangs penetrate, it feels soooooo goooood!' She writhed and groaned.

The man named Karl laughed, revealing teeth even longer than Gerlinde's. Carol was frightened. They know André's crazy, she realized, and they're just as crazy. The horrible idea came to her that this was one of those bizarre blood cults and she their next sacrifice. But she clipped that thought before it could take hold and fury surged. Unable to stop herself she blurted out, 'What do you do for an encore, girlfriend, eat babies?'

Gerlinde stopped laughing but condescended to grant Carol a large smirk before leaving the hallway. 'Come on, Karl, let's get a good seat and catch the audio portion of this show.'

As they left, André gripped Carol's arm firmly just above the elbow and led her to the steps. She was barefoot, her legs scratched and cut. The wound on her right foot seemed serious. I hope I bleed all over their carpet! she thought.

At the top of the stairs they entered the first room on the right, really a room and a half. The smaller area had a dark green couch, a mahogany coffee table and a rose chair near the fireplace. The larger part was taken up with a cherrywood dresser and armoire, a small glass and brass dressing table, and an antique brass bed, over which hung a large abstract canvas in muted colours. Everything was in shades of green and rose, except the carpet, which was teal. Off to one side was a bathroom.

Besides the door they entered by, there was one other, a closet, she suspected. That left the windows, none of which opened. That left the bathroom window, if there was one, although she couldn't see it from this angle. The ceiling was lined with smoke detectors and a sprinkler system, as though fire was a big threat.

'This is where you'll stay for the next two weeks,' André told her. 'You'll have to change your schedule to accommodate me – sleep during the day, awake at night. A servant will bring you meals. There will be food at other times as well. Don't try to leave this room. Anyway, it's impossible. The windows are plexiglass – you can't break them – and all doors leading out will be locked; everything is wired to an alarm system. I have the key to this room.'

'What if something happens to you?'

He grunted. 'You wish.'

He walked towards the fireplace. 'Do you know how to build a fire?'

'Yes.'

'Good. Make one now. And every night before I get here.'

Carol walked to the fireplace wondering what she had gotten herself into. Fear was clawing its way to the surface and she decided to concentrate on building the fire to stifle it. She parted the glass doors, checked that the flue was open then piled small sticks and pieces of newspaper which she crumpled onto the grate. Next to the fireplace were tools – a bellows, a small shovel, a poker.

When she had what she thought was enough, she asked, 'Have you any matches or would you like me to rub a couple of stones together?'

He took a box of long stick matches from the mantle and

handed it to her saying, 'An acid tongue, as caustic as my own. We should get along well.'

She lit the little pile of debris and when it was blazing put on two smallish logs, nudging them into the position she wanted with the poker. Starting a fire wasn't such a bad idea. The alarms would go off, the fire department might come and the sprinklers would, hopefully, keep her from being scorched. She could burn down the door and then . . .

'Don't entertain the idea of burning your way out. The temperature in this house is carefully controlled and the sprinkler system designed to activate at the first hint of a temperature rise. It's also designed to flood every room of the house.'

When the small logs caught she added a larger log, closed the doors and stood. She still had the poker in her hand.

'Take off your clothes!'

He was standing only three feet away and she felt intimidated. A quick rescan of the room told her there were no escape routes she'd missed. He could see she had the poker. What were the chances of hurting him when he was expecting an attack? And what would happen after, if she didn't hurt him enough? Not good odds. She put the tool back into the stand.

Slowly she began removing her rain coat, then folded it over a nearby chair. She was wearing a plain cream-coloured dress with long sleeves, a full skirt and a thin belt. She unbuttoned the dress, undid the belt then slid the dress down, stepping out of it. Slowly she folded the dress neatly and placed it on the seat of the chair. Next she took off the half slip in the same way, feeling embarrassed. His eyes were glued to her breasts as she unhooked her bra. Finally she eased her pants down over her hips. She folded everything carefully, rearranged the items, and then moved the pile to the coffee table, stalling for time.

'I'll take them with me,' he said, his eyes passing up and down her. She could almost feel waves of heat tickling her skin. 'I want you naked, waiting for me,' he said.

She felt shocked and her face must have reflected that.

'This is my fantasy we're acting out, remember? Now undress me.'

She took two steps towards him, thinking, I should tell him I might be a carrier. But how can I bring it up now? What if he hurts me? She'd wait for a better moment.

He was wearing a light leather jacket and both it and his pants were slate, matching the colour of his eyes. She removed the jacket and then the yellow shirt underneath. His chest was muscular and hairy, his shoulders broad; he looked in good shape, like an athlete, and she wondered if he lifted weights. She dropped down and pulled off his low cut boots and socks and then stood up. She was trying to be confidently sensual – this is only a role, she kept assuring herself – but, now that the moment had arrived to deliver on her end of the bargain, she was losing her nerve.

She unbuckled his belt, unzipped his pants and pulled them and his briefs down his legs. His penis was erect. Again, playing for time, she folded each article of clothing and placed the pile neatly on the seat of a chair.

He took her by the shoulders and walked her backward until they were at the bed, then he pressed her down.

Her heart beat wildly and sour fear welled up from her stomach that she swallowed back down. He wasn't hurting her. She had to remember that. It was late. This wouldn't last long. He straddled her chest and with a hand supporting her neck brought her head up. She knew what he wanted and used her mouth, aware again of the waxiness of his skin.

But soon he turned and flipped them both over so that she was on top. He pulled her down so he could lick and suck her while she did the same to him.

This isn't so terrible, she tried to reassure herself. At least he isn't brutal. And we're not having intercourse so the risk of transmitting anything is very low. I'll tell him soon.

He grew firmer and longer as she moved her lips along him. And what he was doing to her felt good. His tongue darted in and out quickly and he licked her where she was swollen and sensitive, then in and out again. She could feel heat spreading up from her lips, burning her thighs, and she knew she was wet, dripping. He's driving me crazy, she thought, astonished by her response.

She took in air through her nose in short, quick sniffs, feeling herself losing control. In moments too fast to remember, before she could stop him, he pushed her over onto her back, turned and entered her, his thrusts long and steady. She just had time to bend her knees and then she was moaning, pulling him close for his final thrust.

He stayed on top of her, inside her, and she drifted off to sleep, a bit dazed. But when he eased away, she opened her eyes a little and watched him through hazy slits. He was moving around the room, dressing, fixing the fire, gathering her clothes in his arms.

'Is André your real name?' she asked in a sleepy whisper.

He turned. She thought he looked different, paler, maybe more human. 'Yes,' he said.

'Why do you think you're some kind of vampire?' When he didn't answer she said, 'Look, I have to tell you something . . .' Suddenly he was gone.

He's not so bad, were her last uncensored thoughts before sleep. He's a little weird, but a good lover, better than Rob ever was. The chances of the virus being passed on in one encounter seemed pretty small. Tomorrow, she thought. I'll tell him tomorrow.

Carol yawned, thinking, this could even turn out to be a nice two weeks.

She woke in the middle of the afternoon. The window in the

bathroom was far too small to squeeze through, although it was the only one that might break easily; she'd already tried to break the two in the bedroom. He hadn't lied. Both were plexiglass, at least the inside windows. Outside were two more sheets of tinted glass. The door was still locked.

She showered, ate some of the fruit, bread and cheese she found on the coffee table, then wrapped herself in a large green bath towel. An early Robert Ludlum and a few magazines in English kept her occupied until evening. Just after sunset, as she was sitting looking at the pictures in an old issue of *Paris Passion*, a burly woman who did not look like the others brought in a tray of food. Stocky and dark-haired, she seemed completely focused on what she was doing. She locked the door behind her, hung the key around her neck and let it drop under her dress. She set the tray on the table.

Carol jumped up. 'Look, you've got to let me out. Help me,' she said slower and louder, pointing to the door.

The woman's eyes showed no understanding; she did not appear to have heard Carol. Either she's deaf or has instructions not to respond, Carol thought.

The woman headed for the door and as she unlocked it, Carol dashed across the room. They struggled. The woman shoved Carol hard inside so she could close the door and relock it behind her.

Carol sighed and plunked down into a chair. She lifted the warming lid off the plate and found a steaming bowl of stew made from veal, potatoes and carrots. There was also homemade bread and a pot of jasmine tea. She ate it all, hungrier than she realized.

After she finished she tried the door. It was locked. For something to do she looked out of one of the double-plated windows. The ocean was so quiet from inside this sound-proof room. The powerful tide had receded leaving the grey waters calm. From one angle she could see the garage. André and a man in a chauffeur's uniform went in and then the silver limousine pulled out. Then she saw Gerlinde, Karl and the older woman leave in a small green sports car. They had all gone and this was the time to make a break.

She picked up a chair and smashed it against a window. It bounced back as if the glass was rubber. She hit the window again. Nothing. Half a dozen more tries told her these windows were built to withstand more force than she could provide. In the process she'd broken one of the chair legs.

Next she tried to pick the door's lock. She bent the tines of the fork and tried to work the lock, but didn't know what she was doing and that, too, proved impossible.

She thought about trying to burn down the door but she had the feeling he wasn't lying about the sprinkler system. And there was the possibility she could burn herself to a crisp in the process.

The hours wore on but he did not return. She checked her watch against the clock chiming downstairs nine times. Ten o'clock then eleven o'clock came and went. She was getting nervous, impatient, pacing the room. She'd already made a fire and was running out of logs.

Carol found herself anticipating what was to come. I must be nuts, she told herself, because I want to see him again. Even thinking about the sex last night sent shivers through her. Why not? she thought. Here's your wildest fantasy. Locked away, a prisoner, abandoning yourself to a rich French lover for two weeks. He's okay, even if he thinks he's a vampire. Taking a little blood wasn't the worse thing she'd heard of. She'd met lots of people in theatre who were pretty delusional, some even made a career of it. And that old man, he probably did die of a heart attack. Besides, she smiled to herself, I don't have a choice, slightly embarrassed that she could even think in such a politically incorrect way. But secretly she entertained the wild hope of letting go here the way she'd never quite been able to with Rob or the two men she had slept with before him. But then none of them had been like André. He was so direct, almost animal-like, that it forced her to feel more physical, which was both exciting and disturbing. The others had all been nice enough, though not exactly passionate. In fact with Rob sex had been based largely on his preferences; mainly oral except when she insisted otherwise. At the time she had felt disappointed, vaguely troubled by a feeling that something was missing and she was settling for less. Now she wished they had *never* had intercourse. I don't have anything left to lose, she thought. Maybe there's something to gain.

But thinking about Rob always brought thoughts of the virus. She had to tell André she might be a carrier. No matter who he was or what he did, it just wasn't fair to him. She would force herself to bring the subject up tonight so he could protect himself.

Just as the downstairs clock struck midnight she heard a key in the lock. She jumped up, feeling foolish, knowing there was a big grin on her face.

André stepped into the room and immediately bolted and chained the door behind him. He stared at her. His look caused her smile to die.

He strode across the room and ripped the towel from her body. 'I told you to stay undressed! Are you defying me already?'

She wanted to tell him that she was doing what he wanted, it was just a towel, but something savage in his eyes kept her from speaking.

He saw the broken chair leg immediately and black anger settled on his face. 'That look!' he snapped. 'It's always there. Which is it, tenacity or rebellion? Over there!' He nodded towards the bed.

Carol began to panic. Her pulse raced and she had trouble breathing. Still she tried to lighten things up, turn his mood around. 'I had a good time last night. Didn't you?'

'My pleasure's the only reason you're here, or have you forgotten? I said, over there!'

Carol couldn't move. Her eyes darted to the poker by the fireplace, not two steps away. Instinctively she turned towards it but apparently he read her mind. With laser speed he blocked her, grabbing her wrist. His hand felt like a bracelet of icy metal, threatening to crush muscle and bone. She looked into his eyes and saw the turbulent grey Atlantic before a storm and intuitively understood the violence that would occur if she resisted. He pointed across the room and she felt a tension in him on the verge of exploding. 'Maybe you like being tied up.'

She shook her head.

'Then move. Now!'

In a daze of fear Carol walked across the room. Out of the corner of her eye she saw him unbuckle the wide leather belt he was wearing.

'On your knees. Turn around!' His voice was inhumanly cold, scaring her to paralysis. 'Back up.'

She turned and moved back until her knees were at the edge of the mattress.

'Head down! This is a crash course in submission.'

She lowered her head but he pushed her face right into the mattress, forcing her bottom up into the air like a perverse offering. Carol felt completely exposed, utterly vulnerable, yet unable to believe what was happening. 'Why?' she asked, trying to keep her voice from quaking, struggling to make sense of this.

'Why what?'

'Why are you doing this? Just because I was wearing a towel?'

'Trying to break our agreement so soon? Just say so. Stop whining and save us both the time and energy.'

'It's not that.' She felt like a child berated for some minor infraction of the rules, an imagined transgression. But she was convinced that if she fought him the outcome would be worse. 'I just want to know why, that's all,' she said weakly.

'I'm sure you do! What if I tell you there's no reason, I'm cruel to women by nature. Can you accept that? Still happy to give yourself "willingly", Carol?' His tone was mocking.

As he finished undressing behind her he said, 'You can influence me, you know.' His voice had a peculiar inflection in it.

She felt set up but asked, 'How?'

'Try begging!'

Again Carol's intuition told her that if she did what he suggested she would regret it. She had already picked up that he despised people who pleaded. She didn't feel she had any choice but to endure what he was going to do and try not to break down. 'I'm not going to beg,' she said in a whisper, barely able to speak.

'You're strong, all right. And controlling. And a bitch, like all women!'

Hard leather cracked across her bare flesh. A loud gasp burst from Carol's lips and her body jerked. But before she had time to really experience the intensity of the pain, the leather smacked her again. For long moments she was too stunned to react. Pain and humiliation piled on top of terror and the combined weight forced tears from her eyes.

The leather stung her increasingly tender skin a third time and she clamped her teeth hard into her tongue, stifling any words.

But the fourth stroke was unbearable and acting brave seemed less appealing. She opened her mouth, ready to let the pleas slip between the sobs, but, to her horror, words refused to form. It was as though a stubborn part of her rebelled at the idea of complete debasement.

Then suddenly something deep within, beyond her control, gave way like a small craft forced off-course by rapids.

As if she had split into two people, Carol heard herself screaming incoherently, crying, hyperventilating, rapidly floating out of her mind.

Later, she remembered at some point he had ordered her to open her eyes. She couldn't see him through the film of tears but heard him remark, 'So, it's tenacity after all. That's too bad.'

When he was finally finished, Carol lay on her side sobbing, head bent low, knees pulled up against her chest, arms protecting her body, curled into a tight ball. She didn't hear him leave. When the darkness gave way to daylight, she didn't hear the maid bringing food. She didn't want to hear anything.

FIVE

Carol stayed in bed all day and into the night, sleeping in fits and starts. She twisted and turned so much that by evening the top sheet looked like a giant white snake entrapping her body. But when she heard a key in the lock she woke completely, to terror.

It was not André but the older woman, the one who looked a bit like him, bringing a tray. Carol watched her place the food down carefully on the coffee table next to last night's tray and cross to the bed.

She sat down and leaned over Carol in order to stroke her hair. 'Poor darling,' she said in a soothing, motherly way. 'I'm sorry I wasn't here last night. André shouldn't have done this to you. He's not adept at mastering his passions. He's insecure.'

'He's a monster!' Carol said.

'Not a monster, *ma chère*. You don't understand. But how could you?'

She turned Carol's head so that they were looking at each other. 'Now what good will it do to stay in bed?

You'll just make yourself feel worse and probably enrage him further.'

'What's the difference,' Carol said bitterly. 'It doesn't matter if I do what he wants or not, does it?'

'Come, my dear,' the woman said, lifting Carol to a seated position with surprisingly strong arms, brushing her hair back from her face. 'You're not a child. You'll live. I'll help you into the bath.'

Carol didn't bother to protest. She felt awful. Most of the night she couldn't sleep. And when she was completely honest with herself, she realized that what was as bad as the physical pain was the pain she felt because of the way he had turned on her. She couldn't understand it. And now she didn't care if she understood. She hated him and didn't much like herself for being so naive as to get trapped in this situation in the first place. She should have taken her chances and fought harder back at the docks. She probably would have lost her life but at least she could have died with dignity.

The woman ran a bath and helped Carol into it. The water wasn't very hot and it didn't hurt her injured skin too much. The older woman used a floral soap to wash her arms and shoulders, her chest and back, and a pleasant herbal shampoo on her hair, just the way a mother would.

'Why are you doing this? You're on his side, so what are you up to?'

The woman paused. 'So distrustful, for one so young. You must have been hurt in your life.'

'I've been hurt right here in this house. Why should I trust you?'

'And why not? I only want to help.'

'Why?'

'Let's just say that I love André dearly. He's like a son to me. I want to see him happy.'

Carol laughed bitterly. 'Well, just give him a whip and

some chains. He'll be in heaven. Or doesn't this cult believe in heaven?'

'You don't understand, dear. He's charmed by you. Fascinated. I haven't seen him like this in a long long time.'

Carol laughed her bitter laugh again. But then she felt desperate. 'Please! Let me go.'

'I can't do that. We cannot interfere with one another. André has found you and only he can decide your fate.'

The woman helped her out of the tub and patted her dry with a soft terry cloth towel. 'I have a natural remedy which will relieve the discomfort.' She pointed Carol towards the corner with a mirror on the side wall. 'Go look in the mirror.'

Carol walked across the room and turned in front of the full-length mirror. Her buttocks were marked with four bright pink stripes. 'You see?' the woman said. 'You'll be fine by tomorrow. The skin wasn't broken.'

'Gee, I guess I should be grateful.'

'Come in and lie down. That's right. This will feel cold at first.'

As the woman applied a thick clear gel, Carol realized that the soreness was diminishing. She could feel how knotted and constricted her body had gotten. She tried to relax. 'What's your name?'

'Chloe.'

'You're like him – you drink blood. You all do, don't you? Like vampires.'

'Words are powerful, Carol. They can frighten or fascinate and should be used carefully. Let's just say that we four are a family.'

'You mean a cult.'

The gel felt cool, soothing, and soon Carol's soreness was gone. She sighed deeply.

'What about the maid. And the chauffeur?'

'They are not part of our family.'

'What do you do, pay them off?'

'They are not . . . how can I put it . . . acutely aware of our peculiar habits. There. You'll be fine now. I'll put some aloe vera on again tomorrow night. In fact I'll leave this here, just in case you want to use it later, all right?'

Carol turned over. She was naked but didn't feel embarrassed in front of this woman. 'Chloe, I'm not sure why you're doing this . . .'

'I told you, dear, I want André to be happy.'

'Well, whatever the reason, thanks. I appreciate it.'

Chloe took Carol's face in her hands and kissed her on the forehead. 'You're very sweet. I can see why he's enamoured. Now,' she said standing, 'I'll leave so you can do what you need to do before André arrives.'

She placed the jar on the night table, walked to the coffee table, picked up the previous night's tray of food then headed towards the door.

Carol suddenly felt terrified at being left alone to wait for André. 'Please, you've got to let me get out of here! He's going to kill me.'

Just before Chloe went out she turned. 'Carol. May I call you Carol?'

Carol shrugged impatiently.

'I cannot let you leave, but if I can make a suggestion? About André.'

'Why not? I can use all the help I can get.'

'Well, it might be better if you didn't mention what happened last night. Don't bring it up, you understand?'

'Right. Let my scars speak for themselves.'

'What I'm getting at is, I don't know exactly what your arrangement with André is, but this I do know. He's peculiar, in a way. More distrustful than you are. Extremely lonely. Bored. Jaded, perhaps. In some respects he's still a child. I think he's at a loss with you. He doesn't know what to do.'

Carol turned away. She didn't give a damn about his loneliness. But she kept quiet and listened to the rest of what Chloe suggested.

'I've known him a very long time, since his birth, and I believe I know him fairly well. The best way to deal with him is in the moment. Forget the past. Don't bring it up because he can be more brutal than you've seen. Just take him in the moment, as he is, the good and the bad. It's the best way.'

'Sure. I've read the psychology books too – men who can't face the fact that they're brutes. Never throw a misogynist's past in his face.'

Chloe sighed. She turned towards the door and opened it. 'I'm only trying to help. Both of you. Do as you must.'

After Chloe left, Carol got up and went to one of the windows. Outside in the twilight the ocean pounded furiously against large immovable boulders. The immense slabs of granite seemed rooted in the ocean floor. Constantly buffeted and ravaged by the violent Atlantic and other more impervious elementals, the rocks looked powerful to Carol but resigned to an eternity of endurance. This room was so quiet it felt like a tomb. Her tomb. Where she was buried alive.

She thought about what Chloe had said and decided she must know something about André; maybe it was the best approach. If I'm not receptive to him, she thought, he'll interpret that as breaking the agreement. He might kill me. Kill me! He can do that at any moment. How can Chloe think he's so fascinated when he keeps threatening me, not to mention what he did last night? He would hurt her at the slightest provocation, or even if he wasn't provoked.

She thought he must be insane, and everyone else in this house too, and that scared her. For all his problems, at least Rob had been relatively normal, ordinary, boringly so. Their life together had been simple and straight-forward, if passionless. And then she realized how strange things had gotten for her to be comparing her former husband – a man who had betrayed her – to a violent blood-sipping lunatic. Maybe I'm going crazy myself, she thought.

She heard the clock downstairs chime ten o'clock. Suddenly she panicked.

Carol hurried to the fireplace and quickly got a fire going then sat down gingerly on the chair beside it. On the table was the food Chloe had brought. She lifted the lid: chicken, wild rice and broccoli. She was hungry but could only nibble at it; her stomach was tight. Nervously, and for lack of anything better to do, she tried the door; it was locked. Everybody has a key, she thought. Everybody but me.

Carol waited pensively, trying to get herself into a mental state where she could pretend that nothing brutal had happened the previous night. But when she heard the lock click she stood and darted behind the winged armchair, feeling a need to keep a barrier between them.

Tonight he was dressed conservatively. He wore a sedate grey suit, grey shoes, blue shirt and blue and grey tie. As soon as he bolted the door he turned, his smile reserved.

'I see you're still among the living.'

So much for Chloe's advice, she thought. He's brought it up.

He walked to the table and lifted the warmer off the plate. 'You haven't eaten again. That's two meals in a row. Trying to starve yourself, or gain my pity?'

He stared at her and Carol shrank under that look. She tried to speak but her throat was dry. Her heart roared in her ears and she thought she might faint. Finally she was able to say, 'I'm not hungry.'

He dropped the warmer onto the plate. 'Good, because I'm not capable of pity.' He came towards her.

Her body began to tremble. 'I'm glad you're afraid of me,' he said, 'otherwise I'd think you're psychotic. I've had my doubts already. You mortals believe you can hide your feelings. Come over here!'

Hesitantly Carol moved from behind the chair. Her legs felt rubbery. She was on the verge of crying.

'I won't bite. Unless you'd like to break our agreement.'

He grabbed her hips, pulling them into his. 'Still think you can give yourself to me? Or do you want to renege?'

'We have a verbal contract,' she said softly, avoiding his intense eyes, focusing instead on the straight line his lips made, afraid she would burst into tears. 'I'll honour it.'

'Modern women are so sensible. Ever think of becoming a lawyer?'

'I tried.'

'And?'

'I failed the bar exam.'

'You could have been a respectable bloodsucker,' he laughed, exposing his teeth, and instinctively her eyes shifted to block out the sight. 'Come on. I can be gentle.'

He led her to the bed. When they got there he undressed and lay down, pulling her onto him. 'You'll be more comfortable on top, counsellor.' He manoeuvred her so that eventually she sat astride his hips. When he had stimulated her, he eased her onto him then moved her up and down until she understood the rhythm.

He stayed longer that night, taking her three times, all in the same position. He was gentle and steady but Carol had to struggle hard to forget the past, as Chloe had suggested, so that she could be in the moment, open, willing, so that she could save her life.

Just before daybreak, as he was leaving, he kissed her lovingly, lingeringly, and then he was gone again. As soon as Carol was certain that she was alone, she finally let the tears flow.

SIX

By the next day the redness on Carol's bottom had completely disappeared. The emotional scars were more persistent.

Each night André came earlier and stayed later. He was always assertive but usually gentle enough. Most of the time he was slow and patient, leaving room for her arousal, although she had a difficult time feeling anything remotely sexual with him. But sometimes he just took her cold, like an adolescent boy unable to savour the sensations. No matter what he did, Carol never fully lost her fear and distrust of him. Twice she had even become actively afraid – both times he made her kneel at the edge of the bed.

When they weren't having sex, André liked to talk. He told her that many of his 'victims' were sailors. 'Bordeaux's an international port, the third largest in France. Every day new ships dock here. A lot of these men are looking for quick sex, with men. I'm not interested in the sex – I just want their blood. We meet, go behind a building, and I take what I need. Most are so eager I don't even have to hypnotize them. Males understand exchange. Females always want more.'

Carol got a bitter sense of satisfaction knowing that at least he couldn't infect her with HIV. We've both probably already got it, she thought bitterly. And he's passing it along to somebody new every night, just like Rob. He's immoral for not mentioning it or using protection, she thought, but then realized that she was too. She didn't have the nerve to bring it up now. Unless he asked her a direct question she was forced to answer, she only listened.

'I've disciplined myself to take just enough, I'm satisfied . . .,' he told her, 'and they live. With iron supplements from the ship's doctor, they're fine. Besides, they leave the city in a few days. Quick, clean, easy. After all, there are four of us here, we have to be careful. Four killings a night, that would be almost 1,500 murders a year in Bordeaux, more than Paris and London combined.'

'But you've killed people, haven't you?' Carol asked one evening when she was feeling especially brave.

He looked annoyed. 'I hate the pleaders. They drive me crazy, begging for sex, begging for me to hurt them or not to hurt them, begging to hurt me, grovelling for their lives, as though their life is some precious commodity. You mortals hold yourselves in high esteem. But to my kind there's the same gap as you feel between you and an insect. You think nothing of crushing one under your shoe. I don't feel anything about crushing you.'

'But your kind . . . you have sex with us . . . mortals.'

'It's on the same level as you fucking a horse, or a gorilla.'

'Then why do it?'

He laughed. 'I'm a pervert.'

Carol usually listened quietly. Often she wanted to ask questions but was too afraid of him to open her mouth. His slant on life was truly bizarre and, despite the madness of such an inhuman perspective, he fascinated the theatrical part of her.

Once she had studied a bag woman for a week, learning her mannerisms, the way she spoke, hoping to bring the reality to a part she'd played. She analyzed André in much the same way. At times she felt as though she'd met a being from another planet with an entirely different set of values, forcing her to observe humanity through his eyes, from an alien viewpoint.

There were so many long hours in the day with nothing to do that, irrational as she knew it was, Carol kept catching herself comparing André to Rob. Inevitably this forced her to examine herself more deeply than she cared to.

Both men were handsome, educated, confident, well-off financially and, controlling. Both were attracted to men, for completely different reasons, if she could believe André, which she was not inclined to do. And both had an oral fixation. Each was callous in his own way. Rob's emotional coolness shut her out completely and betrayed her deeply. André was volatile and cold. Both emotions forced her back and away. But the most shocking commonality was that for Carol each symbolized death, hers, and the unalterability of events.

There was nothing to distract her from such morbid thoughts and she found herself more and more depressed as the days wore on, wondering why her whole life felt wasted. The emptiness had lingered since childhood, a yearning for something she couldn't pinpoint and suspected didn't exist.

On the fourteenth night he arrived just after sunset.

'Put this on,' he told her, handing over a white caftan much like the blue one she had seen Chloe wearing.

He led her downstairs and into a large living room furnished with warm woods and heavily brocaded Queen Anne furniture.

There were five others in the room. The redhead named Gerlinde and the man called Karl sat on a long couch before a large round coffee table supporting an immense black soapstone sculpture of a mermaid riding a dolphin. A tall, exquisitely beautiful woman with brilliant white-gold hair wearing a pale green sleeveless dress that matched her eyes stood beside a slender harsh-looking man with midnight hair, slightly taller than she. A good-looking dark-haired boy, maybe nineteen, sat between Karl and Gerlinde. The group was pouring over an old book the size and shape of an atlas. All of them looked up when she and André came in.

'Sit there!' He pointed to a chair by the fireplace.

'André's instant breakfast,' Gerlinde quipped. There were a couple of snickers.

André went over to the group of what Carol was certain were more of this 'family'. They all had that same strange skin, a not-quite-real radiance. He spoke in French for a few minutes to the harsh-looking man and then left the room. The man then sat down with the others and they apparently resumed commenting on the book which Carol could now see contained ancient diagrams of the solar system.

She turned away and stared at the fire, wondering what this was all about. She knew André was going out to 'feed', as he liked to joke. He told her that he did her a favour by drinking the blood he needed before he came to her, otherwise he would not be able to restrain himself. She realized it was not out of concern for her, but expediency.

Only one night to go, she told herself, then I'll be free of him. Even though he had not been physically brutal since the night he whipped her, still, he obviously enjoyed dominating her. Just the way he spoke to her sounded like a master ordering a slave. She still feared him and knew she couldn't trust him. She was terrified that, after all she'd gone through, he might break the agreement and either keep her prisoner or worse. None of the others would help her and there would be little she could do to help herself.

It had taken her a while to realize that what Chloe said was true, at least about his being fascinated. Every evening he became more comfortable, familiar. After their first sexual encounter he relaxed and seemed to unfold. It was more than his fantastic stories about his existence. Sometimes when he looked at her she caught a glimmer of an emotion in his eyes that bordered on delight. In another place, at some other time, if circumstances had been different, she might have tried to help him, maybe even fallen in love with him, despite the fact that he was obsessed with blood, with being a predator, and possibly even a killer. But the beating had crushed all romantic notions out of her. She was afraid of what he was feeling. Their situation made them unequal and she distrusted what he might do because of his infatuation. Chloe was right about another thing too. Carol did not understand him. But she didn't want to. She just wanted to get out of here alive.

'You're Carol.'

She looked up to see the elegant platinum blonde beside her chair. 'Yes.'

'I'm Jeanette de Villiers. That's Julien, my husband. And Claude, our son.'

Carol was unprepared for such a formal introduction from one of these weirdos and blurted out, 'You have a son? Is he one of this family too?'

Jeanette laughed and sat down across from her. 'Yes. And a daughter. Not by birth.'

Carol wondered what in hell that meant. They were adopted? And then the idea struck that maybe this bizarre cult abducted children.

The blonde looked Carol over slowly, from head to toe and back again. All of them eye me as if they're ravenous and I'm a piece of meat, Carol thought. She shifted in her chair, more towards the fireplace.

'Chloe's description was perfect. You're very pretty. Delicate and strong at the same time. But unhappy.'

'Wouldn't you be if you were a prisoner?'

Jeanette smiled in a peculiar way. 'Believe it or not, I understand. Do you love André?'

'No,' Carol answered without hesitation.

'That's unfortunate. For both of you.'

Carol looked back at the fireplace. They sat without talking, both women quietly watching the dancing flames come to life as magical primitive figures. Nearby, subdued male voices carried around them and Carol felt lulled.

'Go on, take them,' someone said, bringing her back to the present.

Jeanette thrust a large pack of cards towards her across a small walnut table that was now between them. 'Shuffle them a few times, cut them into three piles and pick up the stack that appeals to you.'

Carol did not know what this was all about, but she reached for the cards anyway. As she covered her mouth and yawned, she glanced around. Gerlinde had gone, as had the boy, Claude. Karl and the stern-looking man, Julien, sat talking quietly. The book was no longer in sight. She wondered for how long she'd drifted off.

She recognized the cards as the Tarot. Once she and a friend had gone to a psychic and had their fortunes read. Carol had been told to expect a wealthy oilman to marry her and take her to Texas to live. And that she would mother seven children. Never had a prediction been more inaccurate.

She browsed through the deck. The pastel images of medieval scenes portrayed on each over-sized card jumped out at her. Without thinking much about it, she did as

Jeanette had instructed. When she decided on the pile on the right she handed them back.

Jeanette turned the top five cards over. The first went into the centre, the next to the right of centre, then below, to the left and above.

'Incredible!' Jeanette remarked. 'Are you sure you don't love André?'

'Positive.'

'Then who are you in love with?'

'No one.'

Jeanette picked up the middle card and handed it to her. At the bottom it read, *The Lovers*. The picture was of a man and woman looking blissfully in love, sunshine and a rainbow; heaven smiled on. Without comment, Carol handed it back and Jeanette returned it to its original position.

'Your past is here.' She pointed to the *Five of Cups*, which showed a man in a long black cape. Sorrowfully he looked at three cups that had fallen over, spilling the contents. Behind him were two upright cups. 'He's so caught up in what he's lost that he can't see what he still has, and that's the saddest part.'

Carol stared at the card, thinking that it certainly was how she had been feeling for the last year. Loss and nothing but loss. But if she had anything left she was not aware of what it was.

'This is what's influencing you now. *The Magician*, a powerful dark-haired man who practises the art of transformation. He can be either a creator or a destroyer, and much of the time a trickster but most often he's an alchemist, turning excrement into gold, hate into love or love into hate. This card is what might happen – *The Devil*.' The card seemed to be the opposite of *The Lovers*. Here a man and woman were enchained between a horned monster. 'It means bondage, loss of freedom, enslavement, deception.'

Carol shuddered. Maybe it was an omen; André would

not free her as he had promised. He'd keep her here forever, using her for sex and to fill his demonic need to dominate, drinking her blood, brutalizing her whenever he felt like it, threatening to kill her if she resisted him or even just because he felt like threatening her.

'This last one,' Jeanette was saying, 'is the probable outcome of your situation.' Then she was silent.

'Well, we've gone this far, what is it?'

Jeanette still said nothing.

The door opened and Chloe came into the room. Immediately she joined them. She lay a hand on Jeanette's shoulder and Jeanette, without looking up, placed hers on top. Chloe smiled at Carol who tried to smile back but she was disconcerted.

She looked back down at the card that Jeanette was talking about. It was called *The Empress* and showed a powerful-looking woman on a throne holding a heart-shaped shield. Within the shield was a circle with a cross connected to the bottom.

'Interesting reading,' Chloe said.

'Yes,' Jeanette answered. 'What do you make of the fifth position. The card is clear, but not the context. Here, sit.' She got up and let Chloe take her chair.

Chloe too meditated on the card.

A long time seemed to pass. Everyone in the room was silent. The only sounds were the crackling of burning wood and the rhythmic ticking of the grandfather clock.

Time seemed to slow for Carol. Everything fell into sharp focus.

The harsh-looking man got up and put two new logs on the fire. When he finished he stayed squatting before it, studying the flames. The room smelled sweet with the scent of cedar.

Eventually the man named Julien stood and walked over to his wife. He never once looked at Carol, almost as if she wasn't there. Carol was fascinated by these two. She observed every move they made. The others in the room, Chloe, and Karl who was looking out the window, became silent and still. The scene was like a snapshot, a slice of time, an essence captured.

Carol watched as Julien moved up very close behind Jeanette. He placed his hands on her shoulders. Slowly he slid them down her bare arms. Carol could almost taste the sensations – each pore recognized, every muscle acknowledged. He moved past her elbows, over her forearms and wrists, until his hands overlapped hers. Jeanette's eyelids fluttered and her green eyes looked dreamy.

Their fingers interlocked. Slowly he crossed her arms over her body, his arms moving hers, until he enveloped her, holding her tightly. She closed her eyes. Her head fell back, supported by his shoulder. He nuzzled her hair, kissed her temple, brow, her eyelid and cheek. Slowly he wandered down the side of her face to her jaw and then lower until at last his full lips reached her neck. He locked onto her throat in a passionate kiss and her lips gently parted as she melted back into him. A faint moan of ecstasy escaped her, floating along the sweet-scented air. The sound reminded Carol of an eerie cry she'd once heard brushing the tree tops of a rain forest at daybreak. Primitive. Other-worldly.

Carol shivered. She felt encircled, enraptured, her soul penetrated. She had never seen such abandon and it filled her with wonder and awe and a secret longing.

Suddenly the door opened again. This time it was André, breaking the spell. The room came to life with sound and movement. The clock began to chime the midnight hour.

André looked full, refreshed, and as if for the first time Carol noticed how handsome he was.

Jeanette and Julien parted and were talking to Karl in French. Gerlinde returned and joined them, gesturing wildly and speaking rapidly in both French and German. Claude came in with a fresh-faced teenage girl. They were having a lively argument in English about whether the Atlantic, the Pacific or the Indian was a more interesting ocean. Only Chloe was removed from the international hubbub. She continued silently staring at the cards, unmoving.

Carol watched it all, on the one hand fascinated, on the other feeling left out, alien, alone. No one paid the slightest bit of attention to her which she both resented and felt grateful for.

Eventually André left the others. He spoke with Chloe briefly then motioned for Carol to get up. She felt more upset than usual that he was treating her like an inferior, a pet. I'm being silly, she told herself. Nothing has changed. Tomorrow I'll be free. What do I care what he does?

As they were leaving the room, Jeanette called out, 'Wait a minute!' She picked up one of the cards from the table – the one nobody would interpret – and gave it to Carol. 'You'd better take this with you.'

Carol followed André up the stairs and into the bedroom. He locked the door, turned and stared at her.

She instructed herself to stay calm. He won't steal my blood – not tonight anyway.

'Take that off!' he demanded.

As she removed the caftan, he took off his clothes. With a slight nod he motioned for her to come to him. She could read his signals now, what he wanted and how he wanted it.

When they were lying down he entered her immediately, but didn't begin moving right away. His arms went under her thighs, lifting them until her knees were almost above her head. His hands locked her wrists to the bed, capturing her like a Monarch butterfly pinned to a board. Only when he had her helpless and immobile did he begin moving slowly. She listened to the sounds of his flesh against her wetness, surprised that the sensations caused by the friction excited her.

He stopped and tasted the inside of her mouth, meeting her tongue with his, their kisses warm and moist. Then he moved in and out of her. She felt the heat increasing. He paused again to suck one of her nipples, bringing it up firm with his lips.

She found herself moaning, beginning to desire him. He moved again, then stopped for more kisses. Then more movement, then teasing her other nipple. They went on and on as the night faded, he building her up, holding back, tormenting her, controlling her, fanning the flames inside her.

Carol was losing herself, slipping away. Only the passion remained, tumbling her over and over, a blazing force causing her body to quake uncontrollably with an intense unfamiliar longing. But each time he almost satisfied her he pulled back, forcing her to new breathless heights.

She forgot that she hated and feared him. She forgot who and what he was, what he had done to her and could still do. All that mattered was that if he would only fulfil her she knew she would give him anything.

'Do you want me?' he whispered, licking her nipple, the roughness of his tongue thrilling her.

'Oh yes!' she whispered back unashamed, her body quivering in agreement.

'Badly?'

'Yes.'

'Beg me!' He took her nipple between his lips.

'I want you.' Her voice was soft, low, panting, her body trembling and on fire. 'I want you so much. Please, André, take me now. I'm yours.'

Before she realized it, the pleas were out. In sudden horror her eyes snapped open wide. She saw him above, his face colder than it should have been. But he looked startled, caught in his own game between wanting and despising her, her fate hanging in the balance of his conflict.

For an eternal moment the universe seemed to pause; neither of them moved nor breathed. And then something shifted. He was swayed to one side, but she didn't know what had moved him. All she really understood was that he became hard, direct, unavoidable as he drove deeply into her, deeper than ever before.

She cried out, screaming his name again and again as he ravished her, possessing her, forcing her to embrace an ecstasy she had never dared dream of.

And afterwards, as they lay holding each other, she knew exactly how her face looked because she'd seen that look before in Jeanette, that look of complete abandon.

SEVEN

The following night, shortly after sunset, they left the château in André's limousine. As they reached the highway, Carol turned to look at him. From profile he was gaunt, his features exaggerated. She knew he wanted blood.

They drove for twenty minutes before he said anything. 'Sit closer to me.'

She moved over but joked, 'Our contract's expired.'

He faced her, his eyes flat pinpoints, piercing her. 'Our contract expires when I say it does!'

She didn't argue. She wasn't home free yet.

Just like on the ride from the city, he put an arm behind her, pulling her head back. He kissed her long and passionately, running a hand slowly over her face and throat like a blind man memorizing her features, finally letting his cool finger tips rest on the throb of her jugular.

Carol submitted to his kisses, sinking into them. She entertained the fantasy of what it would be like to live with him, to spend the rest of her life wallowing in passion. The idea thrilled her and she met his desire with her own.

He's really not so terrible, she told herself, the memory of his brutality taking second place to other, more pleasant recollections. I can change him, I know I can. He's already infatuated. I can grow to love him, even if he has a few problems. It'll be easy. I don't have much to lose.

The wild idea suddenly came into her head to propose another deal. She'd stay with him for a month, see how it went. Again, she'd insist that he refrain from taking her blood and she'd have to tell him she might be a carrier. And this time too he would have to agree to nothing violent. He'd go for it, she felt sure.

They crossed the more modern bridge, Pont de Cubzac, and then turned onto the road along the harbour and were almost at the spot where the taxi had driven her to only fourteen nights before. His lips came down onto hers again, a moist insistent pressure, sending shock waves through her vagina. And when their lips parted their eyes locked.

Carol had already opened her mouth, about to tell him what was on her mind, when he said, 'Don't come back here. Ever!'

Her limbs went numb, her brain froze, her heart shattered from the coldness.

The car stopped and he got out. He did not look at her.

Without a word he shut the door and walked away quickly, heading back along the wharf.

Immediately the limo drove off. They crossed the Pont de Pierre which led to the downtown core and Carol was deposited in front of her hotel. Zombie-like, she walked up to her room, packed and checked out.

'The bill's been taken care of, Mademoiselle. And this was left for you,' the clerk said as Carol cleaned out her safety deposit box.

Inside the large envelope she found a one-way ticket to Philadelphia. She flagged a taxi, instructing the driver to take her to Mérignac Airport. There she bought a ticket to Madrid. The ticket to the United States she threw away.

It was three weeks later that Carol began feeling ill. At first she thought it was just a reaction to the spices used in Spanish cooking, then she thought it might be a reaction to a perpetually broken heart. But soon she was vomiting daily and forced to find a doctor. He ran a series of tests. The results shocked her. After she pulled herself together, the first thing she did was to buy a plane ticket back to Bordeaux.

Part II

'You have the devil underrated
I cannot yet be persuaded
A fellow who is all behated
Must something be!'

– Goethe

EIGHT

'Inspector LePage, please cut the pretence. I know you know who he is, what he is and how to get in touch with him.'

The detective took a drag on his Gitane. They sat side by side on stools at the counter of a small coffee bar, at the quiet end, where they wouldn't be overheard.

'If I could find André myself, I would,' Carol continued. 'I've spent the last three nights down by the docks on both the right and left bank, and when I wasn't there I was walking the streets looking for him. That's the only reason I phoned you.'

'Why are you so interested in finding this André, Mademoiselle Robins? Less than two months ago you did not care enough to remain in the city, against my orders, to aid in our investigation of what you insisted was a murder. Now you seem to want to locate the alleged killer yourself, in actuality a man who simply tried to make your acquaintance. Is this a vigilante action or masochism?'

Carol felt exasperated. 'Look, I told you, I really don't care what your relationship with him is, what kind of deals the police have going. But I have to find him – soon. I need your help. It has nothing to do with the murder, and it was a murder, even if it was accidental.'

'Insinuating that I have made a deal with an alleged murderer is a serious accusation, Mademoiselle. But for the sake of argument, assuming I knew of this Monsieur André, why should I help you locate him?'

She'd been trying to convince LePage for the last hour and he hadn't budged. He wouldn't admit to anything but just asked her more and more questions. Carol hated to do it but she played her trump card.

'The main reason you should help me is because what I want to see him about is important. If I don't find him and it's too late, he'll discover that you didn't help me, and, well . . .'

Inspector LePage took another drag on his Gitane, squinting to avoid getting the smoke in his eyes. She could see him contemplating the ramifications of angering a wealthy madman. It wasn't only that what the doctor in Madrid had told her could be vitally important to André, but she also needed his help; she felt desperate. Threatening the policeman was self-preservation.

'Why don't we leave it at this?' she said. 'I'll be at the harbour tomorrow night, near the docks on the right bank, from nine until midnight.'

'A dangerous area, Mademoiselle. You take your life in your hands.'

'Thanks for your concern.' She picked up her bag and stood. 'If he gets this information, I know he'll be grateful to you.'

The policeman remained seated, continuing to chain-smoke, watching her through the white-blue haze. She knew she had him. Years of legal and theatrical training made her a shrewd judge of character. She also knew when to make an effective exit.

*   *   *

It was a warm May night, hot but not muggy. The sky was clear, sprinkled with stars and a full moon.

Carol wore a cool white summer dress and flat shoes. A bleached canvas shoulder bag holding essentials hung across her body. She'd waited in the shadows of a fish warehouse near where his car had been parked before. Although the street had little vehicle or pedestrian traffic, she wanted to hide. It *was* a dangerous area and there were probably worse things than self-appointed vampires prowling the night.

The taxi would be back to pick her up at 12:05. Carol checked her watch: 11:30. She'd been there since nine and her legs ached from standing. And she was beginning to feel discouraged. Maybe he's not coming, she thought. Maybe LePage didn't pass on the message. She wondered too why she hadn't seen his car on the three nights she'd scoured the city. She also thought that what she was doing was crazy. More than likely he would just take her blood outright, which was what he had wanted to do all along. But none of that mattered very much now. She felt depressed, desperate, and the idea of dying quickly at his hands wasn't completely unappealing.

Ten minutes before twelve the silver limousine drove up and parked half a block from where she stood. The driver killed the ignition and the lights went off. The car sat there, no one getting out.

Carol exhaled, suddenly feeling nervous. She forced herself away from the shadows and under a street light. She walked towards the rear of the car, her leather soles tapping loudly against the cobblestones.

The driver got out, closed the door, lit a cigarette and headed up the street in the other direction. As she reached the limo, the rear door swung open, blocking her, as though after all her trouble she might just pass on by. Carol peered inside. André sat in the middle of the seat.

'Get in!' he said.

When she was seated, he reached across her and pulled the door closed then turned on the inside light. He looked at her and she at him. There was a long pause.

'I told you not to come back here. Are you a fool or crazy?'

'I need to talk to you.'

'Get over here, next to me!'

'I didn't come for that.'

'I don't care why you came back.' He grabbed her arm, yanking her closer. Immediately his lips and hands were all over her. He reached up under her skirt, tearing her panties away, then pulled the dress over her head, ripping the top in the process. At the same time he was kicking his Pumas from his feet and pulling his T-shirt off.

'Don't do this! Listen to me.'

His mouth stopped hers. Carol struggled but he was impossibly strong. He pressed her back against the seat, trapping her arms, meanwhile getting his pants down quickly. He forced her legs apart, pushing one up under the back window, the other onto the floor. In the confines of the car he attacked like a deranged animal. He ejaculated immediately but then stayed on top of her. Both of them were sweating and breathing heavily.

Carol was terrified. She berated herself for being so naive as to put herself in his clutches again. Now, she thought, he'll probably take my blood. I'll die here, at the hands of a demented monster who thinks he's in a Gothic melodrama. Her fate seemed bitter and undeserved. Well, she decided, I'm not going down without a fight.

'I'm pregnant.'

For a couple of seconds he held his breath. Then he pushed himself off her saying, 'Congratulations!'

He pulled up his pants and snatched at the grey T-shirt, dressing quickly. 'Is this confession supposed to elicit pity or something?' He slid his foot into his left shoe and tied the laces tightly, angrily. 'How could I take the blood of a pregnant woman? I told you once before I don't feel pity.'

Carol pulled her dress over her head. 'It's yours.'

He was tying the laces of his right shoe and paused briefly but then continued. '*Merde!*'

'It's true.'

He sat back and turned towards her. 'You're incredible. First of all, it's impossible. I can't impregnate you. Secondly, you probably just don't want to face the fact that you're such a slut. You don't know who the father is, so you've deluded yourself into thinking it's me. But you'd fuck anything that can get it up. Nice try, though.'

Carol felt as though he had stabbed her in the heart. Without bothering to reply she reached for her shoulder bag and pressed the door handle.

'Unlock the door!' she said coldly.

He didn't move.

She looked at him. 'You're right, I was an idiot coming to you for help. Just let me out.'

He laughed. 'Not on your life.'

She hated him so much in that moment that she burst into tears.

'Yes, now tears. I love to see women crying, trying to create guilt. But your tears mean nothing to me. We're two different species, I told you that before. There's no love lost between enemies. You know you'd kill me if you got the chance, which you'll never get. But I can kill you, easily.'

Carol just cried harder, her emotions a potpourri of fear, pain, frustration and anger. 'You son of a bitch!' she screamed. 'You're a delusional, pompous jerk. You couldn't be more callous if you were a real vampire. I don't know what you are and I don't care. You can do what you want to me, I don't care about that either. But you're wrong. This is your child and I just want to get rid of it. Now, kill me and get it over with. I'm tired of life and sick of your nasty, adolescent games. I hate you!'

She collapsed against the door, swept by waves of strong emotion.

It took ten minutes for the storm to pass. Every time Carol nearly brought herself under control a new rush of pain flooded her and she sobbed uncontrollably again. But finally she was just sniffing, dabbing her eyes with a tissue, when she heard him ask in a civil tone, 'How pregnant are you?'

'A month,' she sobbed.

'What makes you think I'm the father?'

She gave him a look backed by the total disgust she felt. 'Because you're the only man, not to mention the only monster I've slept with for over a year.'

She started to cry again.

'Even if you believe this is the truth, why come to me? You know I just want your blood.'

Carol felt so frustrated, so upset, so wild, she could hardly speak. 'Because I want an abortion,' she said, her voice high with hysteria.

'So get one.'

'I can't. I couldn't get one in Spain, they're illegal. I don't know how things work in Europe. I can't even speak the languages. I thought you'd be able to help me.'

'Go to Sweden. Or back to Philadelphia.'

'No! I won't go back there!' she said adamantly. She felt like a little girl throwing a tantrum and could imagine herself stamping her foot.

'Then have the baby. Many single women do.'

'I can't,' she sobbed.

He sighed. 'You mean you don't want to. Look, it can't be my kid. And I don't care about this shit. You're making a big deal out of nothing. Have the baby and keep it or give it up for adoption or go home and get an abortion. You can always return to Europe, if this is where you want to be. What's the problem?'

She felt completely alone in the world. How could she convey this? And he wouldn't care anyway. He'd just say he was more alienated then she and he survives. She should grow up, face reality. In fact, what he suggested was perfectly logical – go back and get the abortion then return to Europe. But her logical side wasn't functioning all that well, obviously, or she wouldn't be here now. Her feelings, which had never been more overwhelming, confused her, drenching her in fear and loneliness, leaving her unsure of what to do or how to do it. The outcome was more tears. She hugged herself. All she seemed able to do was cry.

At some point he reached over and pressed a few buttons on the phone. She heard a beeping sound outside the car. About ten seconds later the driver got back in. They pulled away. Soon they were on the highway heading towards Soulac-sur-Mer.

NINE

André left her in the living room seated on a couch opposite Gerlinde, who put down her magazine to say, 'Welcome back. Is he that good a lay?'

Carol didn't answer. She was barely holding herself together. She felt terrible, so frightened and alone. And now I've probably gotten myself into a worse mess, she thought.

'You ain't lookin' so good, kiddo,' the redhead commented. 'Been crying? André being his usual cold sadistic self?'

Carol looked at her. She didn't trust this one. 'I'm just not feeling well.'

'How come?'

'I . . . I don't know. It's nothing.'

'Ummm.'

Gerlinde came over and sat next to her. It felt as if the temperature in the room lowered a couple of degrees. 'Hey, I'm not your wicked stepsister. I know I have a big mouth, but there's some sugar with the shit.' She smiled a crooked little grin. 'Like a drink?'

Carol shook her head.

'It's not blood. Believe me, if there was any spare blood around, I'd drink it myself. We've got some sherry.'

She stood and went to a table beside the window. From a cut glass decanter she poured the sweet amber wine into a small glass, then walked back and handed it to Carol. 'Bottoms up. Whatever you've got, this'll cure it. I used to drink the stuff myself.' Gerlinde sat down beside her again, smoothing out her fuchsia leather skirt.

Carol sighed deeply. She sniffed the contents and took a small sip.

'See? Sherry. Honest!'

Carol took another sip before placing the glass on a coaster on the table in front of them. Suddenly tears welled from her eyes, her chest heaved and she was sobbing again.

Gerlinde wrapped a comforting arm around her and Carol found herself crying on the shoulder of a woman who, only a few weeks before, she had detested. Gerlinde stroked her hair. 'Hey, what's up?'

Carol blurted it all out.

The redhead looked stunned. 'André an incubus? No way! Listen, kiddo, it ain't possible. I mean, André can't do it. He just can't.'

'I know,' Carol sniffed. 'He told me that. But he's the only one I've been with.'

Gerlinde just shook her head in disbelief. 'Man, I can't believe what I'm hearing! Are you sure you're pregnant?'

'Yes. I made the doctor repeat the test.'

'Another immaculate conception!'

The door opened and André came in followed by Chloe. Carol stayed in the safety of Gerlinde's crook. She noticed a look on André's face that she interpreted as disgust.

'Hello, Carol. How are you?' Chloe asked, her face soft, her smile warm and remote at the same time.

'I don't know,' Carol admitted. 'Upset. Pregnant.'

'Yes, André told me.' Chloe sat opposite the two women. André took up a position across the room, as if intentionally trying to keep a distance.

'Carol, who's the doctor you saw in Spain?'

She thought for a moment. 'I don't remember his name. Mendez – something like that. Wait! I've got some pills he gave me because I've been throwing up so much.'

From her purse she removed a small plastic container of blue and white capsules and handed them to Chloe, who read the label.

'Gerlinde, how's your Spanish?'

'*Mejor que mi Aleman*,' the girl said.

'Can you talk like an American trying to speak the language?'

'See, Seen your hah.'

'Will you call this doctor? Tell him you're Carol's sister. She's with you in France and you just want some details. Find out what he knows?'

Gerlinde stood, ruffling Carol's hair. 'Chin up.'

As she passed André she punched him macho style on the arm. 'You devil!'

He scowled at her.

Chloe reached out her hands and hesitantly Carol took them. Then Chloe looked into her eyes. Those blue orbs were so relaxing. Carol felt tension leaving her body. She sighed. She was tired. So tired. She had a sense of Chloe being a mother, comforting her, inviting her back into the womb so that she could just relax and forget everything that was bothering her. I can rest, she thought. I need rest. I can be at peace.

Gerlinde's voice dragged her back to reality. 'He said she's preggers, maybe a month. A little low on iron, but otherwise strong. He did an ultrasound. Looks like a foetus, alright. No problems he can see.'

'Fine,' Chloe said.

Carol sat back against the couch. Visually things were unusually bright.

Chloe turned to André and spoke in French.

'What did you say?' Carol asked.

'I said that you are definitely with child. Besides what the doctor told Gerlinde, I can feel it, and see it in your eyes. Who the father is, that's another question.'

Suddenly Carol felt like crying again. She wanted to get up bravely and tell them, thank you very much, but she was going to leave now. None of them believed her, and she could understand that, and she shouldn't have come back for their help. She would make her way, go back to Philadelphia and have the abortion. She was sorry to have put them out.

But she couldn't move. Physically and mentally she felt depleted. Emotional exhaustion and depression crushed her.

'André said you want an abortion. Why?' Chloe asked.

'I don't want to have the child.'

'Why not? You're young. Strong. Probably healthy. Do you dislike children?'

'I . . . I don't know. I've never thought much about it.'

'So how come?' Gerlinde asked.

Carol hesitated. 'He thinks he's a vampire – not human. He's sick. I don't know what that means. I don't want to give birth to anything with defective genes. And there could be complications. I might die.'

'With an attitude like that, you might die anyway.' André spoke for the first time.

Carol suddenly realized that she had offended them. She didn't care about André so much, but the women had been kind to her. 'I'm sorry,' she said to Chloe then turned to Gerlinde. 'I didn't mean it the way it sounded. I'm just afraid.'

'And a liar!' André crossed the room quickly. He grabbed her by the hair, pulling her to her feet. 'It's written all over your face. What's the real reason you don't want to have the kid?'

Carol started to shake.

'Answer me!'

'I . . . I may have something.'

'What's that supposed to mean?'

'Something I can pass on.'

'Which is?'

She was embarrassed to even say it, the implications were so dreadful. 'HIV. I've tested negative twice but I'm probably a carrier – my ex-husband has AIDS. The baby would likely come down with it.'

They were all silent. Carol looked from one to the other. Chloe seemed concerned and Gerlinde shocked. André's face had turned livid – and furious.

'You little bitch!' he said in a tight low voice. 'So that's why you were so eager to let me fuck you. You thought you'd infect me, kill me with the virus.'

Carol felt stunned. 'No, that's not what . . .'

'What a set up! Even if I had decided to take your blood you thought you'd get me.'

'I wasn't trying to infect you. I wouldn't do that to anyone! I tried to tell you, several times . . .'

'You lying . . .' He raised his hand, about to smack her, but Gerlinde stepped between them.

'Cool it, kiddo! You have just leaped to a gigantic conclusion.'

He shoved Gerlinde out of the way. But immediately Chloe said, 'André! Stop!'

'Stay out of this,' he warned them. 'She's mine. It's my right to do what I want to her. Neither of you can interfere.'

Chloe began talking to him in French. She was explaining

something in a calm voice. The more she said the more he argued. But at some point what she was saying affected him and he became silent. Both he and Gerlinde were staring at Chloe with startled looks on their faces, listening with rapt attention.

Carol had no idea what was going on but she was grateful to Chloe. She knew André had meant to seriously hurt her. But this whole place, all of them . . . It was like suddenly waking up to find herself imprisoned in an institution for the insane. She was beginning to feel reality slipping from her grasp.

When Chloe finished, Gerlinde flopped into a chair. 'I don't believe this!'

Chloe said something else to André in French and immediately he grabbed Carol's arm and pulled her across the room.

As they were going out the door, she heard Chloe tell Gerlinde, 'I'll have to let Jeanette know she was correct about *The Empress*.'

He almost dragged her up the steps, taking her to the same room she'd stayed in before. Without a word he shoved her inside, closed the door then locked it from the outside.

Carol was alone the rest of that night. Just before sunrise the maid brought a tray of food. Next to a plate of liver and spinach sat a bottle that read: *Vitamines et Minéraux Multiples Comprimes*.

TEN

As soon as the sun had set the following evening, the maid arrived again with more food. Carol, for all the chaotic events of the night before, had slept well, late into the afternoon. She felt refreshed and hungry and was still eating when André came in.

He sat across from her, watching her. Tonight she felt stronger, not so vulnerable. She took her time eating. He could just wait for her. When she finished, she put down the knife and fork, dabbed at her mouth and sat back.

Minutes passed. Neither of them spoke. She poured a cup of camomile tea into a turquoise and white china cup with a gold rim and drank some. More minutes went by. She felt as if he had her under a microscope, examining her closely, no doubt searching for imperfections.

'I've decided you'll stay here until the child's born. Once the birth takes place you'll leave. The baby remains.'

Carol put down her cup and saucer. 'I don't want to have the baby. I told you, I want an abortion.'

'What you want is irrelevant.'

'Another ultimatum? Your way or death, right?'

'Just my way.'

'Don't you get tired of controlling the universe? It must be tedious acting out the role of Satan all the time.' She was feeling brave. She didn't want to put up with any of his patriarchal crap.

'This is the deal. You stay, have the kid, then go. That's it.'

'What do I get out of this "deal"?'

'Your life.'

'Maybe that's not enough anymore.'

'I don't recall offering you a choice.'

'I'll escape. Or abort.'

'Try either one and I'll chain you to that bed for the next eight months.'

Carol was quiet. He had her over the proverbial barrel and they both knew it. 'Why do you want the baby? You don't even believe it's yours. Do you want to drink it's blood?'

'You're such a stupid bitch. I'm surprised you haven't provoked someone enough to murder you by now.'

'Always threatening. Why? You're so powerful, physically and in other ways. But you act like a kid with a toy hammer; you've got to smash everything you see.'

He stood and walked across the room to the window. His back was to her as he pulled the heavy drapes aside and looked out. 'You can do this the easy way or the hard way, it's all the same to me.' He turned around. 'But you'll do it, that I can guarantee.'

Carol chewed on her lower lip, wondering what he was getting at.

As if reading her thoughts he said, 'The easy way is this: You stay here, behave yourself, take care of yourself, make yourself available to me, the way it was before, and eight months from now you deliver a baby. The next day you're gone.'

'And the hard way?'

'Same as the above, except I use force. And you won't like it.'

He walked to the door and held it open. 'Think about it. Do yourself a favour.' He left.

A few minutes later Carol tried the door. It was locked.

Around midnight André returned and took her downstairs.

Gerlinde, Karl and Chloe waited in the living room on the couch nearest the fireplace. André took a chair opposite the others.

'Sit down next to me, Carol,' Chloe said, patting the smooth fabric.

Carol sat. She looked around. The four were watching her closely.

'We want to talk with you, about what's going on. I know you must be confused.'

Carol exhaled and her shoulders fell forward a bit. She felt tired again. And depressed. But it was good that Chloe was so kind, otherwise she knew she might have tried something foolish. She felt almost suicidal.

'What's happened to you, your pregnancy, is very very unusual. Extraordinary, really.'

'Mondo weirdo,' Gerlinde said.

'Legend has it that only once in a great while can one of our kind reproduce through birth,' Chloe continued. 'A male impregnates a mortal female. It doesn't seem to work the other way around.'

My God, Carol thought. Mortal female? They think they're gods. They're all seriously disturbed.

'It happens so rarely,' Chloe continued, 'only every few hundred years, that when it does we have a hard time believing it. None of us in this room existed the last time a birth occurred. And I'm the only one here who's heard the legends.'

'A divine child,' Karl said.

A demon child, Carol thought. 'Why does it happen?' she managed to ask, wondering why she was humouring these crazies.

'No one knows,' Chloe said. 'All we can guess is that the conditions must be right, the male and female, the time, the chemical balance, the circumstances, maybe even the moon. We just don't know. But what we do know is that such a child is very special to us.'

'Will it be, you know, a blood drinker, or whatever you people are?' She couldn't believe she was saying this. But the whole conversation seemed so unreal.

'The baby will be half-mortal and half-immortal. Whatever is the major influence in his or her life will decide.'

'In other words,' Karl added, 'if the child is raised by mortals it will probably live out a mortal existence and then die a natural death. If brought up by our kind, it will likely be immortal. In either case, just before the age of puberty it must choose. If it decides on immortality, it's lifetime will halt at the age it wishes to remain.'

'You can see, Carol,' Chloe was saying, 'that because of the rarity of such a birth, we want the child to stay among us, where he or she naturally belongs. And since you don't want the baby anyway, here's what we propose.'

Carol sat back listening. They sounded as reasonable as lawyers and she had to keep reminding herself that this was madness. And she couldn't shake the feeling that she was surrounded by vultures, ready to pick her bones clean, eat the foetus right out of her body.

'Stay with us until you reach term. We'll take good care of you, help you in any way we can. After the baby is born you can leave freely, with no regrets, no concerns. The child will be given more love than he or she will know what to do with. Your job will be finished and you can begin your life fresh.'

'What about the virus? The baby will probably have it.'

'Our cells have mutated,' Karl told her. The child may or may not develop antibodies, we don't know. That's another reason why it should stay with us. It will consume only blood, initially through us, reinforcing the cells like ours, cells immune to mortal diseases.'

'And what kind of danger's involved for me?'

'No one here will harm you.'

Carol looked at André. He crossed his arms over his chest defensively, looking smug. 'I mean, in terms of the birth,' she continued. 'If this isn't an ordinary child, it can't be an ordinary birth.'

Chloe shifted slightly but Carol did not miss the movement.

'This will be difficult, won't it? I may die giving birth.'

'No one knows what's involved,' Chloe said. 'As I told you, this is the first time for the four of us. We've sent out word to our community. If any of the others know more, they'll be in touch.'

'Great! You want to keep me here, a prisoner . . .'

'Not a prisoner, kiddo,' Gerlinde said. 'We can all be one big happy family.'

'Sure,' Carol glared at her. 'Except I'm the only one who can't leave.'

'Just for eight months,' Chloe reminded her.

'At the end of which I might die bringing another nut, probably a genetically-programmed killer, into the world. Thanks but no thanks!' She stood. 'I'm not going to do it. And you can't make me. You can torture me or chain me to the wall, but I won't do it. I'll starve myself, if I have to, and if you force-feed me I'll throw up. Or I'll kill it with hate. I'm through being intimidated.'

Her entire body quaked. She felt turbulent, violent, despondently impulsive. Her eyes darted wildly to the large picture window. She envisioned hurling herself through it.

They were on ground level, so she wouldn't die from the fall. But she could easily see herself crashing through that shatter-proof glass . . . *She heard it shatter and felt herself thud against the ground. She grabbed up handfuls of shards. Quickly she sliced open the veins in both her wrists, severed the ones behind her knees and slashed at her throat where she hit an artery. In seconds I'll be dead and they can't save me!*

'Hold on, kiddo!' Gerlinde gripped Carol's shoulders firmly and looked her in the eye, forcing her away from this ghoulish fantasy and back into the reality of the room. 'It ain't the end of the world. You're falling off the deep end.'

Somehow Carol knew that Gerlinde understood what was going on inside her. Suddenly she felt exhausted again, frightened and sad, completely overwhelmed. Before she knew it, she was bawling like a baby in Gerlinde's arms, crying over and over, 'I can't! I can't do it. Don't ask me to. I can't!'

The two women sat with her. Karl fixed her a cup of herbal tea. They waited it out with her, all but André, who stayed aloof. The three of them talked to her, letting her know she wasn't alone, they would do everything they could to help her.

She knew they were creating the illusion that they were on her side. The real truth was she had no choice.

After a while she told them, 'I don't want to do this, but I guess I have to. But I've got some conditions. If you meet them then I promise not to try to hurt myself or the baby.'

'What are your conditions?' Chloe asked.

Carol looked at her. 'I want freedom. I want to be able to go outside. I'm not going to be locked up in here for eight months.'

'I'm sure we can work something out,' Chloe assured her.

'I want a doctor to check me out regularly, just to make sure nothing's going wrong.'

They looked at one another. 'It will be difficult but we can arrange that.'

'And I'll need some things: clothes, books, movies, I don't know what yet.'

'No problem,' Gerlinde said.

Carol looked at André. His eyes met hers. 'And he has to promise to leave me alone.'

There was silence. Chloe spoke in a soothing voice. 'Carol, dear, I told you before, in our world, you belong to André. He has final say over these terms. And one of the things we do know about such births is that the male must have input.'

'What are you getting at?'

'You gotta screw him,' Gerlinde told her.

'No! I refuse!'

André laughed.

'Carol, let me put it this way,' Chloe said. 'The child you carry will automatically feel your influence. I have a book you might want to read – *The Secret Life of the Unborn Child*. It documents cases of how a foetus is affected by its mother before birth, intrautero. There is also strong evidence that when the father is present he has an equally powerful effect. In the case of this child, because it is so split between our world and yours, and because we want to guide it into our world as much as we can, André must have even greater access to the foetus, so that his effect will be strong and clear. He and the child must bond.'

'I don't know what you're getting at,' Carol said, afraid that she did.

It was André who answered her. 'She means that I'll have to spend as much time as I can stand being with you until the baby arrives. Among other things, my son's going to feel my power surrounding and protecting him. He needs to know I'm here.'

'Think of it as a love affair,' Gerlinde said, hugging Carol.

'A loveless love affair,' Carol mumbled. And thought, with a demon lover.

ELEVEN

On Carol's second night back at the château, André came for her just after sunset, when the remaining pink in the sky still reflected along the surface of the calm Atlantic. She was just finishing another meal of liver, spinach and turnips.

'Hurry up!' He looked deathly thin and pale, like a wax figure. His cheeks were hollows, his grey eyes flat. He seemed preoccupied. Carol suspected he was thinking about blood.

About five minutes later she finished. 'Come on,' he said, eying her from head to toe when she stood with a look of mild distaste.

They waited outside for the car, Carol on the steps, André walking impatiently up and down the gravel driveway. It was very hot and she was already perspiring.

The front door opened and Gerlinde stepped out. She wore a loose lemon- and lime-coloured shift, cut at an angle, baring one shoulder. 'Hi, kiddo,' she said, her thin lips smiling a slightly crooked smile.

'Hi!' Gerlinde too had that hollowed out look, anorexic and pale.

For a few seconds Gerlinde watched André pacing and then remarked, 'He's no good before his first cup.'

'The chauffeur. And the maid. How come they don't know you guys are . . . different.'

'We have our ways. Hypnosis, is probably the nicest way to put it. They can still do their job, they just don't make the connection that they only see us at night.'

'Is that what you're going to do to the doctor too?' And the police, Carol thought.

'Sure.' Gerlinde's voice was a bit strained.

'Listen. Thanks for being so nice to me.' Carol touched her arm. 'I don't know what I would've done without you there.'

A peculiar look came over the redhead. Suddenly her eyes seemed to catch fire and Carol was mesmerized. They reminded her of a piece of fruit she'd left on the patio one summer. Two days later, it began moving. It had taken her a moment to realize the fruit was covered with larva.

Gently Gerlinde pushed Carol's hand away. 'Hey, I'm not much before my first cup either. Keep a distance, honey. You smell like a fine blend to me.'

A green sports car with the hood down pulled up. Karl was driving. He, too, looked pale and drawn. Gerlinde got in, waved and they drove away. Within seconds the silver limo stopped beside the house.

André held the door for Carol and got in right after her. The car drove off immediately.

During the forty minute trip to Bordeaux he didn't look at her once. He seemed agitated, and Carol was smart enough to keep quiet. But as they drove along the harbour street on the left bank she asked, 'Can I get out and walk around until you come back?'

He eyed her briefly, turned away and said irritably, 'Don't be ridiculous!' As soon as the car stopped he was out and hurrying towards the wharfs.

Carol heard the driver's door open and close. She tried the back doors, both of which were locked. There was obviously some kind of sophisticated mechanism for locking and unlocking them that she didn't understand. She sighed and flicked on the inside light, hoping to find something to read. There was nothing. She sighed again. At least it's air conditioned, she thought.

For a while she amused herself by exploring the little doors and drawers in the limo. There was a full mini liquor cabinet, a tiny refrigerator, empty except for ice cubes, a little closet with small plates, cups and utensils that looked as though they'd never been used, two spare seats, a radio, a tape deck and a pile of modern cassettes, a TV and VCR with two video movies – the new James Bond and a French film called *La grande bouffe*. She turned on the television – all the shows were in French – and made a half-hearted attempt to concentrate on a sit-com.

Everything's happening so fast, she thought. Only a month ago I thought I was free and now I'm a prisoner again, being forced to have a monster baby. And I brought this on myself. I don't even understand why I came back. Three days ago it made sense. Now the whole thing seems like a bizarre nightmare.

Canned laughter burst from the speakers.

She had no feeling for the child inside her. But Carol had never really wanted children. Earlier, before the marriage ended, she and Rob talked about it. Neither felt ready. They were too young. And a baby was inconvenient. Carol hadn't even taken the bar exams and Rob was still building his reputation. Maybe, a couple of years down the road, they'd both said. Now she was glad they'd waited. But she'd never felt a real desire. She didn't look at babies on the street thinking, how cute, wish I had one. The two children that had been part of their circle of friends seemed bearable for about three hours at a stretch. But she'd often thought, thank God I can go home now.

A man yelled '*Merde!*' and there was more laughter. The station broke for a commercial – soup was being ladled into bowls by a woman in a frilly white apron who looked like she was having the time of her life.

She didn't want to have this baby, that's the one thing she was positive of. But she had the feeling there wasn't much she'd be able to do about her situation. She felt okay right now, but lately she'd been so ill, vomiting daily, that she was weak all the time. And emotionally she was a wreck. She'd feel settled, balanced for five minutes and then, wham, she was off the deep end, as Gerlinde had put it. It scared her to think that last night she had come so close to considering suicide.

On the small screen she watched a preview for a made-for-TV movie. A woman dressed in black cried while another woman comforted her.

I wish things were different, she thought. That I hadn't been exposed to the virus. That André was normal. And he was nice to me all the time. She wished he wouldn't berate her, demean her, brutalize her. Maybe he would treat her better now that she was pregnant. He'll have to, she thought. He won't endanger the baby. I can bargain a little for what I want.

Carol heard the driver's door open and close and then the rear door opened. André got in. He looked alive, filled out. He switched off the TV and the light, picked up the phone, punched the buttons and spoke to the driver. She understood the words, Royal Medoc. On the five minute trip into the downtown, he turned in the seat, studying her in silence.

When they reached the hotel, André got out first. While he talked through the front window, giving the chauffeur instructions, he gripped Carol's upper arm securely. The minute the car was gone he turned towards her, pulling her close. He took her face in his hands. 'Put your arms around me,' he said softly.

The street was crowded. Out of the corner of her eye Carol saw people glancing at them, smiling, nodding approval, assuming they were lovers. She formed a split-second plan to scream for help as loud as she could.

'I'm only going to say this once,' André said, so seriously that her attention became riveted to his face. 'Don't do anything stupid, although I'm sure you'll find that difficult.'

He kissed her gently on the lips. 'If you get out of line I'll hurt you more than you've ever been hurt before, baby or no baby. You'll have to redefine the word pain. Understand?'

Carol nodded. He smiled at her, kissed her again, then draped an arm around her neck tightly. On the way into the hotel, he nodded at several passersby and exchanged *bonsoirs*. He's deranged, she thought.

They stopped at the desk to pick up the key to her room then went right up. As soon as they were inside he flipped on the lights and said, 'Take that dress off and give it to me!'

Carol froze for a moment, then put down her purse and undid the safety pins she'd used to hold the sun-dress together where he'd torn it two nights before. She slipped the dress down over her hips, folded it carefully and handed it to him. Immediately he ripped it to shreds and threw it in the trash can. 'Don't wear anything this ugly again, not while you're with me. Take everything else off too.'

Carol removed her panties, also torn, and her shoes.

'Lie down and spread your legs!'

'Don't talk to me like that!' she blurted out.

He laughed sarcastically and crossed his arms over his chest. 'Like what, the whore you are? What did you expect? You planned to give me AIDS. Did you think I'd find that endearing?'

'I didn't plan anything. I figured if you could get it you

probably already had it, because of all the sailors. At least you couldn't give it to me.'

'Then what was the big tease about not taking your blood?'

'In case you weren't immune, I wouldn't give it to you. But that's what I thought at first, before we had sex. But then I didn't want to die, that's all. I tried to tell you so many times. I came back to tell you.' She was completely flustered.

'Right!' he sneered.

André went to the closet and took out her luggage. He pulled her dresses, skirts and blouses off their hangers, one by one, tossing them haphazardly, with disgust, into the suitcase. 'You dress like a cleaning woman with the taste of a chambermaid.'

When the closet was empty of her things, he sorted through what was in the bureau, picking out an olive M*A*S*H T-shirt and tan cotton army shorts. Except for her hairbrush, toothbrush and make-up bag which he put into her shoulder bag, everything went into the suitcase.

He tossed the T-shirt and shorts at her. 'Put these on.'

She went to the suitcase to get underwear but he stopped her. 'Nothing underneath, just the shirt and shorts.'

She dressed then slipped on the same flat shoes she'd worn earlier.

'Turn up the cuffs,' he instructed.

Carol rolled the cuffs on her shorts up twice.

'More.'

She did another fold.

'Twice more,' he instructed.

The pants were now very short. Too much of her bottom showed. 'I can't go out like this. I'd be embarrassed.'

'Typical mortal angst. You're all a bunch of egomaniacs.'

While she sat on the bed waiting, he phoned the desk. Within five minutes a bellhop was at the door. André gave the boy some money and instructions in French. Then he told Carol, 'I'll lock your suitcase away at my place so I don't have to look at these rags. You'll get it back when you leave. Come on!'

The small elevator was crowded but they squeezed in. Immediately his arm went around her waist. He slid a hand down her backside and up under the shorts, in clear view of the other passengers.

Carol felt totally ashamed. She knew her face was flaming. He acts like a rebellious teenager, she thought. Erratic, constantly trying to embarrass and humiliate me.

He paid the bill while she cleaned out her safety deposit box. As they were leaving the clerk called out, 'Mademoiselle! I nearly forgot. A letter. It arrived for you yesterday.'

She reached out to take it, but André intercepted the envelope.

He glanced at both sides quickly before pocketing it.

They got in the car and drove two blocks to a hair salon.

The owner, a short handsome man with an affected manner, greeted André warmly, kissing him on both cheeks, calling him, '*Ma belle bête noire.*' Most of the staff said hello to André too. The owner looked Carol over with what she thought was disapproval, ran his hands through her long hair in a professional way and quickly had her washed and sitting in a chair before a large mirror. She realized she could see André in the mirror and was surprised. He almost had me believing he's a vampire, she thought.

While the stylist pinned sections of her hair up, preparing it for cutting, André sat on the edge of the counter flipping through a style book. The two men consulted together frequently, with lots of laughter and mock-arguments accompanied by wild hand-gestures, and at last seemed to come to an agreement.

Within half an hour Carol's hair had been snipped into

a short, smart, modern style that showed more of her face than she normally exposed. The stylist massaged in gel and blew her hair dry while using his fingers to shape it. He sprayed the end result into place. A pretty young girl came by and made up her face with vivid colours, outlining her eyes in kohl so that they appeared very round, and her lips in a dark red pencil. Carol glanced in the mirror thinking, I'm a teenager again!

Their next stop was a clothing store on the chic rue Ste-Catherine. André made her try on several outfits, out of which he bought three skirts, all similar, four tops and an oddly-cut summer pant suit the colour of watermelon. Her T-shirt and shorts were packed in with the new things. She was now dressed in a very short black leather skirt and a red and white horizontal striped tube top, no underwear. He hung a silver chain belt around her hips. It was made of wide links interlocking with smaller links, and clasped at the front onto a flat sharply-angled piece of metal that resembled a padlock with a stylized keyhole. An old-fashioned key hung from one of the links. Overall she looked like a modern Apache dancer.

Next they went across the street and he bought her two pairs of shoes with three inch heels and thin straps around the ankles.

She wore the red ones, her flat shoes packed with the black patent leather pair.

On the way back to the car she said, 'A month from now these things won't fit.'

'A month from now the style will be *passé* and I'll buy you something new.'

He made another brief stop. When he came back he had one long silver earring, shaped like a pair of handcuffs, which she put on, and a red studded leather wrist band with a large red stone imbedded in it.

'Turn around,' he said. He hooked something around her

neck. It fit snugly, although he fastened it so there was just room for her to breath. She touched it. 'This is a dog collar!'

'Try not to bark too loudly.'

When they next got out of the car, he snapped one end of a six foot chain on to a ring on the front of the collar and the other end on to a loop in the waistband of his pants which already had one half of a set of handcuffs hooked on. It's like he's walking a dog, she thought, which depressed her. But soon she was too disconcerted to be depressed.

They strolled slowly along the length of a promenade in Le Vieux Bordeaux, André holding her tightly around the waist, the chain attaching them. This area of town seemed frenetic. Trendy types, artists and actors brushed shoulders with hookers, drug addicts and derelicts, a general assortment of odd characters. On the streets people juggled, sold handmade jewellery, paintings and hot Walkmans, walked pit bulls and chihuahuas and performed mime shows. Bag ladies dressed in faded orange or yellow crêpe de Chine begged for coins; musicians hooked up to mini amplifiers played loud grating music; artists sketched caricatures in pastel charcoals on the sidewalk itself; exquisite older women costumed in expensive attire flirted with bisexual hustlers dressed to draw attention to their genitals; Tunisians smoked aromatic tobacco in long pipes; couples gyrated to music blaring from the open door of a nostalgia shop/night club, and they all seemed to know André. Many of the women kissed him passionately, and some of the men. Everyone examined his newest acquisition – Carol.

She felt awkward, embarrassed, picked apart, ignored and then paid too close attention to, not to mention trapped.

They all had something to say about her. And she couldn't understand one word of it.

André seemed to be taking in everything with a lot of enthusiasm. He's obviously very popular, she thought. Right at home with all the other nuts. He savoured the attention, smiling with the pride of a collector when these creatures of the night fussed over Carol. She just wanted to crawl into a hole somewhere and hide.

After what seemed like hours, he led her to a little café on a small street off one end of the promenade near La Grosse Cloche, a large Gothic eighteenth-century bell tower featuring a big clock surrounded by graceful figures. They sat outside, in a prominent place. André chatted with people at nearby tables and called to others who were passing. He ordered a spinach salad for Carol plus another piece of liver, which was served with *pommes frites*. At one point, while André was busy talking, the waiter asked her in broken English if she wanted something to drink.

'*Vin*,' she said, adding, '*rouge*,' two of the dozen or so French words she knew. But when the wine came, André made the waiter take it back and bring her a glass of milk instead.

About four in the morning they left the café. He took her hand as they walked down to the river and crossed the Pont de Pierre. André pointed out spots of interest along the way, just as if she was a friend visiting the city. Le Monument des Girondins, l'Hôtel de Ville, and the Gothic Cathédrale Saint-André with its nearby Tour Pey-Berland. 'See the gold statue of the virgin at the top of the tower?' he nodded. 'The virgin and St André's are linked by an underground passage.'

Eventually they recrossed the Garonne and walked along the left bank taking the same path that Carol had taken, the path where the carpenter had died. Tonight the water level was higher. They passed that spot and headed further west beyond the large ships, away from the downtown core. It was still very warm out, but the humidity had dropped a little so Carol wasn't as uncomfortable. But she felt tired. 'Can we stop for a while? My feet hurt. It's the shoes.'

André turned towards her and pulled her close. He examined her, apparently pleased by the new look, then kissed her lips. A couple passed behind them going west.

Soon he was kissing her passionately, aggressively. He pulled the tank top down, exposing her breasts, and lifted her skirt up to her waist.

'Don't!' she said, trying to cover herself. But he was all over her.

He turned her around. 'Hold on to that.' He nodded at the street light post.

Carol heard a whine in her voice as she said, 'Why here, now?' but she was too exhausted to muster a strong protest. And what does it matter any more, she thought.

He took her from behind, grasping her hips, entering her vagina slowly, moving rhythmically up into her. The sky above was clear, the moon full. Below she heard water splashing against the dock, and both of them breathing. She was surprised that her vagina was moist, and more than amazed to hear herself moaning with pleasure.

TWELVE

The rest of her second month and throughout the third, Carol settled into her pregnancy, and life at the château. Many evenings she went into the city with André, or they walked along the beach, other nights she spent downstairs talking with Chloe or Gerlinde, and Karl, when he was around. For a prisoner she was being treated well enough, although she was bored with the daily rations of liver and/or spinach they fed her.

Carol was still leery of André because he was so unpredictable. Yet it wasn't all bad. Sometimes she even found herself enjoying the time she spent with him.

One night he brought her six Bird of Paradise. They showered together, laughing under the spray. But when Carol stepped out of the shower, while he was towelling her off, the sickness she felt daily hit hard.

She noticed her ashen face in the mirror. 'You'd better leave me alone in here,' she warned him.

The words were hardly out of her mouth when she began violently throwing up. She grabbed the towel-rack for support but it broke away from the wall and she fell, heaving so hard she was crying too. André caught her and held her while she vomited dinner into the toilet.

He was so gentle Carol could hardly believe it. He wiped her face and gave her water to rinse out her mouth. And then he carried her to bed. Once he'd tucked her in carefully and turned out the lights, he got in beside her.

The sickness always frightened Carol. André seemed to sense it and stayed until dawn, holding her in his arms, kissing her, stroking her hair as she cried. He told her funny stories about the characters he knew at the promenade, 'vampire groupies', he called them, breaking up her tears with laughter, distracting her from the nausea. Carol was grateful and told him so.

The following night he walked in as she was changing. 'Feeling better?'

'Yes.' She was wearing one of the new skirts he'd bought but no top. She no longer felt self-conscious about being naked in front of him.

'Leave that on,' he told her. He sat in an armchair and took off his shirt. 'Come over here.' He pulled her down onto his lap. 'I brought you some books. Pick one. I'll read you a bedtime story. Inspirational. Some of our best French authors.'

He handed her three paperbacks. She glanced at the titles – *Justine*, *The Story of O*, and *The Claiming of Sleeping Beauty* – then looked at him with what must have been a startled expression on her face.

He threw back his head and laughed, his long teeth exposed. 'I love shocking you.'

'A.N. Roquelaure is Anne Rice's penname, and she isn't French, she's American.'

'She's French in spirit, counsellor, and that's good enough under the Napoleonic Code.'

He pulled her close, sucking her earlobe, running a hand up the inside of her thigh. 'You're so fuckable.'

'Is that an insult or a compliment?'

'What do you think?'

Overall he was treating her all right, considering she had no choice but to be here. He still tried to embarrass her when they went out and constantly ordered her around. But at least he wasn't physically brutal and had stopped threatening her. Sometimes he seemed almost human.

'Here, lean over the footstool and I'll massage your back,' he said one night.

Carol knelt in front of the chair where André sat, resting her arms on top of the footstool and her head on her arms. His thumbs worked the muscles along her spine.

'That feels really good,' she murmured.

They were silent for five minutes or so. He changed his movements to an enfleurage, broad strokes from her waist up to her shoulders. 'Where's your family?' It was the first time he had shown any interest in her life.

'My real dad died when I was three. He was from Québec. That's where I was born. But my mother is an American. She was up there for a holiday and they met and fell in love, I guess. She never talked about him much. Anyway, I know he was from a little town in the Gatineau Hills. I've never been there. His name was Desjardins. I guess that makes me half French.'

'It makes you half Canadian,' André said.

'Anyway, my mother remarried right away and my stepfather adopted me. That's why my name's Robins. He wasn't around much. He was a salesman, always away on business, and I don't think I saw him more than six weeks a year, if that, so I never really knew him. I didn't feel close. My mother was always unhappy. I don't know. It was a funny family, I guess.'

She felt the tension in her body ebbing. Now that she was

revealing it, her past seemed less intimate, more unrelated to the person she now perceived herself to be. 'My mom fell apart when my dad died – he was killed in a car accident – and she never really recovered. She kind of went downhill, and when I was at law school she had a stroke. She's been in a nursing home since. Paralyzed. She doesn't even recognize me – the doctors say her brain is damaged and she'll never come back. Fortunately she had enough money that the interest pays for it.'

'Brothers and sisters?' He kneaded the muscles in her neck and she sighed.

'I was an only.'

'You must have some relatives.'

'Oh, there are aunts and uncles floating around on my mother's side, but we're not close. I exchange Christmas cards with one cousin, but that's about it. I don't like my adoptive father's family. And I've never met my real father's relatives. All my grandparents are gone. Maybe it's different in France, but in the States families are pretty scattered.'

He was now massaging her scalp, rubbing the thin muscle across it in small circles, then wider and then the whole head.

Carol felt completely relaxed. Peaceful.

'I was married,' she mumbled.

'And?'

'He liked women and men, and a lot of them. That's how I was exposed to HIV.'

André ran his fingers through her hair, from the scalp to the ends. It was so soothing.

'I thought I loved him, and maybe I did, I don't know anymore. We've been divorced for over a year.'

'That's why you hadn't slept with anyone else?' He had stopped touching her with his hands but his calves rested against her hips, continuing the contact. She turned her head to the other side and sighed deeply.

'I guess so. That and the virus. I just felt, I don't know, kind of raw inside. Betrayed. And I couldn't stand the idea of being hurt like that again.'

They were silent, Carol drifting off to sleep. She heard the clock downstairs strike eleven times. 'What about you?' she asked softly. 'Ever been married?'

André stood. It was so abrupt a movement that she opened her eyes. He went to the closet, opened it and pulled out a vermilion dress he'd bought for her recently. 'Put this on. I'll take you to dinner. And then, if you like, we'll go to a club.'

One evening Carol was sitting in the living room alone when Chloe came in.

'Hello, Carol. You're looking well. Are the teas helping with your nausea?'

Carol put down her book and sighed. 'I guess they're helping a little. I haven't thrown up in two whole days. But I still feel queasy sometimes, like now.'

'I have something for you.'

'Not more liver, I hope.'

Chloe laughed. 'No.' She handed Carol a small rectangular box. 'From Jeanette. You remember her, don't you?'

'Sure. She read my Tarot cards, except for the last one.'

'Well, she was confused. And so was I. That card usually has to do with fecundity. The Empress is the earth mother who connects heaven and earth, spirit and flesh, through love. Both she and those around her are unconscious of her powers. Neither of us could see the connection. Of course, now it's obvious. Open it.'

Carol looked at the exquisite box. It was lacquered gold and silver leaf patterns over polished ebony. The patterns formed mask-like faces. The box was tied with wire-thin silver and gold ribbons. Inside she found a two-inch piece of clear rock shaped like a wand. She held it up to the light. 'What is it? A crystal?'

'Smoky quartz. Many believe it's as old as the earth itself. It's been used for healing purposes and for personal protection for centuries. Of course, recently there's a big interest in rocks and minerals and other geological materials, much of it, to my mind, a bit on the superficial side. But Jeanette is seriously interested in the occult, mysticism and related subjects. The colour within is called a phantom and signifies that this crystal is especially powerful.'

Carol peered through the quartz. Inside a swirl of darker grey resembled a little figure.

'She sent a note,' Chloe said, handing over a small envelope. Carol opened it and read aloud:

Dear Carol,

You're a special girl. I knew that when I first met you. Chloe sees it too. André is very, very lucky to have found you and you've got to realize how honoured you've been to be able to increase our line in this way. All of us can only be grateful. I've sent this piece of quartz because I've found it comforting. I kept it with me all through a difficult dark period in my existence, when I was so bent on revenge at any cost that I didn't believe I'd ever be happy again. I know the crystal's energy. That's why I'm giving it to you, so that it will help you bring this new life into the world. Julien and I hope to be there for the birth.

Much love, Jeanette

Carol was touched by this woman she didn't know, a woman who was a blood drinker. When she looked up she felt tears in her eyes.

'Jeanette's special herself,' Chloe said. 'She travelled a long hard road. Some never even begin the journey, let alone find the right path.'

Carol sighed. She didn't feel so distant from Chloe now. It suddenly didn't make much difference what she was. Maybe they had more in common than she thought.

'Chloe, what are you, and Karl and Gerlinde and André? If vampire isn't the right word, what is?'

'Not everything can be described in a word.'

'You're not dead, are you?'

Chloe laughed. 'That's a very convenient way for mortals to understand us. Death is just a change of form. What happens to us is more along the lines of a transformation.'

'Would you explain that?'

'Well, if you had read the old alchemical texts, which, of course, very few even know of let alone have seen – naturally they're all in Latin and Greek – you might understand the nature of transformation. In a real sense it's a magical process. Just think of your pregnancy. A sperm and ova come together, two separate things, and create a third thing, distinct, neither one nor the other but encompassing both, changing both. That's transformation, when one thing changes into another because it is penetrated by an influence beyond understanding. Call it magic, God, life. I believe they're all the same.'

'You can say the word "God"?'

Chloe laughed again. 'And why not? Do you really believe we're spawns of Satan? We're just beings of this earth, with our powers and our limitations. We're like mortals but greater than mortals. We too have our strengths and weaknesses.'

'André doesn't seem to have any weaknesses.'

Chloe shook her head. She took one of Carol's hands in hers. 'Oh he has. It's just that you can't understand them. Our way is so different from yours, although we look like your kind and, to a large extent, act like your kind. But there is no mistaking us. From your end you can't clearly see the differences. But from ours, well, sometimes we can hardly remember the similarities.'

Carol thought about what Chloe had said. 'Is it painful?'

'Is what painful?'

'This change. The transformation.'

'I suppose change is always painful, in some way. In order to move to another house you must leave the one you're familiar with. You may be leaving something behind you can't bear to part with.'

'Doesn't it bother you, drinking blood?'

'No more than it bothers most mortals to eat a cow or a pig or even a dog in some instances. And mortals have been known to eat each other. Perhaps it bothers us less because we're more aware of what we do. And too, for most of us killing is a choice. Restraint is difficult to learn but in the long run it's a good safeguard. And it humanizes us.'

'Humanizes? I thought you're superior to human beings. I get the idea you, well, André anyway, despises us.'

'We are superior, as humans are because consciousness makes you superior to other animals. But we need to remember that we share the same earth with you. It's enough that your kind sleep-walks through life, refusing to acknowledge the existence of, the essential equality of, other creatures. Such mindlessness may well destroy us all. Those among us with any awareness are driven to responsibility. We refuse to share the guilt of unconsciousness.'

Carol thought for a moment. 'Chloe, there's one thing I just don't understand. You're pretty stable. So is Gerlinde. And Karl. But André, he's all over the map.'

'It seems that way to you because you're so close. The nature of your relationship is symbiotic.'

'I don't feel close to him. And how's it symbiotic? Okay, he wants my blood, but what do I get?'

'A good question to ask yourself. What are you getting?'

'Nothing that I can see. I feel like André and I are from different planets.'

'That may be how you feel but there's something else working. He was only able to impregnate you because of a psychic connection. You may not see or understand what it is. Maybe no one can. But it's there, between the two of you, I'm sure of it.'

'But he's back and forth. Kind one minute, an infantile despot the next. A benevolent dictator at the best of times, a callous bastard at the worst. Why?'

'André is young. I've told you that.'

'But Gerlinde said she's the most recent convert in the house and was made or transformed or whatever you call it in the fifties. I don't know exactly how old André is but he's been around at least as long yet he acts like a kid.'

'André is a child, in many ways. I've known him from birth. His father and I were very close. I loved his mother too.'

Carol stared at Chloe. 'Who made André a blood drinker?'

'I did.'

'Why?'

'I think you will need to ask André that.'

'Who turned you into one?'

'I couldn't tell you.'

Carol was a little startled that she was actually talking as though they *were* vampires. Certainly Chloe believed everything she said. The idea that it could all be true suddenly struck Carol for the first time. What if they were another species? Like vampires. She was silent for a while, but finally asked, 'You told me none of you can interfere with André . . .'

'We cannot interfere with one another.'

'Why not? If you're all so conscious, how could you sit back and let André hurt me?'

'That was some time ago, Carol.'

'I'm not just talking about the physical, and you know it. You're avoiding my question.'

Chloe stared at her for a long moment. 'You see us as a group and in fact we call ourselves a community, but that community is made up of strong individuals, fiercely independent. Our code of non-interference is imbedded in our genetic make-up – we cannot go against our basic nature. Many animals are the same way. It's not uncommon.'

'It's because you see us as food, isn't it? Like two dogs fighting over a bone. The weaker one backs off, the strongest one gets to eat.'

'That's a stark perception, Carol, but I cannot tell you it's entirely unfounded. If you were one of us, things would be different and you would see things differently. But you're not one of us. I'm not certain I can explain this to you. But what are you really concerned about?'

Carol thought for a moment. 'What's André's problem?'

'I'm not sure he has a problem, just growing pains.'

Carol shook her head. 'If there's any pain in his growing, it's what he inflicts on me.'

Chloe patted Carol's hand before releasing it. She stood. 'I hear the car. I'll make some fennel tea and send it up later. That should help your stomach before you sleep. And Carol, try not to worry so much. It won't do you any good.'

'You mean me or the baby?'

'I mean you and André and your miraculous creation.'

A minute later Carol heard the car's tires on the gravel driveway. There was silence then a door opened and closed. She marvelled at Chloe's acute hearing.

'What's that?' André asked as soon as he came in.

'It's a piece of crystal Jeanette sent me. To help with the delivery. And other things. That's a phantom inside.'

He held the quartz in front of the lamp. 'Looks like a foetus.' He handed her back the wand.

Carol returned it to the gilt, silver and ebony box and closed the lid. Carefully she retied the ribbons. When she looked up, André was watching her, his smoke-grey eyes intense and incomprehensible. He reached out a hand and said softly, 'Come upstairs.'

THIRTEEN

By the fifth month Carol's belly was big, her breasts large and her nipples constantly sore. The larger she got the more pressure there was on her kidneys and she had to urinate frequently, which was sometimes inconvenient. The sickness had stopped but she still felt tired a lot of the time and irritable and generally emotionally unstable. But despite all this she had blossomed. Often her cheeks were rosy, her eyes bright and she looked filled out. She knew she was now more of a woman and less of a girl.

One evening in September when the humidity had dropped, which Carol felt to be a gift from the gods, she and Gerlinde headed into Bordeaux for a late movie. They went in the green Mercedes, the top down. Gerlinde drove, her short red hair blown all over by the wind. She was wearing a bright chartreuse sleeveless dress with a mini skirt and was what Gerlinde herself would have termed a 'knockout'. Carol leaned her head back against the headrest. She felt good. Really good.

'You know, kiddo, I envy you,' Gerlinde said suddenly.

'Me? Because of the baby?'

'Yeah. I mean, I'll never have that experience – giving birth.'

'Do you want a baby?'

'Well, I'll have yours.'

Carol sat up. 'What do you mean?'

Gerlinde glanced at her. 'Well, you know, when you leave. We'll all be raising the kid. I guess I'll be like a mother.'

Carol was a little shocked. It just struck her now, although of course she'd known all along that she would be giving up the child. The idea had not bothered her until this moment. She told herself she was just being sentimental; how could she form any attachment? But what Gerlinde said grated.

'Hey, kiddo, wanna hear some stories about my immoral mortal existence?'

'Sure,' Carol said, laughing at this girl who looked younger than herself. 'Tell me about the fabulous fifties.'

'Well, they weren't all that fabulous, at least not until I got hep. Know the term?'

'You mean hip? It's from the sixties, right? The Beatles, the Stones, you know, the hippies.'

'No way! I'm talking *hep*. The word goes back to the twenties and thirties and the black jazz musicians in Chicago. You oughta ask André about it. Those were some of his favourite times. But he likes the present too.'

This was one of the few things Carol had learned about André's past. All he ever talked about was his life now, and the others carefully avoided her questions or were just more interested in talking about themselves.

'Anyhow,' Gerlinde continued, 'I was twenty and in Berlin and it was 1958, and there were terrific joints downtown to go to where painters and writers and musicians went – we called it a scene, imported direct from New York. The Artists' Hut was one and The Other End, I think that's how it's translated from German. We were beats, the beat generation. Beatniks, the mags called us.'

Carol looked across at Gerlinde and laughed. 'I can see it. You dressed in black pantyhose.'

'What pantyhose? They hadn't been invented yet. But I wore the uniform, a black garter belt, black underwear, black stockings with seams – straight black skirt, tight black turtle-neck sweater and, you guessed it, black stilettos. It was *de rigueur*. I wore my hair long then, straight down my back to my waist, parted down the middle, and heavy eye make-up, white lipstick and chunky lucite earrings. And I acted cool, which is to say intellectual.' Gerlinde laughed. 'I'll tell you, kiddo, I had so much fun then. Of course, youth always creates some kind of scene for itself, like the hippies, the punks, the new-wave kids. But this scene was more exclusive, at least in Berlin. It wasn't that big – there couldn't have been more than a hundred of us at the most. Naturally we were outside the mainstream, that's a must. The guys wore black too, and berets, and played the bongos at the clubs, recited poetry that made no sense and the rest of us would sit there, coolly snapping our fingers. That's the way we applauded.'

Carol laughed. 'Were you an artist too?'

'Sure. Wasn't everybody? I still paint. Hey, if you're interested, I'll take you to my studio and show you my stuff sometime – it's just across the hallway from your room.'

Carol shifted uncomfortably. 'I'd love to see your work, but André told me not to try to go into any of the other rooms on the second floor.'

'He's such a tight-ass. I'm not supposed to take you there because he doesn't trust you. He thinks you'll tell people about us when you go, not that anyone would believe you. "Château of the Vampires"', she said with a Transylvanian accent.

Carol giggled.

'André thinks the less you know, the better. But how earth shattering could it be if I show you a couple of canvasses.'

'How did you meet Karl?'

Gerlinde smiled her crooked little smile. 'He was a beat, or that's what he told me at first. I had my own pad. Oh, Carol, it was fabulous! Everything was red or black, the walls, what little furniture I had. I made a table out of a door – the knob was still on – and the walls were plastered with all kinds of art work – my stuff and the paintings and drawings of friends. I loved that place!' she cried enthusiastically.

'Anyway, I met Karl at *The Other End* one night. I noticed right away that he didn't drink – beer or anything. He had a great line, though. He was writing a book, the story of creation as seen through the eyes of the first single-celled life form, which, of course, kept changing because the life form kept dividing. He told me he needed to fast so he could always stay in contact with the microscopic world. He was an intellectual, an existentialist, and he raved about Gide and Kafka and Camus and this French guy, Alfred Jarry, who wrote *Le Surmâle*, that's Supermale, and was into something called pataphysiques, which I've never been able to figure out – has something to do with what is but not the real way it got there. I thought Karl was cute and a little nuts. And he was a terrific lover, fun to be with, and different – most of the guys then were either too square or real dopes. I didn't find out he was the way he is until two years after I'd met him.'

'Two years? Didn't he try to take your blood?'

'Sure he tried. And sometimes did. I was a wild kid and ready to do anything at least once. He convinced me that if he took a little of my blood our sex-life would be even better, and the germs in my body would mix with his and he'd have these terrific insights into the germ world and it would help his writing. Well, I was a sucker for art then.'

Carol was killing herself laughing. She wiped the tears

from her eyes. 'How did you find out he was, you know, a vampire?'

'One night he just confessed. Of course I didn't believe him, even though I knew he was really weird. I mean, in two years I'd never seen him eat or drink – except for water and my blood – and he only came by at night. Also, he wouldn't tell me where he lived. But by then he was my main course, as we used to say, and I just accepted him. Everybody in our scene was strange so he wasn't that odd, really. And he was amazingly romantic. He used to tell me I had bedroom eyes.' Gerlinde batted her lashes a couple of times.

'Anyway, we went to see this new British film that was all the rage – Christopher Lee in *Horror of Dracula*. Afterwards I joked, 'Hey, Karl, maybe he's a relative of yours'. He looked at me kind of funny and then told me what he was and that's why he'd been taking my blood. Of course I thought he was kidding. I went around calling him *der Nosferatu* – that's German for the undead – for about a week after that. And then one night he made me listen to him. He showed me his teeth which, believe it or not, I had never realized were so long. He explained his life, in detail, and little things started to make sense. He was so intense. He told me he wanted me to be with him, like him, for eternity and that he could make me that way but he would only do it if I agreed. He said he'd give me time to think about it. If I said okay, great. If I said no, he'd leave and I'd never see him again because it would be too dangerous to stick around with someone knowing what he was, and too painful for him because I'd be near and he couldn't have me and I'd grow old and die. I tell you, kiddo, when he left I was shaking like a leaf.'

'I can imagine,' Carol said. He's so different from André, she thought. Karl was nice to Gerlinde, unthreatening. She wondered what was in her own karma that she'd hooked up with such a sadist.

'Well, two weeks went by, hell for both of us,' Gerlinde continued. 'I thought about it and thought about it. I couldn't decide if I was nuts or he was or what. I tried talking to my girlfriends but they just laughed in my face. He's neurotic, Blanche, they said. *A Streetcar Named Desire* was big then too. Anyway, he came back because he couldn't stay away and I realized I'd missed him as much as he'd missed me and, well, our hormones were working overtime and we made out and screwed and it was great and then, well, one thing led to another and I said yes. It's kinda like a marriage.'

'Have you ever regretted it?'

'Not yet. I've got everything I want.'

'But doesn't it bother you sometimes – the blood I mean. I've seen you when you're hungry. You look starved and in pain. All of you look that way, although I haven't seen Chloe hungry.'

'Chloe's better at controlling it than the rest of us. She's been around longer. But no, it doesn't wig me out. It's not too different from eating food.'

'I've never been hungry enough that I'd think about killing,' Carol said.

They stared at one another.

'I've never killed anybody,' Gerlinde said.

'But you live off human beings.'

'Look. If you were in the woods you'd have to catch something and kill it to survive, right? You wouldn't think twice because it's different from you – lower on the food chain. But there's all these steps between you and the food, so when you get a slab of hamburger you don't even recognize it as meat. We don't have so many systems in place. We've got some, though, frozen stuff, just in case. But I tell you, it tastes a hell of a lot better right from the old vein. It's like the taste of spinach picked fresh from the garden, which I used to be crazy about, and canned stuff.

You guys can't even tell the difference anymore, you're so used to it. But we still can.'

'Ugh!' Carol said, sticking out her tongue. 'Please don't mention spinach in any form. That and liver. If I never see either one again it'll be too soon.'

They arrived in the city and parked. The theatre was a repertory cinema on the elegant Place Gambatta and the film, *Casablanca*, which they'd both seen before and had loved.

'Want some popcorn?'

'No, thanks. Maybe a drink, though, but I'll probably have to pee.'

Gerlinde bought her a Perrier and they got seats in the middle, halfway down. The two women attracted a lot of attention.

Gerlinde, of course, was mesmerizingly attractive and drew plenty of looks from both men and women. And Carol too, despite her pregnant state, looked good. She wore new clothes that André had gotten for her – another short skirt and an oversized top that disguised her stomach.

As Sam played *As Time Goes By* for Rick, Carol leaned over. 'I hate to do this to you, but if I don't get to the bathroom quickly they'll make us mop up the floor.'

'Do you know where it is?'

'Back by the candy counter?'

'Yeah. Go on.'

Without you? Carol almost asked. But something made her stay silent. She eased her way along the aisle and hurried to the back, just making the door marked '*femmes*'. It was the first time she'd been out of range of any of them. When she came out of the washroom, impulsively she turned and ran out of the theatre.

This is crazy, she thought. Gerlinde will surely find me. And I feel mean, betraying her trust like this. But Carol didn't turn back. She wasn't quite sure where she was in the city but just kept going, as fast as she could.

A few blocks away at an intersection she stopped to catch her breath. This area seemed familiar. She looked in all four directions. To the left, maybe two streets away, she saw the promenade in the old part of town that André loved to frequent. Without any hesitation she ran in the opposite direction. She asked directions once, calming herself to enter a store, but the clerk didn't understand her, so she braced herself and asked a policeman.

'What's the best road to Paris?'

'*Paris?*'

'Highway. Auto. Burrrrr,' she made a sound and mimed turning a steering wheel.

'*Ah, la route de Paris?*'

He pointed in the direction she had already been going in and said a couple of sentences. She heard the words 'Pont de Pierre'.

'How long? *Un, deux, trois?*'

He nodded understanding. '*Cinq rues.*' He held up five fingers and counted them off to be sure she understood.

Carol thanked him profusely then hurried away. When she got to the bridge she crossed it, walking, nearly running, until she reached the highway. There was a complicated overlap of roads and it took a while to get on the right one, the road with the sign that said *Paris, 250 kilometres*. As soon as she held out her thumb a car stopped. Inside sat a middle-aged couple, tourists. 'Do you speak English?'

'Nothing but,' the hefty woman said. 'Y'all goin' to gay Paree? Hop in then. We're headin' there ourselves.'

Carol was so relieved she almost cried.

The couple, Judy and Bill Harris, Americans from Texas on a month's holiday, drove her all the way into the city. She concocted a story because the truth seemed too bizarre and she didn't want them to think she was crazy. She told them she was travelling alone, a stupid thing to do, and that she had been robbed in Bordeaux and needed to get back to Paris to find the girl she'd been travelling with and borrow the money to call home. Yes, she was pregnant. They wanted to know about the father.

'He's dead. I'm alone.'

It sounded so ridiculous they believed her. They bought her dinner and handed her fifty dollars. Carol was more than grateful. She hugged them, took their address, and promised to repay the money.

She found a phone and immediately placed a call to Philadelphia.

'Hello.' It was Phillip's voice. He sounded exhausted. She had only called because Rob and he were living together and she didn't know who else to ask for help.

'Phillip, it's Carol. I'm in France. This is an emergency or I wouldn't have phoned. I need to talk to Rob.'

There was a pause. 'I guess you didn't get my letter. Rob died four months ago. Carol, I'm not in any shape to help anybody. Whatever it is, babe, you'll have to deal with it yourself.' He hung up on her.

Carol felt frantic. The shock of Rob's death left her stunned. But she had no time to grieve now. Her first priority was to find enough money to get back to the States. She thought through her friends and realized that she'd let them all slip away in the last year and a half. She wasn't sure if any of them would help her now.

It took an hour to reach the information operator in Philadelphia, but finally she got the number of an actress at the theatre company where she had worked, a woman named Mary Skiving, a woman she had considered a friend until she found out Rob had been fucking her.

Mary was surprised to hear from her, but turned a bit cool when Carol asked to borrow five hundred dollars. 'Please, Mary, for God's sake, help me. I know this doesn't make sense, but I'll explain everything when I get there and I'll pay you back, right away, I promise. I'm desperate. The US Embassy's closed Sundays or I'd get help there. I don't have any money or even a passport. If I don't get out of France today something terrible will happen to me. I know I sound paranoid but I'm not. Just help me, please. I don't know who else to turn to.'

Finally, reluctantly, Mary agreed to wire the money in the morning, when the bank opened.

Carol spent that night sitting in the telegraph office on the Place de la Bourse. Because she didn't have any ID, it took longer for the money to be released. Finally, at two the following afternoon, she had cash in her hands.

Carol took a taxi to Charles-de-Gaulle Airport and booked the next available flight to Kennedy, which would not depart until ten thirty p.m. – she put herself on stand-by for an earlier flight. She had forty dollars left over. It was going to be a long wait, but there was nothing she could do about it.

She camped out in the airport near the ladies room in order to make frequent trips. She tried to sleep, but the seats were too uncomfortable and her back ached. Eventually, though, she managed to doze off and dreamed . . .

A pack of four wolves circles her. Terror! One large wolf. Gaping jaw, sharp teeth. Grey eyes, the pupils pinpoints. Those eyes mesmerize. She spins in a circle, looking for a way out, feeling dizzy. An aeroplane appears. She begins to board, but instead of the steps going up they lead down, under the ground. She turns, struggling to run back up, but the steps become a ramp. She slides down fast, faster, plunging towards darkness. Right into the mouth of the grey-eyed wolf!

Carol jolted awake, slick with sweat, her heart pounding loud in her ears. She glanced at the clock, trying to orient herself. Eight p.m. She was being paged over the loudspeaker.

FOURTEEN

'I'm Carol Robins,' she told the woman at the Centre d'Information who was busy with two phones and three irate Frenchmen. The woman looked blankly at Carol for a second then pointed towards a door.

'Is it a call?' Carol asked. Because if it isn't I'm not going in there, she thought. She knew it was dangerous booking under her real name, but she'd have a hard enough time getting into the States without a passport. A fake name would just be one more thing to explain.

The woman struggled to be pleasant to one of the businessmen who was yelling at her. A third phone rang. 'Is there a call for me?' Carol interrupted.

The woman gave her a hostile look and pointed. 'In there. Mary Skiving.'

Carol made her way to the door. She opened it and walked in. Gerlinde stood by the window, arms folded across her chest. 'Bad move, kiddo.'

Carol sucked in her lower lip. She left the door open. 'How did you find me?'

'Easy. The cop you talked to about getting to Paris? He talked to an inspector and, well . . .'

Carol knew that could only be Inspector LePage.

'We knew you were broke so you'd have to wire someone for cash. I talked the guy at the telegraph office into telling me who sent you the dough. Then I called the airport and found out you're booked on the ten thirty and flew right up.' She shook her head from side to side and Carol thought she looked sad. 'Trust ain't that easy to build but it sure is a breeze to knock down.'

'Gerlinde, I didn't want to hurt you or betray you.' She took a few steps into the room. 'But I can't do this. I just can't go back. I'm sorry.'

'Not half as sorry as you're going to be!' She turned at the sound of André's voice. He slammed the door closed and moved towards her slowly. His eyes resembled the eyes of the wolf she had just dreamed about, mesmerizing. She felt like prey that had been patiently and methodically trapped and now the predator moves in for the kill. His tense body looked close to being out of control. She had never seen such black rage on anyone's face. The grey of his eyes had turned steely and hate-filled. His lips had parted, exposing the tips of menacing fangs. Carol was horrified by what she saw and at the same time unable to do anything to defend herself.

'Salope!' He slapped her so hard she fell onto the floor.

'Hey! Hold it, André! You'll kill her or hurt the kid. Get a grip!'

'Fuck you! I know how to handle this, you don't. You're the one who was stupid enough to let her escape.'

'Maybe so, but what you're doing is only going to make things worse. Just cool your heels a bit. Wait 'till we get back and talk to Chloe, okay?'

Carol was jerked to her feet. She felt groggy, stunned and couldn't see very clearly. But she saw his face in her face;

his darkness penetrated her. He grabbed her by the throat and shoved her up against the wall.

'You better listen to me, bitch, because you're out of chances and I'm out of patience. The three of us leave here and you keep your mouth shut. The slightest move or gesture, if you even think about escaping again, first you can watch what I do to anybody you involve and then you can experience first hand what I do to you. And you'd better believe that I'll do it slowly and painfully and you'll be begging for death.'

He shoved her towards the door.

'Just a minute,' Gerlinde said. 'Let me wipe the blood from the kid's mouth.' She used her finger and licked it.

They walked through the airport, one on each side of Carol, holding her arms securely. She felt dazed, unable to comprehend how she could again be trapped by him. She went over and over in her mind what she had done and what she should have done differently.

André bought three tickets and they caught a late flight to Mérignac, arriving in Bordeaux just before midnight.

Outside the airport it was drizzling. The silver limo pulled up to the entrance immediately. Gerlinde got in, then Carol and finally André. As soon as the door closed they drove off.

On the flight as well as now in the car no one spoke. André faced front in a silent rage. Carol cowered in the middle. Gerlinde stared out the side window. At one point, as they neared the house, the redhead tried to talk to Carol but André cut her short.

'Shut up!'

'Hey, babe, this is Gerlinde here. You don't hold any papers on this model.'

'But I own her,' he said, meaning Carol, his voice intimidating.

Gerlinde stayed quiet.

Carol was despondent. Tears pushed their way out of her eyes but she was afraid to make a sound, afraid André would hit her if she did. She bit down on her finger to stifle her feelings. But things were bleak. She didn't know just what would happen but she did know that she'd really messed up. Four more months with them and now I'll be a prisoner with no rights and have to deal with André's wrath besides, she thought gloomily.

When they reached the château, the three immediately went into the living room where Chloe and Karl waited, both looking serious. André shoved Carol into a chair.

'Carol, why?' Chloe asked immediately, her voice distant, her look cool, as though she, too, was hurt and disappointed.

Carol shook her head, afraid to speak, afraid she would cry. She knew she would get no sympathy.

'What's the difference why?' André said angrily. 'She ran away, we found her and now we keep her locked up until the birth. And after that,' he looked down at her, 'a little revenge.'

'Carol,' Chloe said, 'you gave us your word.'

'I told you I wouldn't hurt myself or the baby. I haven't,' she explained in a small voice.

'But you ran away.'

'She's scared to have the kid,' Gerlinde said.

'Why don't you just shut up!' André turned on Gerlinde. 'Screw off!'

'You're as crazy as she is.'

'If you didn't scare her half to death she wouldn't have run away.'

'Obviously I haven't frightened her enough since she didn't think twice about using you.'

'What did you expect? You try to control her every move. No female of any species would put up with that for long.'

'You think you can empathize with her but she manipulated you, just the way she's manipulated all of us. You cunts are all alike.'

Before Carol's eyes, Gerlinde's face changed. Her face seemed to narrow and pale, her features became exaggerated, her eyes glistened. Her lips spread apart and two razor-sharp teeth emerged. A low hiss came from her. Suddenly Gerlinde slashed André across the face with her nails. Carol didn't see him move, but instantly Karl was between them, keeping Gerlinde back with one hand and holding the other up to André. 'Let it go,' he said to André.

André's body quivered with tension. Before Carol's startled eyes the gashes on his cheek were already healing. He spoke in a low strained voice, 'You'd better keep her under control, Karl, or she'll have your balls on a silver platter, just like Ariel.'

'Look,' Karl said, reasonably to both of them, 'we have a problem here we should be directing our attention to and that's how are we going to deal with this for the next . . .'

'I told you,' André cut him off harshly, 'we lock her up. She belongs to me and that's what I want so that's the way it will be. *C'est fini!*'

He grabbed Carol's arm, hoisted her to her feet and pulled her across the room.

'André, don't hurt her or you'll hurt the child,' Chloe warned, but he only laughed bitterly.

He was using such force that near the top of the stairs Carol fell, but he just dragged her up the rest of the steps and along the hallway. While he opened the door she got to her feet. Once inside the room he locked the door, ripped her clothes off and shoved her down onto the bed. Within seconds he had her handcuffed to the brass posts. Now she let the tears flow freely; there didn't seem any point in holding back.

'Get used to it! This is how you'll live for the next four months. I'll keep you chained here like a dog. You'll eat, sleep and live in this bed. I'll fuck you as often as I have to to keep the baby alive. And whenever you get even an inch out of line you'll have me to deal with. You couldn't play it easy with me. Well now we'll play hardball!'

He slammed the door on his way out. Carol sobbed uncontrollably.

FIFTEEN

Over the next four days Carol plunged from misery to despair. During the daytime she cried herself to sleep. At night she endured being used sexually. Throughout it all she was handcuffed to the bed on her back, unable to even turn onto her sides. Apparently André did have free reign to treat her any way he liked because she saw none of the others, only the maid – who seemed hardly aware of her – and him.

Food was placed on the pillow next to her face and she ate with only her mouth, feeding like an animal. She ate almost nothing. He let her up three times each night to use the bathroom, but it wasn't enough and during the day the bedding became saturated with urine that she was forced to lie in. Every evening the maid turned the mattress. The room stank.

But worse than all the pain and discomfort was the aching loneliness. André never talked to her now, not even to threaten her. Carol talked to herself to stay awake and sang herself to sleep. She tried to remember movies she had seen, books she'd read and conversations she'd had, but she wasn't an excessively introspective person by nature and found it painful. This was not like the year she'd isolated herself. This was his doing. She was going crazy and knew she had to try to save herself.

Five nights after she had been returned to the château he cuffed only one of her wrists to the bed, which meant she could sit and stand. She took this as a sign. He was at the door, his hand on the knob.

'I think all this is hurting the baby. I need exercise. Can we make some kind of deal?' She tried to keep her voice calm, reasonable, the way a lawyer would present a fact, without self-serving emotion. They were the first words she'd spoken to him.

He turned. In that moment she realized she had either taken the wrong approach or that any approach at all was a mistake. His eyes hardened and his flesh paled; it appeared more stretched across the bone; a gargoyle mask. A low animal sound seeped out of him. When Carol saw his teeth she screamed.

In a flash he was on her, choking her. She struggled to pry his powerful fingers from her windpipe. Her scream cut off, she could only thrash wildly, desperate to breathe.

As they pulled him off her, she dragged in air. Her throat felt crushed. It took all three of them to hold him. She could clearly see him struggling to get at her, a demon from Hell, unleashed, bent on her destruction.

Terrifying sounds came out of Carol's mouth, something between a shriek and a yell. It was as though a voice far off, and not her own, made all this racket. The bed filled with excrement and the food tray overturned, adding to the mess.

'Geez, her neck!' she heard Gerlinde say.

'Bring me some warm water. You'd better call the doctor, too. Karl, take André out of here!' Chloe instructed.

The women worked on her for half an hour while Carol convulsed, frothing at the mouth. When the doctor arrived he gave her an injection that knocked her out almost immediately. She heard Chloe ask, '*Le bébé?*' but she didn't hear the answer.

When Carol woke she felt dead. Or more, that something inside her had died. She lay in bed watching and listening, an invisible barrier separating her from everything that went on. She floated somewhere just outside her skin. It wasn't uncomfortable and she decided to stay right where she was.

Every night all night long Chloe and Gerlinde and sometimes Karl sat with her. She never saw André now. The three of them gave her injections, cleaned her up, talked to her, tried to feed her and get her out of bed and generally discussed her condition in worried voices. They made efforts to bring her out, but Carol did not respond.

'Carol, why don't you try to get up tonight?'

She stared at Chloe, who seemed to be covered in a thin layer of gauze. Her face was soft-looking, her voice concerned. It meant nothing to Carol.

Gerlinde appeared behind her. 'Come on, kiddo. You're okay. Snap out of it. We just want to help.' And then she said to Chloe, 'I think this is serious.'

Carol wouldn't chew. They hooked her up to nutrients that flowed intravenously and also force-fed her, tilting her head back, inserting a large funnel into her mouth and then pushing puréed food, like baby food, through it, the way geese are fed to enlarge their livers. They had to change her sheets all the time because she wouldn't move, even to the bathroom, although she was no longer locked to the bed. She viewed them from a far-off place, a place with no attachments, no emotions, no worries, no fears, where nothing mattered. She felt no wants, needs or regrets. She drifted in limbo, unaware if days or weeks had passed.

One night Jeanette appeared in front of her. She looked down at Carol, her face full of concern. 'She won't respond,' Chloe said.

'Yes, I can see. I'm glad you asked me to come. How long's she been like this?'

'Almost a month.'

'What's the doctor say?'

'Shock and depression,' Gerlinde said. 'And she almost had a miscarriage – she was bleeding for a day, but now he thinks that part's okay.'

Carol looked at the faces of the three females hovering above hers. Their words didn't seem to relate to her. What they said sounded funny even, and she was tempted to laugh, but then the impulse passed and she closed her eyes.

Jeanette talked to her off and on during the night but Carol had no desire to respond. Towards morning she heard Jeanette say, 'Look, I don't know what to say about this. But you're right. She could lose the baby. I'm going to phone Julien – he's back in Austria with Claude and Susan – and ask him to come here. I think he might know something the rest of us don't. Anyway, *I'll* feel better if he's here.'

The next night the tall, austere man named Julien came into the room. He stood beside the bed and looked at Carol for a long time without saying a word. His eyes were dark orbs, severe, cold, like black pits leading to oblivion, and Carol could hardly stand looking into them. Her own eyes grew heavy and she had to close them. Every once in a while she opened them again. He was still there.

Later she heard a voice, but she didn't know whose, say, 'Get André in here.' Fear, like a battery being jump-started into life, quivered inside her.

She heard many voices now, whisperings, murmurings,

hissing sounds, sounds of snakes slithering in the grass, worms crawling through corpses. Then words, out of context, 'Punish', 'Bitch', 'Betrayal', 'Drain', 'Baby', the word 'Love' came up again and again, but she didn't know who said what and none of the words meant anything. Someone mentioned hypnosis. Someone else, Chloe, she thought, said, 'The resistance is too deep.' She heard Julien's voice and André's voice and occasionally Karl's. They were speaking French, Julien calmly, steadily, André in tones rising and falling with anger.

Someone reluctantly took hold of her limp hand. She didn't open her eyes. There seemed no need to. Whoever it was sat beside her on the bed, then touched her face. Suddenly she knew it was André. Her heart began to pound quickly, erratically, her breathing became ragged and shallow. Fear washed over her, the first complete emotion she had felt in a long time.

The others were still in the room, she could sense them, but the silence was palpable. He said nothing, just held her hand and stroked her for what seemed like hours while her heart raced along, threatening to overstep its abilities and plunge her into a permanent sleep.

At dawn he picked her up and carried her downstairs. They turned left, through what must have been the dining room, into the kitchen where she had made tea occasionally and then down more steps. She didn't know where she was, but felt afraid to open her eyes to find out.

It was cool here, it felt dark. She heard a key click and the sound of a combination lock, like the kind on a safe, being spun. A door creaked open.

He laid her down and covered her with a quilt, then locked one of her wrists to something wooden, a horizontal bar near her head.

She felt him lie down next to her, up against her. She had an urge to scream, to move away, but was frozen, afraid, her heart thudding heavily in her chest, her breathing stifled, suffocated.

Later, when she felt brave enough to open her eyes, she found herself in complete darkness. The air was cool but not cold on her face; the quilt kept the rest of her warm. She could still feel him up against her, but something had changed. She moved her arm slightly and then she understood. This was his place. It isn't a coffin, she thought, but he sleeps here in the day, like the stone cold dead.

SIXTEEN

The following night André carried her upstairs to the living room.

'Julien has another idea I think is a good one,' Carol heard Jeanette tell the others, listening with her eyes closed.

'He thinks we can't let her keep withdrawing, it's dangerous. We'll tie this loosely around her waist and around the waist of one of us. We can take shifts. At least physically she'll always be connected to someone. Symbolically it's an umbilical cord. But André, you'll have to do most of this.'

Carol heard André arguing in French, his words fast and furious. Julian answered him.

Jeanette tied something around Carol, a rope maybe. 'When you go out of the room you take her with you, everywhere,' Jeanette continued.

'Do you want me to take her up to my victims and introduce her?' André asked sarcastically.

'Stop complaining,' Gerlinde said. 'This is all your fault anyway.'

'No, it's your fault. If you hadn't been suckered she couldn't have run away and . . .'

'All right, you two. I'm sick of this argument,' Karl said.

'Ditto,' Gerlinde added.

'I think we've got to try this,' Jeanette said. 'If she stays withdrawn it will definitely hurt the baby. As it is, I'm afraid that every five years the child will go through a trauma.'

'How come?' Gerlinde asked.

'Well, there's this theory.' It sounded to Carol as though Jeanette had sat down. 'Whatever happens in the womb is reflected throughout a mortal's life, in cycles. For example, if you're born prematurely, then things tend to always feel premature for you.'

'Look,' André interrupted, exasperation in his voice. 'You still haven't told me what I'm supposed to do with this millstone while I'm hunting down blood. I can't drag her around with me.'

'André, since you're her main connection, you're going to have to find a way to alter your attitude,' Chloe said.

'*Mon Dieu!* . . .'

'I'm serious. Of course, it's your choice, but there's no point in doing this if you hate her. She'll feel that and stay withdrawn.'

Carol wanted to tell them that even if he stopped hating her she'd stay withdrawn. She felt safe and comfortable where she was, and she'd never trust him again.

'Chloe's right,' Jeanette said. 'Julien, you know what's going on, tell him.'

Julien's voice was warm and rich, a complete contrast to the way he looked. He was also the opposite of Jeanette. Carol had wondered how the two of them could be together, they were so different. He spoke in English, and she thought he did that so she would understand.

'As we discussed last night, I believe you capable of a variety of emotions, each intense and perhaps many volatile.

You know some of my history and may realize the extent to which I comprehend your situation. If you have felt *l'amour* for this one, I suggest you either resurrect it or accept the loss of the offspring. In my experience, where hate and power rule, there love is lacking. But the results of hate and power are identical, the soul dies. *L'âme se meurt.*'

Carol didn't know why, but if she were going to trust any of these vampires — and she now believed that's just what they were — he would be the one. He spoke from a deeper place than the others. And although she didn't understand what he meant, she instinctively felt his integrity.

The room became silent. Finally André said, 'I want to go out. Will somebody come along and stay with her for a while?'

'I'll come,' Karl said.

Carol felt a tug on the rope around her waist. Then she felt herself lifted. 'Bring a blanket,' André called over her head.

Soon she was in the car, between the two of them. On the drive into town they spoke together in French. She slept and woke in fits and starts. Karl stayed with her while André went to the docks. When he returned, Karl got out of the car.

'Don't wait for me. I'll be down here for a while. Send Gerlinde to meet me at *le Caveau*,' he said, then closed the door. On the return trip to the château André mostly ignored her. But twice he touched her hair and face. Both times a chill passed through her, a chill of terror.

For the next six weeks André stayed tied to her, taking her with him from room to room, place to place. Occasionally one of the others would fill in, but the job was definitely his. Many nights they just lay together in her bed or on a couch where he read or listened to music or wrote reams of what looked like poetry, balling up nineteen out of every twenty sheets of paper in frustration, throwing the failed attempts into the trash and binding the few that he kept in a large cloth book. They watched TV like a regular couple, Carol propped up against him, a life-sized rag doll, wrapped warmly in blankets. During the day he took her to his bed below the house and she lay next to him in complete blackness while he slept.

His room was odd. It was dark most of the time, although occasionally he lit a fire. She never really got a very good look around, but what she did see was intriguing. The place had an art deco feel, silver, black, grey, with chevrons along the walls and angled furniture. The headboard of the bed was black lacquered wood with inlaid silver. Above it hung an Edward Gorey sketch, black and white on grey, of a large dark-winged creature with enormous teeth flying through the night carrying in its arms a victim, a big-eyed pale humanoid of indistinguishable gender. The drop of red at the victim's throat was the only colour in the sketch, or in the room. There were also two couches, tables, books, music, a large fireplace, everything except windows.

Sometimes he lit a hurricane lamp, although she knew the place had electricity because he'd turned the lights on once. But most often he brought her down just at dawn, when he was ready to sleep.

Out of boredom she'd begun walking again, and eating of her own volition. She read books, watched movies, did everything but speak. She refused to communicate verbally with any of them. It was her last stronghold against what she now realized to be the truth – they were all monsters, undead creatures that lived off people like her.

But they continued to talk to her. Even André was starting to converse with her again, although there was an edge to his voice. He also resumed having sex with her. He was not particularly gentle and certainly not romantic, but at least he wasn't brutal. He made efforts to stimulate her so that most of the time what he did didn't hurt. Often he entered her vagina from behind. She was never sure if he thought it was more comfortable for her, if he was trying to humiliate her or if he just couldn't stand to see her face. She never complained but she never let herself enjoy it either. She refused to actively participate.

In her seventh month Carol came down with a fever. It hit without warning. She was in the limo alone with Gerlinde, who was listening to music on a Walkman.

Suddenly Carol felt chilly. Her teeth began to click together and her body shook. Gerlinde looked at her.

Carol watched Gerlinde's face change shape. She started to resemble a brown bear, and then her features re-formed into the way she normally looked. Carol's flesh became burning hot, her lips parched, sweat pouring down her face.

'Hey, kiddo, you're not ill, are you?' Gerlinde asked, her voice worried. 'Here, lie down.' She moved over and made Carol recline, taking her head onto her lap. There was a blanket in the car, and Gerlinde covered her with it and with her own coat. But Carol was cold again, cold into the bone, and shivering.

The door opened and André got in. 'What's up?'

'She's sick. A fever and chills.' André took off his coat too and put it over her, but now Carol was hot again, burning, hallucinating.

'Momma, please let me stay home from school today. I don't feel well,' she said in a little girl's voice.

The car was driving along the highway at a fast clip. She looked around, unsure of where she was. 'Can I have some water?'

André poured some from the tap in the mini bar into a plastic cup. Gerlinde held her head up while she took a sip.

'I'm so hot,' Carol said, trying to brush the coats off.

'Leave them on.' André held his hand on top so she couldn't remove them.

'What a mess,' Gerlinde groaned. 'Just when she was coming out of it. Why do mortals have to get sick all the time? You'd better call home.'

'Rob?' Carol said. She watched him pick up the phone. He turned his blond head and gave her that brilliant smile. She started to cry. 'I didn't know you were dead. Phillip told me. Why didn't you tell me? You never said goodbye!'

She hyperventilated. Suddenly she shivered. 'Cold. I'm so cold.'

André punched a couple of numbers into the phone. 'Carol's sick. I don't know, a fever. High, I think. Get the doctor out. We'll be back in five minutes.'

She was carried up to her room. They piled five blankets on top of her, although the house was warm. Someone made a fire. Carol was only vaguely aware of what was going on. She kept flipping from the present to the past, from burning hot to freezing cold. Hands touched her and voices surrounded her. She remembered seeing the doctor at one point.

'The baby's not going to live,' Carol told him.

'Do not worry, Mademoiselle. Lie quietly and relax. I am giving you this to bring the fever down.'

'My baby's dead. You're not telling me, but I know. It's so hot in here. Open the windows. Please!'

The fever lasted all night. They plied her with liquids, most of which she threw up. They kept her covered with blankets, even though the sheets were drenched with sweat.

'Help me!' she cried when she was cold. 'I'm freezing to death. My bones are cold and I can't get warm.'

When dawn broke, André took her downstairs with him. He plugged in a small room heater and built a fire in the fireplace.

Carol was convinced she wouldn't last the day. She knew the fever was higher than before, her spans of being clear mentally grew increasingly shorter. She saw the end of her life rushing towards her, a life that had not been a happy one.

She looked at André, who was lying beside her not sleeping. The back of his forearm rested across his eyes.

'Kill me,' she whispered. He lifted his arm and turned his head. 'I'm dying anyway. Just this once do something for me.'

He looked startled. 'You're not going to die. You'll be okay tomorrow.' But he sounded unnerved.

'Then make love to me and let me die that way. You've made love to me before, I remember. Just love me this once because no one ever has, and I know you don't but I want to believe it. I want to die believing that someone cares for me.'

'You're hallucinating.' He seemed stunned.

'Make love to me as if you love me.'

He hesitated, but then moved the blankets away from her body. She shivered with cold. 'This isn't a good idea . . .' he began.

A strangling sound came out of her mouth and she grabbed his arm in a vice-like grip. Her eyes burned feverishly, her brain was on fire and she felt crazy.

He touched her body, slick with sweat, and lay on top of her, perhaps as much to warm her as for any other reason. His movements were sluggish, his limbs seemed stiff. He kissed her lips, her hair, the sides of her face and her nipples where the sweat ran in large drops. Slowly he caressed her, penetrating her. She laughed and cried and most of the time didn't even know he was there but talked to the ghosts from her past, telling them all her secrets, the feelings she'd stored up and had never been able to convey.

She wove in and out of reality. But when she was there,

with him, a bitter-sweet awareness of him trying to love her stabbed at her heart. She sobbed uncontrollably; her barren life stretched out before her like a vast unforgiving desert she had wandered. And that arid heat only served to burn away all her illusions.

He wrapped her again in the blankets and held her close all day, she deathly weak, he immobile as a corpse.

SEVENTEEN

The fever broke. The next evening Carol felt weak but alive. The level of tension in the house dropped.

'Kiddo, for a while there I thought you were a goner,' Gerlinde laughed, tucking a blanket around Carol, who was propped on the longest couch. 'Welcome back to the land of the living, or a reasonable facsimile.'

'It's good to be back,' Carol said. 'I feel exhausted but okay.'

'Well, you'll still need to take care of yourself. We don't want a recurrence,' Chloe said.

'God no!' Jeanette agreed. 'We'd run out of ideas.' She stood next to Julien, an arm draped over his shoulders. He held her around the waist.

Everyone was happy, excited, glad Carol had recovered. They crowded around her, all except André, who hung back. He said almost nothing. The look on his face was peculiar. Soon he left the room and she heard the car pull away.

'Well, you're into the eighth month now,' Jeanette said. 'All this will be over for you soon. You must be glad.'

Carol had thought about this all through her with-drawn state and into her illness. There didn't seem to be an easy way to break it to them. 'I want to keep the baby.'

Silence filled the room.

'I know this is awkward, but it's mine. I'll stay here, if you like, or go away. But I want the baby.'

Chloe sat down and looked at her.

Gerlinde whistled. 'Never a dull moment here at Hotel Transylvania.'

'I don't think you know what you're saying,' Jeanette said. 'You're probably still a little feverish.'

'She understands perfectly.' Julien stared at Carol with those same frightening eyes. But Carol thought she detected something else in them, something that may not have been approval but wasn't rejection.

'Carol, that's impossible.' Chloe interrupted her thoughts.

'We've explained why the baby must grow up with us,' Karl said.

'And,' Chloe added, 'your influence would only distort things. It would be torture for the child, being torn in two directions. It will be difficult enough for him or her to decide which path to take. Ours is superior and we want to encourage that. You're just experiencing natural maternal feelings, but they'll pass.'

'No, they won't!' Carol said adamantly. 'I didn't just decide this tonight, I've been thinking about it for months. I won't part with my baby. There's nothing you can do to make me.'

Everyone fell silent again, apparently unable to think of anything else to say, except for Gerlinde. 'I'll break out the plasma.'

When André returned, Chloe took him aside and told him the news. He wasn't nearly as surprised as the others nor, oddly enough, as negative.

'There's only one way,' he told Carol, 'and I don't even know if I'm for it. You'll have to become like us.'

'Become a vampire?'

'I wish you wouldn't use that word,' Gerlinde said. 'It gives me the creeps.'

'The process is relatively painless, at least for you,' André said.

'But I don't want that. I want to be the way I am and raise my child to be human.'

'Out of the question!' Karl said.

'Think about it,' André told her. 'You've got time. We've all got time to decide. It's the only way.'

Carol noticed Julien watching the scene from a removed but interested position. Their eyes met. She had the feeling he saw something that no one else in the room did, including her.

Throughout her eighth month and into her ninth, the physical discomfort became incredible. Carol found she couldn't sit or stand for long periods and felt constantly restless. Her back ached continually.

She rarely left the house now except for a daily walk along the beach. Because she was so uncomfortable, she spent days in her room rather than with André, so that she could move around. During the evening hours she was either downstairs with the others or alone with him.

Their sex life had discontinued; no position was comfortable and Chloe voiced fears that the baby might be injured. But they had plenty of physical contact and talked a lot, more than before. Some change had come over him, something inexplicable, and Carol had no idea what it was. He was kind to her, which was all she cared about. He did everything he could for her, little things like backrubs and holding her and generally exhibiting a caring when he talked to her that she hadn't experienced from him before. He was as protective and concerned for her welfare now as he had once been threatening. Carol would never have called what was between them love, at least from her end. But she had to admit to herself that a certain closeness had developed and she was starting to see him in a fuller light, despite the fact that she now understood that he was something entirely different from her. He was showing her more than his defensiveness.

But the nearer Carol got to the delivery, the more worried she became. 'What if the baby comes in the day, when I'm alone?'

'The labour will be at least twelve hours. We'll call the doctor to be with you if we can't be,' Chloe reassured her.

'But what if something happens? Complications.'

'I have a strong sense everything will be all right,' Jeanette said. 'You've gone through the worst of it. You're strong and this is, after all, just a baby. Our cells are different from yours, but there are similarities too. You're not delivering an ogre.'

Carol went into labour at six o'clock on New Year's Eve. The women stayed with her throughout the night and the men were nearby. André was more nervous than she would have expected. He popped in and out of the room constantly, agitated, excited.

'Daddy of Darkness,' Gerlinde kept calling him, making Carol laugh during the contractions.

The pain was more extreme than anything she had known, excruciating in fact. Chloe had taught her how to breathe through it but she needed constant coaching because she had a tendency to hold her breath when it got bad. She found she couldn't lie down much, but preferred to either be on her knees or squat with the help of two of them holding her up.

'That's the way we did it in my day,' Chloe said, lifting Carol up into a squat.

Carol groaned out the words, 'When was your day?'

'The early nineteenth century. I was born here in Bordeaux in 1803.'

'Did you have any children?' Tears and sweat dripped off Carol's face and Jeanette wiped the moisture away.

'Yes, ten.'

'Ten? You went through this ten times?'

'I went through it twelve times but two of my babies were still-born.'

'And the others?' Carol gasped.

Someone said, 'Breathe,' and she began panting.

'The others lived their lives, some brief, some long, and then died.'

'What about your husband?'

'He died too.'

Jeanette massaged Carol's lower back but she could barely feel it. Contractions hit about thirty minutes apart.

'Kiddo, I don't know how to break it to you, but we have to go now. The sun's coming up,' Gerlinde said, kissing her on the cheek. 'I'm sorry.'

'You're going to leave? All of you? You can't leave me!'

'The doctor's downstairs, he'll be with you throughout the delivery,' Jeanette said. 'If you want, maybe Julien will stay too. He's the only one of us who can tolerate being awake in the day. Do you want me to ask him?'

'Please!' Carol said. Things had been going okay because she didn't feel alone. Panic set in.

'In this warmer is a bottle of blood,' Chloe instructed. 'It's at body temperature. If the baby comes before sunset, feed some of this to him or her. Don't worry, there shouldn't be any problems with digestion. Just make sure you don't give the child any of the colostrum from your body.'

Carol nodded that she understood.

One by one they left her. 'Chin up, kiddo. This'll be over before you know it and then you'll have a squalling baby bloodsucker to deal with.' Gerlinde kissed her and Carol laughed.

'Remember, feed the child only blood,' Karl reminded her. He touched her face gently.

Chloe hugged her. 'You'll be fine. There's no sign of complications. The doctor has said so and I can tell. Remember, I've had much experience.'

There were pink-tinged tears in Jeanette's eyes as she hugged Carol. And Carol found herself crying. The crystal wand lay on the table beside the bed and throughout the night, off and on, she had held it just because it reminded her of Jeanette. She picked it up now.

The others left so that she and André could be alone. He cupped her chin in his hand. 'I'd be here if I could. We all would.'

'I know,' she cried.

He kissed her face all over and then her lips. Carol threw her arms around his neck, wanting him to stay. 'Hold me,' she sobbed, and he did, until light that must have been from the sun broke through the tinted window in a pencil thin opening between the drapes. He removed her arms and backed towards the door, blowing her kisses.

Carol was alone for half a minute before Julien came in. Immediately he sealed the opening in the heavy drapes. His movements were stilted and very slow. He turned off all lights except for the one near the bed and sat in a chair in the darkest corner of the room. 'The doctor will attend you shortly.'

'Thanks for staying with me,' she said.

'I have never witnessed a birth. It will be an experience, for both of us,' he told her.

Another contraction hit and she tried to remember to breathe. She grabbed onto the top bar at the foot of the bed, groaning and panting in short breaths until the pain passed.

By three in the afternoon Carol was on the point of collapse, almost hoping that the child would simply die or she would die or preferably both of them, and quickly. But just as she was ready to throw in the towel, he came into the world.

He was tiny, red and shrivelled, covered in mucus. The doctor cleaned him off, cleared his nose and mouth and, once the placenta was released, placed him on Carol's stomach. He did not put drops in the closed eyes nor sever the cord right away, as per Chloe's instructions.

The infant's dark hair curled in wisps, more the colour of André's than her own. His little hands bunched into tiny fists as he lay still, sleeping off the trauma of birth, comfortable on top of her.

She couldn't keep from touching him, marvelling at him, hardly believing he had come from her body. His skin felt soft, warm, a little moist, and he was so fragile and helpless there was no question of her not loving him. Without thinking, she put him to her breast. She noticed Julien watching her silently, but he said nothing about the pre-milk. The baby's little lips puckered automatically and he sucked in the nourishment with a look of total contentment on his face. More than ever she knew she couldn't part with him.

At sunset the others filtered into the room. They washed and dressed her and congratulated her. Everyone wanted to hold him.

'Has he had any blood yet?' Chloe asked.

'No, not yet,' Carol said. She didn't mention the colostrum.

Chloe fed him the warm blood and he swallowed it as eagerly as he'd drunk from Carol, which both alarmed and confused her.

When André came in he was mute. He held the child, staring at him in much the same way Carol had. And when he glanced at Carol she could tell he too was in awe of how he could have had a part in creating such a tiny perfect being.

The baby, now wrapped in warm cotton clothes, was placed in Carol's arms and she drifted off to sleep. When she awoke, André was lying beside her and the baby was gone. 'Where is he?'

'Gerlinde's got him downstairs.'

'I want him!'

'Later. You're exhausted. You need to recover. They'll take good care of him.'

'You'll give him back?'

'Tonight, yes. And tomorrow night. But after that . . .'

'After that what?'

'After that you've got to decide if you want to stay or go.'

'I just want my baby. I want to be with him. I won't give him up.'

'Then you'll have to go through the change. I've decided I'll do it.'

'No, I don't want that!'

He sat up abruptly. 'Carol, I told you, it's the only way. We can't let you raise him as a mortal. He stays here with us. If you want to stay you have to change. Otherwise, you'll have to leave.'

She started to get out of bed.

'Where do you think you're going?' As he pulled her back she struggled.

'I want my baby! Nobody's going to stop me!'

'Stay here. I told you, Gerlinde will bring him back in an hour or so. Turn over. I'll rub your back.'

'You're lying to me! You won't give him back.' Her voice rose; she felt out of control.

André snapped, 'I don't lie. I don't have to. I said you'll get him back later and you will. I've been straight with you all along. You're the one who's been decep-tive.'

She struggled against him but he was a wall. Finally he

just pressed her down firmly against the mattress, his face over hers. 'Stop it! Now!'

Carol wailed. Chloe hurried into the room.

'What's going on?'

'She's hysterical.'

Chloe gave her an injection of something and within a minute Carol felt calmer, duller, as though things didn't matter so much.

'Gerlinde will bring the baby soon,' Chloe assured her. 'But you get some more sleep first, all right?'

André said nothing, just watched her, his eyes laced with distrust.

She nodded. Her words slurred, 'And can I have him tomorrow? Please. Just tomorrow?'

'Yes,' Chloe answered. 'Then we'll see.'

Carol closed her eyes. You'll be the ones to see, she thought as she drifted off, because I'm not going to part with my baby or let myself be turned into a vampire.

EIGHTEEN

They gave Carol the baby that night and the next, as promised. Just after sunrise the following day, when the two of them were alone, Carol reached beneath the mattress for the dinner fork she'd hidden there. She went to one of the windows and began hacking at the putty holding the plexiglass into the window frame, a job she'd started two days before. In her condition the work went slowly and was tiring; she pulled up a chair so she could sit while chipping along the bottom and sides. The old putty flaked. Rotting wood allowed her to pry the frame away in spots.

She slammed the chair against the slightly curved plexiglass. The inner window had been inserted concave, so that it could not be popped in from outside, for security. Likely it hadn't occurred to the installers that someone would want to pop it from the inside out. She bashed the plexiglass again and again until it smashed against the outer tinted glass, which finally shattered. Cool air streamed into the room. If an alarm had been triggered, it was silent.

She fed the baby, then dressed him warmly and bound him

tightly to her body. She dressed herself in all the clothes she could find and wrapped a blanket around her shoulders.

By sheets tied together Carol lowered herself and the baby out the window and to the ground. Quietly she skirted the garage, not wanting to alert the driver or the maid, either of whom might be peering out a window. Inside she found four cars but couldn't see any keys. She gave up that idea and headed quickly down the gravel driveway on foot, immediately regretting that she only had two pairs of socks and her flat summer shoes to wear. Eventually she came to the highway.

It was January and cold out. A thin layer of snow, the first she'd seen in Bordeaux, covered the ground and the pine trees which had been planted to counteract the sandy soil. Dense air created fog off the Atlantic that shrouded the vineyards. Another pair of socks doubled as gloves, but her hands were cold too. Very few cars came by but whenever one did she stuck out her thumb. Because of the fog, they didn't see her until they were long past. She knew she looked ragged and strange, no coat, dressed in layers of summer and fall clothing and a blanket; the baby was completely hidden. No one stopped.

At a service station she used the bathroom and fed the baby – her body was now producing milk. She washed out his soiled diaper and put it on the radiator to dry. There had only been one spare in the room, the rest were elsewhere in the house; she had to make do.

They rested for over an hour in the warmth. Carol was chilly but the baby seemed to be okay. She had to take care of herself or she wouldn't be able to take care of him.

She finally got a ride, almost to Bordeaux and, about noon, as she approached the city, she got a short lift past the downtown to the outskirts. She wasn't sure where to go. She didn't want to head for Paris again because they would think of that right away. But where else? She decided to try for the ferry to England at Le Havre and got directions at a gas station. She would keep out of London so they'd have a harder time finding her. She didn't want to think too much into the future.

Carol got two long rides. She felt like a waif standing by the road, baby in arms. By late in the afternoon it began to snow, forcing her into another service station. Even though the owner didn't speak English, he took pity on her. He gave her coffee to drink and half a stick of bread with a piece of meat in it and let her sit in the office. She fed the baby, changed him again, tried to warm up and worried about the sky, which was growing darker.

Reluctant to leave the security she'd found, Carol pulled herself up and got back on the highway. She saw a sign ahead: *Rouen*. Further along another – *Le Havre* – *150 KM*. She was almost at the ferry. She had no idea how she'd pay the fare without money, but refused to worry about it. There were too many other things to think of.

The baby didn't cry. She kept him well covered and warm, close to her heart. He seemed content. She peeked at him often, each time knowing he was more than worth the risk she was taking and that no sacrifice was too great. 'We're together,' she told him. 'That's all that matters.'

As darkness took the sky, snow fell heavily. She knew she must have looked like a bag lady because traffic was heavy but cars refused to stop.

She was just fifty kilometres from the ferry but had to rest once more. The birth had exhausted her. Her legs ached and her feet and her hands had numbed. And the baby needed to be fed and changed again.

She took an exit, one of the ones with a service station half a mile from the highway, the only building on the road. But when she neared the building she almost cried. The side facing the road looked okay, but the rest had been boarded up and the exterior had blackened from fire. She didn't know what to do, keep on this road and try to make it to the closest town or go on to the ferry. She needed to stop, but didn't know how she could. Suddenly the baby began to whimper.

'Hush, my little darling,' she whispered. 'I'll figure this out, somehow.' She rocked him gently and sang him a little song her mother had sung to her about all the pretty little horses.

It occurred to her that if she could pry one of the boards away from the garage they could at least get out of the cold and snow for a while. She pulled on the two by four but it wouldn't budge. She thought she just might manage to squeeze through one window. She pulled the remaining shards of broken glass away and struggled through the opening.

Inside, the place smelled charred. Carol walked carefully among the debris in the blackness. Something scurried past her foot, then she banged her shin and yelled out. The baby whimpered again.

She felt along the wall and finally came to a counter of some kind. Below that she touched a metal box on the floor. She tested it with the weight of her leg, reasonably sure it would hold her.

She sat down, exhausted. It was cold in here too, but not like outside. Her toes and fingers had lost feeling and she recognized that as a bad sign. She rubbed them, trying to bring back the circulation. Eventually they began to hurt, pins and needles, and she felt pretty sure she'd be okay.

Carol opened her many shirts and guided the baby's lips to her breast. He drank with a lot of energy, apparently hungry. She was hungry herself, weak, depleted, afraid she was bleeding a little too. But she didn't want to stay here in this dark, dirty place with little warmth. And it wasn't safe. She didn't know if any place was safe, but getting out of France would be a major step towards feeling secure. 'Just a rest, that's all we can afford,' she told her baby. 'We'll be in Le Havre soon.' If luck was on her side, which so far she felt it hadn't been, they would get a ride right to the ferry. And then? She directed her attention to rubbing her feet.

She pulled the dirty diaper off the baby and put the clean dry one on, all in darkness, by touch. She tossed the soiled one away; she couldn't wash it and didn't want to carry it. And then she picked herself up and crawled out through the window, heading back to the highway.

She had almost reached the ramp when a car screeched off the exit and raced towards her – it was the silver limo!

Carol ran for the entrance ramp, stumbling in the snow, but the car was on her. André jumped out.

She tried to run in the other direction but he caught her.

'Let me go,' she screamed. 'I'll kill you if you try to take him!'

She fought him as he pushed her into the backseat.

Gerlinde and Karl were there, both looking pale and upset.

Tears of frustration poured from Carol's eyes. She clutched the baby to her. 'You'll have to kill me to get him because I don't want to live without him.'

No one said anything while she sobbed. Finally she wiped her eyes. 'How did you find me this time?'

'A man at the service station. You asked him how far to Le Havre,' Karl said. Red eyed and hostile, she glared first at him, then Gerlinde. Finally she turned to André. His mask-like face hid emotion.

'Let us go, please!' she cried to him. 'I'm begging you, even though I know you hate being begged. I'll get on my knees if I have to. Please, if you're capable of mercy, show me some.'

'I can't do that,' he said, his voice even, compressed.

'Then make me into a vampire. I won't leave him. I'll do anything to be with him.'

'I can't do that either.'

She felt shocked to her bones. 'But why? You said you would, I just had to make a choice. I'm choosing.'

'We can't trust you. I can't trust you. You've let me down too many times.'

'*I've* let *you* down. What are you talking about?'

'Your lies make you dangerous.'

'Gerlinde, help me!' Carol pleaded with the redhead.

'Kiddo, I would if I could. Everybody agreed, you'd put us in danger.' She looked away.

André picked up the phone and spoke in French to the driver. They were on the highway again, heading towards the ferry.

'Where are you taking me?'

'We'll put you on the early boat, give you some money, you can go where you like,' Karl said.

'No! I won't leave him. I'll kill him before I hand him over to you.'

'Karl!' André nodded at him. The two held Carol. She struggled ferociously, screaming, trying to bite them, but André held her head back by the hair. Gerlinde unwrapped the baby and took him away from her.

The baby whimpered and Carol screamed.

At the dock, Karl got out to purchase a one-way ticket and Gerlinde took the baby into the washroom to feed and change him.

Carol sat alone in the car with André. She couldn't stop sobbing. 'I promise I won't do anything to hurt any of you. Please, don't do this to me. Make me into one of you so I can stay. I'll do anything you want. Anything. Please!'

'It's out of my hands,' he told her. 'The others have a say now too. We have to protect ourselves and the child. But even if they said yes I wouldn't agree. I couldn't,' he added.

'How can you be so heartless? How can you face yourself?'

He said nothing, just took a large wad of money from his wallet and tucked it into her shirt pocket then handed her a short jacket. 'Put this on.' She didn't move so he stuffed her arms into it. 'Karl's taken your suitcase on already. Your passport's inside. I'll give you an injection so you'll stay calm.'

She looked at him in horror. 'You're going to kill me with an overdose of drugs so you can steal my baby!'

'It's only a simple tranquillizer, to relax you.'

They struggled, but he soon forced her face down onto the seat and held her tightly while he injected the valium into a vein in her neck. It took effect almost immediately. Her breathing grew heavy. She became incoherent. He turned her head and made her meet his eyes. And where the drug stopped, André's power began; he eliminated a slice of her memory.

They walked her onto the ferry, the red-headed woman charming the ticket taker, flirting in French. Carol was propped up in a corner. She saw and heard all that was happening but could not move or speak. Silent tears poured down her cheeks; she had no idea why.

'Good luck, kiddo,' the woman said, almost crying herself. 'I'll take real good care of him, I promise. We all will.'

Take care of who? Carol wondered.

The woman and a man left, but the man with grey eyes stayed until the whistle blew. He stood and looked at her one last time, almost reluctant to leave, as if he wanted to say or do something. But then he too was gone.

The drug began to wear off as the boat reached Portsmouth. Disoriented, Carol disembarked and presented her passport to the customs official. A red-faced man asked, 'Reason for visiting England?'

'I . . . I don't have a reason,' she said. She did not know what she was doing here or why she had come.

'Are you on holiday, then?'

'Yes,' she said automatically.

Passport returned, she found the nearest bench and sat down to think. She felt as if she had been in a car accident and shock had set in. She was stunned without understanding why. She tried to calm herself and clear her mind so she could think about how she got here.

Obviously, I just passed through the arrival gate from France, she thought. She had no memory of ever being in France and yet she had just stepped off the boat from Le Havre. And her ticket said so. She looked down – she was dressed strangely, old summer shoes, a hunting jacket, and underneath layers of clothing, none of which she could recall owning. This must be a dream, she thought. What else could it be?

Her body ached, particularly her stomach, which looked a bit swollen. She felt exhausted, as if she had been through some colossal physical undertaking, like running a marathon. Suddenly she became terrified. Nothing made any sense. It was as though she had gone to sleep in her bed at home in Philadelphia and woken in another time and place. How could that happen?

Panic set in. She opened her suitcase and rummaged through it, looking for clues. She recognized every piece of clothing, every toilet article. Under the hunting jacket, inside a shirt pocket she found a large sum of cash – in US dollars. She didn't count it, but just a quick flip through told her there was a lot more money than she had ever had in one shot in her life. She searched her shoulder bag and discovered her passport. At least I haven't lost all of my memory, she thought. She recognized her name and the photo and her home address. The date stamped inside indicated she'd arrived in Paris – an arrival she did not remember. A quick look at a newspaper told her about nine months had elapsed from when she had supposedly entered France until now. Nine months. Long enough to have a baby. Why did I think that, she wondered, and suddenly, inexplicably, tears flooded her eyes and washed down her cheeks.

'Dearie, are you all right?'

A soft-faced old woman bent over her.

'No. No, I'm not all right,' Carol sobbed. 'I don't know where I am or how I got here.'

'Why, you're in Portsmouth, of course. At the ferry dock. You arrived on that very boat out there – I was on the same one.'

The woman handed Carol a tissue, which she dabbed at her eyes. 'I can't remember getting on the boat.'

'That's not surprising. You were so tired you could hardly keep to your feet. Your friend helped you on board, he did. Sat with you until the boat left.'

'Friend?'

'Yes. Frenchman, by the look of him. Not bad looking. Him and the couple with the baby.'

Carol shook her head rapidly, as if trying to deny something, but what? She burst into tears. 'I don't remember any of that. I don't even know why I'm crying.'

By the time security arrived, Carol was out of control. An ambulance took her to a local hospital where lithium carbonate was pumped into her continually for nearly a week. Different people asked her a lot of questions: about the money; about having given birth recently; about a relative in the US who might be contacted. She had no answers for the first two questions, but for the last she told them to phone Rob.

During her second week at the hospital, the fog she floated in began to lift enough that she got a grip on where she was and why she was there.

One morning she sat across the desk from a psychiatrist, who introduced himself as Dr Stanton – his name-tag confirmed that. He said, 'Apparently you've recently given birth, yet you have no memory of that experience. Why do you suppose that is?'

'I don't know that I've given birth,' she told him.

He looked at her seriously. 'You've been examined, Miss Robins. There's no doubt about it.'

Carol's hands trembled and clasped together.

'It appears the baby was born out of wedlock, perhaps still-born, or died after birth?'

Carol felt panic well up. 'I . . . I don't know.'

'Did you sell the baby?'

She felt too horrified to react. 'Have you phoned Rob? My ex-husband?'

'I telephoned last week. You realize, of course, that he died last May.'

Carol looked at him dumbly. 'Rob's dead? No, I didn't know.'

'A Mr Phillip Mullins assured me he wrote you a letter informing you of the death – through American Express.'

Carol said nothing.

'He also told me you telephoned him from Paris four months ago where he gave you the same information. And you sounded desperate.'

'I don't remember.'

'Repressing unpleasant memories is common, particularly when guilt is part of the equation. You were found with a rather large sum of cash – ninety thousand US dollars or thereabouts. About forty thousand pounds.'

Carol didn't know how to respond. She just didn't remember. This was like the time she had undergone anaesthetics for dental surgery. One minute she was counting backwards from ten and had reached eight, and the next second she was awake. Not only was there no memory of the two hours during which the surgery took place, but it was as though that time span did not exist. She hadn't even dreamed. Her brain had simply shut down and time ceased to be. But this was worse, far worse. Nine months of her life was missing. Rob was dead. Apparently she had given birth to a child and acquired a large sum of money, in France, a country she had no recall about visiting.

'Miss Robins, I can't help you. First off, you're not my patient and hence cannot stay in this hospital. Secondly, you are a visitor to Britain. This is neither the time nor the place to undergo an extended period of therapy. I strongly suggest to you that you return to Philadelphia and seek psychiatric help there. I can provide you with the name of a competent therapist trained in memory retrieval. I don't believe any more can be accomplished from here, and it would certainly benefit you to be in familiar and no doubt comforting surroundings.'

Carol had another week to think about it before the hospital released her. The week after that she was on a plane for Philadelphia. But the lack of feeling about France or what might have occurred there held the same space in her heart as would a memory itself. Her body was returning to the United States, but the rest of her had not left Europe.

Part III

'We are all in the gutter, but some
of us are looking at the stars.'
– Oscar Wilde (*Lady Windermere's Fan*)

NINETEEN

'Carol, I want you to focus on this gold pendulum. Watch how the light flickers off the metal. Your mind is relaxing, your eyelids are growing heavy. Let them close. That's it, continue to breathe easily and naturally. Picture in your mind the Ocean. The Atlantic. Calm. Eternal.'

The tranquil voice of Rene Curtis blended with the serene image of the ocean Carol had just formed in her mind. The same image she had created weekly over the last eight years of therapy during sessions with Dr Curtis.

'Good. You're relaxed and safe. Tell me where you see the ocean from. Where are you now?'

Carol looked out the window at the grey water. 'I'm in the room. In the house.'

'The house in France?'

'Yes.'

'Where in France is that house located?'

'I . . . I don't know.'

'Describe the room, as you have before.'

Carol saw herself turn. She related the colours of the

two-sectioned room. The fireplace. The furniture. The bed. Suddenly she felt nervous.

'All right, just relax. Breath deeply. You're safe. I'm here with you. Tell me about the bed.'

'It's large. A brass bed. The sheets and duvet are floral.'

'You have slept in this bed.'

'Yes.'

'And had sex in this bed.'

Again Carol felt nervous. 'I . . . I had sex in this bed.' This was all ground she had covered before, remnants of memories revived after years of hard work.

'With who?'

'I . . . I don't remember.' She felt frightened and just wanted to get away.

'All right. Take in deep breaths, through your nose and out your mouth. I'm not going to let anyone hurt you. Tell me what else you remember about this bed.'

Carol in her mind stood and stared at the bed. 'It's mine,' she said, but she still didn't know why she felt that.

'I want you to walk over to the bed and run your hands over the sheets. Will you do that for me?'

Carol nodded. She moved towards the bed and her finger tips touched soft cotton percale for the hundredth time.

'Sit down on the bed.'

Carol sat. The mattress sagged a little beneath her. All this felt very familiar.

'Carol, lie down on top of the bed.'

That sour fear again, rising from her stomach.

'You're perfectly safe. We're just remembering, as we did the other times. Lie down.'

Tentatively Carol lay on top of the comforter. She stared up at the textured pastel ceiling. The mattress beneath her felt firm. It held her up. She did not immediately fall through space as she had on other occasions when Rene had brought her back here through the power of hypnosis.

'Good. How do you feel?'

'Afraid.'

'Of what?'

'Him.'

'Who?'

Carol shook her head. She ran her hands along the sheets and under the soft pillows until she touched the cool metal bedstead. The moment her fingers reacted to the cold, she reacted emotionally. Her breathing quickened. 'He chained me here. To this bed. He kept me a prisoner and used me!'

'Yes, you've remembered that before. Did anything else happen in this bed?'

She gasped for air, feeling like a fish out of water, unable to breathe, unable to swallow. The room spun into darkness. A black hole sucked at her, drawing her, spinning her like water swirling down a drain.

'Carol, stay with me! What else happened here?'

She screamed.

'Carol! Carol! Listen to me. You're with me, in my office. Open your eyes.'

The moment she opened her eyes she felt safe again. Sweat glued her blouse to her body and her hair to her neck and forehead. Her heartbeat was too fast. But she remembered.

She turned to Rene Curtis. 'I had a baby in that bed.'

Rene nodded. 'A boy or a girl?'

'A boy, I think. I don't know why I think that.'

'It's all right. We'll go with your intuition. What happened to the baby?'

Carol shook her head.

'Was the baby born dead?'

'No.'

'How do you know that?'

'I don't know.'

'Did the baby die later?'

She shook her head again.

'Do you remember where that house is located?'

Carol cried, overwhelmed with grief and hopelessness. 'No. No I don't. I'll never remember.'

Rene Curtis rubbed her arm gently and smoothed her hair back, then picked up the ever-present 'Fifty-is-Killing-Me' mug filled with icy liquid and sipped. 'You'll remember. You've come a long way. Eight years ago you didn't even recall going to France and now you've put quite a few pieces of the puzzle together. It just takes time. We're dealing with major trauma.'

'Time,' Carol said bleakly. She felt, for some reason, that time was running out.

She thought back over the eight years since she'd returned to Philadelphia and all the things she'd had to cope with. Rob's death, and, just after her return, Phillip's. And then the death of her mother. Psychotic breaks meant she couldn't work in any high stress position. She'd found a job at the Emerald Theatre, doing sets and props for plays before they went to Broadway, or just as they left for a tour. With Rene's help, she'd invested the eighty thousand dollars that remained at a good return rate. The interest paid for the therapy, which had progressed slowly, at least from Carol's perspective. It had taken her a long time to trust Rene – to trust anyone. What memories they'd managed to retrieve had begun coming back over the last three years, and those fragments unearthed only through gargantuan efforts.

She lived a quiet, uneventful life, at least in the real world. No close friends. All her non-working time was spent doing therapy or reading. Every night when the sun set, an inexplicable terror climbed over her and clung to her body until the sun rose. And in this room she faced demons and terrors on a weekly basis that no human being should have to encounter. Without Rene she knew she couldn't have done it.

A year ago she had tested positive as an HIV carrier.

They told her she might never contract AIDS – but there was no way to be certain. That alone gave time a sharp focus. But there was something else, some other reason why time felt crucial, that she couldn't identify but which kept her pushing ahead. Carol worked intensely in her sessions to break through the solid granite that entombed all that had happened to her in France, in that house on the Atlantic Ocean, with a man she could not remember, other than knowing she was deathly afraid of him. Still, one thing she now knew for certain was what had been confirmed by half a dozen doctors who had examined her: she had given birth to a baby during her time in France. And she could confirm that experience herself, through a recaptured memory. But where was that child now?

'I'm afraid that's all we have time for today,' Rene said.

Carol blew her nose and sat up. 'Thanks, Rene. I guess we made a little progress.'

'A big leap, I'd call it.'

Carol headed to the coat rack beside the door and began slipping on her boots.

'If you hold on, I'll go down with you.'

They took the elevator together to the main floor. Rene, a stylish woman with blonde hair and slim hips in her early fifties, had an easy attitude that Carol admired, even envied; she took good care of herself and seemed to live a happy and charmed life.

'Well, I'm off to dinner with "the girls",' Rene said. 'Old college friends, and I do mean "old". God, how time flies. We meet once a year and eat too much and drink too much,' she held up a long brown paper bag, 'and never get to talk enough. They're all looking pretty used, to tell the truth. Not me, of course,' she laughed and winked, the skin at the corner of her eye crinkling.

'What's in the bag?' Carol asked.

'Wine.' Rene looked at her. 'Why?'

'I don't know. What kind.'

'Red.' She opened the bag and took the bottle out. She read the label and turned it so Carol could see.

It was as though a gust of hot air hit, nearly knocking Carol off her feet; she fell against the mirrored back wall of the elevator.

'Carol, what is it?'

'That's where the house is!'

Rene looked at the label again. 'Bordeaux? Are you sure?'

'I'm positive.'

TWENTY

Six months after Carol discovered where she had been kept prisoner in France, other memories emerged at an accelerated pace, including – a street that resembled a circus; the Royal Medoc Hotel, where she may have stayed; and something about an old man being murdered, at night, and a lot of blood. When the Emerald Theatre closed for the entire month of August, with Rene's blessing Carol took her first vacation in eight years. She went back to Bordeaux.

As she strolled the streets of the downtown, of the harbour, little almost-memories made her brain itch the way the biting mosquitoes infected her skin. And as she scratched at the recollections, they swelled and became more prominent. So many things looked familiar; déjà vu continually caught her off guard.

She stayed at the Royal Medoc Hotel. Of course, there were no records from eight years before, and few of the staff that had worked there then worked there now. None of those who had recognized Carol.

During her years back in Philadelphia she had studied

French, sensing that she would be returning to this country some day; now the language came in handy, although she could speak and read far better than she could understand.

Bordeaux was not on the Atlantic Ocean but near it; she must have been kept outside the city itself, but where? She bought a detailed map of the region and studied it, searching for clues, but none were apparent.

Carol went to police headquarters her second day in the city. It took a while to explain what she wanted once she found the right person, but finally she managed to convey that she needed to research an old case: the murder of a man in Bordeaux approximately eight years ago. At night.

The word officious had never taken on such a full meaning as when she dealt with French bureaucrats. She knew that without the contact people in high places that Rene's connections had provided, all this would have taken far longer, or been impossible. As it was, it took a week to get permission to search the records, another three days to scan computer records of murders and violent crimes for the time period she was in France, and another four days to muddle through the procedures she must follow to actually handle those records not on computer. And after all of this searching, she came up with nothing.

If she had witnessed a murder, that murder was not recorded in the police records of this city. Either the murder had been committed elsewhere, her tortured psyche had fabricated it or, the most frightening scenario, the files had been expunged. She wanted to speak with any police investigators who had been in charge of homicide that year. Eventually she had an appointment with an Inspector LePage.

They met in an interrogation room, a stark drab setting with only a table and three chairs, and nothing more. The moment Carol saw LePage she remembered him.

'We've met before.'

His face and the tone of his voice betrayed nothing. 'I could not say, Mademoiselle. In my line of work I meet many people.'

'No, I'm sure I've met you.' He had aged but looked essentially the same as the snapshot now restored in her mental photo album. Even his mannerisms were familiar.

He lit a cigarette and watched her through the haze of acrid smoke he blew in her direction. Then finally, in that same impassive voice, said, 'I am a busy man. How may I help you, Mademoiselle?'

'Inspector, I was in Bordeaux eight years ago, between April and early January. I believe I witnessed a murder. An old man was killed.'

'Did you report this crime at that time?'

'I may have, I'm not sure.'

'I see.' He walked out of the office, leaving the door open. Within a minute he returned with paper and pencil in hand. 'I will take your report.'

'I'm not here to report a murder, Inspector, I'm here to find out if it *was* reported.'

He placed the paper and pencil on the table.

Before he could say anything more, Carol said, 'Look, I know this sounds strange, but I've lost much of my memory of the time I was in Bordeaux.'

He crossed his arms over his chest, the cigarette caught between his lips.

'I believe I was held captive here, for nine months.' She didn't want to tell him more than she had to; he looked sceptical enough. 'I also believe I may have witnessed a murder. There's nothing in the police records to indicate that an old man was killed, but that's what I remember.'

He tilted his chair back and stared at her, squinting his eyes through the smoke curling up his face.

'I needed to talk with someone who was around then, who may remember.'

'Mademoiselle, if the murder is not listed in the police files, I do not see how I may help you.'

'Do you recall a murder about eight years ago? An old man? Killed at night? By the water. A lot of blood?'

'No.'

He answered too quickly. Did that mean he thought she was crazy, or that he was hiding something? It could mean he just didn't remember.

'Maybe an attempted murder then.'

'Mademoiselle Robins, if you have searched the records and have not found what you are seeking, I do not know how I may contribute to your cause.'

This was getting nowhere. He wasn't going to help her. She stood. 'Inspector, I'm not sure what you do or don't know but I need to tell you this: something happened to me here in Bordeaux, so horrifying that I can't recall most of it. It's eaten up my life trying to remember.'

'Sometimes the past is best left where it is.'

'And sometimes it's important to dredge it up. It is for me. If anything comes to you that you think might help me, I'm staying at the Royal Medoc Hotel.'

She thought she saw his eyelid twitch.

That night Carol put in a call to Rene at her office – the five hour time difference meant it was only three in the afternoon in Philadelphia. She told her all that had transpired.

'Tomorrow I'm going to rent another car and drive along the ocean again – it's not far from Bordeaux. I'll try the north shore this time. Maybe something will come back to me.'

'Carol, how are you doing emotionally?'

'Not bad. Not as bad as I thought. I wish I had more time here – my plane flies out in three days. There's something here, Rene, I can feel it. I know I've been here before. I remember LePage. I remember so many things. I just can't put it all together.'

The familiar and comforting sound of ice clinking against Rene's mug calmed her. 'If you need me, call. Anytime. My service can page me, just leave a number and when you can be reached. And Carol? Be careful. Whatever happened to you there shocked you into repressing the memory of it. Take it slowly.'

Saturday morning Carol rented a Peugeot and took highway D1 northwest. Vineyards lined the road, the vines pregnant with ripe grapes trellised in neat rows. This was her third trip along the coast in the last two weeks and each time she had an unmistakable feeling of having seen all this before, over and over, through a couple of seasons. And yet she also realized this scene was typical wine country, depicted in brochures and travel magazines and on postcards. Specifics, though, confirmed her experience.

As she approached the resort town of Soulac-sur-Mer, something about the name affected her emotionally. Like a homing pigeon, she turned in that direction by instinct.

As she drove along the coast, the grey-blue ocean over-lapped the image she visualized during hypnosis. The houses were old and solid, again, familiar-looking wood and stone structures with large entrances and dormer windows. Many were visible from the road, but many were not, and she drove down smaller gravel roads and into private driveways. Nothing clicked until she turned down one curving road that lead to a large fieldstone château.

Carol slammed on the breaks. It was as if a ghost suddenly materialized in front of her. This was where she had been kept. She knew it as surely as she knew her own name.

When she calmed enough to think clearly, she stepped on the gas pedal gently, inching the car along. No vehicles blocked the driveway but the doors on the enormous garage were closed. She had to be careful.

Her body trembled. I should go back, she told herself. I

shouldn't be here alone. This could be very dangerous. I don't know who I'm dealing with. But she had come too far and had been through too much to retreat now.

She left the keys in the car, the door open and the engine running, in case she needed to get out of here fast. She knocked at the front door. No one answered.

She moved to one of the front windows of the three storey house and peered in. An empty room. As she moved around the main floor, looking through windows at empty spaces, no drapes, no furniture, she recognized the infrastructure: the shape of rooms, doorways, fireplaces. The garage too was empty. This château had been abandoned.

Back at the house she tried to break a window. The outer windows, tinted, broke easily, but the inner windows were apparently shatterproof. Both the front and back doors had been bolted securely. After an hour of trying, she realized she couldn't do this today.

Carol drove back to Bordeaux and stopped at a real estate office. An agent looked up the house on her computer. It had been empty for just over seven years. It was not for sale. The owner was a number, a corporation with the head office in Switzerland, the building managed by a local management firm.

Carol glanced at her watch. It was too late in the day to contact the management company and too late in terms of Carol's return flight to take the legal route. She stopped at a hardware store and made a few purchases.

First thing in the morning she returned to the house at Soulac-sur-Mer. Gaining entry was easy – it was as though she remembered doing this before: chipping away at the window frame, gouging out putty. The window refused to pop inward but after hours of work she managed to pry it out.

Even the air inside the house smelled familiar. She explored the main floor; in her mind she could see the layout of furniture in this room and remembered a large sculpture of a girl riding a dolphin that sat on a round coffee table. The room felt dense with memories, all of which pressed at her brain for admittance. She went up to the third floor first and decided to work her way down to the basement where the idea of being below ground in darkness unnerved her.

Nothing on the third floor rang a bell. Maybe she had never been here! That thought confused her, especially because the living room swelled with images. The second floor registered the same as the third. Almost. Similar doors leading to similar rooms that meant nothing to her – it felt like she'd never been inside them, just like the floor above. Until she reached the last room.

When Carol stepped inside, she broke the seal of a part of her brain that had been locked away. Memories pulsed with the speed of light, overwhelming her. Her body slid to the floor. She hyperventilated. Flashes of a fire in the fireplace; the window she stared out so often; the bed, its placement, waking and sleeping, where and how she had been chained to it. Suddenly her body ached. She convulsed and deep moans poured from between her trembling lips.

She clearly remembered them: Chloe; Gerlinde; Karl; Jeannette and Julien and their children. Her baby. Her tiny vulnerable infant with dark wisps of hair, puckered skin, sucking milk from her breast. Sucking a bottle of blood! And then, as if an invisible door suddenly crashed open in her mind, a face seared its way out of the darkness and into her consciousness. Black hair with grey at the temples. Unnaturally pale skin. Teeth like fangs. Steely eyes emitting unrestrained fury.

Carol screamed as all the doors banged open at once, splintering, slicing her soul with too many shards of memory, too fast. She felt herself fragmenting. She could not stop the screaming of a dozen voices.

TWENTY-ONE

'All right, Carol, let's go back to the room again, from before the Bordeaux police found you in the house and sent you home – thank God they didn't charge you with breaking and entering! Tell me everything that happened. Leave nothing out.'

'Rene, we've been over this a million times since I got back. I don't even know where to begin. It's as though it all came to me in one big explosion.'

'It's going to take a while to sort everything out, but if we don't keep at it, we'll never cement the pieces into their right places. Let me just refill my mug and we'll begin. I've got an extra hour free today, if you need it.'

Over the next months Carol told Rene about meeting André, about returning to Bordeaux when she discovered she was pregnant, and running away twice. And how he had taken her baby away from her and used drugs and a powerful form of hypnosis to lock her away from her own experiences. And through it all, as Carol worked through the intense emotions connected to each layer of her ordeal, one burning thought kept her sane, a thought she often repeated to Rene: 'I'm going to find my son and get him away from that nest of vampires.'

'Carol, we've discussed this ad nauseam. I think you've made them into vampires. It's a quick and easy way to identify what's repellent to you. There are elements of truth in this vampire thing but we have to crack the symbolism. It's a metaphor. Your first instincts were likely correct; they're a blood cult. Maybe into black magic, that sort of thing. This André impregnated you, probably drugged you. Even when you remember the entire thing, you may not know why.'

'Rene, I'm not wrong about this. And I know how fantastic it sounds. Maybe vampire isn't the right word, but what they are isn't human.'

'Their *actions* are inhuman.'

'*They* aren't human. It's not just that they drink blood, and the things André did to me. I don't know how to convey it, Rene. They're like a super species, with their own rules and codes that have nothing to do with what we human beings do.'

'And you find them appealing as well as repellent.'

Carol's jaw tightened. 'Whose side are you on?'

'Yours, of course. But Carol, I've listened for months as you've gone over this material again and again and to tell you the truth, you make them sound, well, attractive.' She took a sip and ice cubes clicked against the ceramic mug.

'No. That's not true. Physically attractive, maybe, but they're killers.'

'We're all killers, aren't we?'

'You sound like Gerlinde.'

'All right, let's look at this logically. They use hypnosis, but so do I. Am I a vampire?'

'Do you drink blood?'

'Bloody Marys.'

Carol felt frustrated. 'Well, *they* drink blood.'

'All right, which ones have you seen drinking blood? Gerlinde? Karl? Chloe? The ones from out of town?'

'No. Just André.'

'And that was when?'

'On the dock. The night he killed the carpenter.'

'It was dark. The police said there was no evidence of that. And you checked the records – there was no murder. They told you they drink blood, but does that make it so?'

Carol said nothing but she felt hostile.

'Do they live forever?'

'I don't know. They live a long time.'

'You only believe that because they told you they live a long time.'

'I think they do. There's something archaic about them, the way they think and act, as if they're from another time. Gerlinde, for example. It's as though she's really from the fifties.'

'Well, maybe she is.'

'Oh, Rene, she'd be your age and she looks like she's in her early twenties.'

'Who's her surgeon?'

'I'm serious. And there's one in particular, Julien. If you saw him – it's as though he really is from the Middle Ages. And there's something more about him. It's as though he possesses some ancient wisdom . . .'

'Maybe they've found the elixir of youth, and maybe this Julien is the leader of the cult,' Rene said. 'Often happens, the leader's a Svengali, possesses enough charisma to get the others to obey.' She sipped from her mug and crossed her legs. 'You know, Carol, with the fear of being HIV positive that you had at that time, isn't it possible you needed them to be eternal? You wanted something to exist that does not die?'

Carol stared at her therapist. 'Of course it's possible, don't you think I've thought about that? But doesn't everyone dream that?'

'Well, I suppose . . .'

'I mean, wouldn't you like to live forever? Never age?'

'You betcha. But that's unrealistic. We all must face . . .'

'Please, Rene, don't give me rhetoric. How do you really feel about dying?'

'Say, who's the therapist here?' But she stopped and considered the question. 'I suppose if I had a choice . . .'

'You'd go for eternal life.'

'I'm afraid cosmetic surgery is the closest I'll get. Unless I meet one of your vampires.'

Carol sat up and looked her therapist squarely in the eye. 'I've decided something. I'm going back to Bordeaux.'

'Can you get the time off from the theatre?'

'Not a vacation. I'm going there permanently. At least until I find my son.'

Rene shifted uncomfortably. 'Carol, I don't think this is a good time to think about doing this. In fact . . .'

'I've made up my mind. Rene, you've got to understand. I need you to understand. I'm thirty-four years old. I'm HIV positive, and that's likely to change – for the worse. I can't stop thinking about my son. I don't have time to do any more therapy.'

'Then maybe it's time to put it all behind you and get on with your life.'

'I can't do that either. I feel if I don't act now I won't be able to act. It will be too late.'

'Because the virus might become active?'

'That, but more because my son will be nine years old in another year.'

'What does that have to do with anything?'

'I don't know, but I have a feeling I need to find him fast and I can't say why.'

'Carol, I wish you'd reconsider.'

'I've considered this since I came back from Bordeaux. I have to go.'

'Well, it's against both my professional and personal advice, but you know that. Will you promise me one thing? Promise you'll keep in constant touch with me? I want letters every month, updates, and a phone call every once in a while. We've been together a long time now – close to nine years. I care about you as a person, not just as a client. You're almost like a daughter to me.'

Rene's words touched Carol. Her therapist had been more of a mother to her than her own mother had been. 'I know that, and I'll keep in touch. And you can always find me through AmEx.'

'These people are dangerous. You should go to the authorities.'

'I tried that. They pay everybody off, or use hypnosis. I have to do this my way. And alone.'

'What will you do when you find them, *if* you find them?'

Carol shook her head. She didn't know *what*, but she knew she would do something.

It took Carol three months to prepare for Bordeaux. She placed the principal of her investments into an accessible account, cleared up her mother's small estate and researched as much as she could on methods of locating missing persons. She even consulted a detective who gave her tips on searching records in Europe and, equally important, what *not* to waste time on. By the time she left Philadelphia, she was in good shape mentally, physically and emotionally. In her heart she knew that if it was the last thing she ever did on this earth, she would find her son.

TWENTY-TWO

Carol immediately headed for Bordeaux. The day she arrived, she called Inspector LePage. He not only refused to help her but wouldn't even see her.

After that initial failure, she had a minor success. The management company that looked after the château gave her the number of the corporation that owned the house – 8320. The head office was in Switzerland and Carol flew there the following morning.

She found Zurich immaculate, orderly and utilitarian without the predominance of chrome, glass and concrete of many large North American cities.

Eventually she located the government records – the owners of corporation number 8320 were John and Jane Doe, their address a derelict building. Why am I not surprised? she thought. The Swiss were a polite, tight-lipped people. André and the others had really covered their tracks.

Carol bought a Volkswagen van, which she slept in and ate in to conserve funds. It was a meagre arrangement but

suited her needs. She planned to spend as long as it took –
until her money ran out – systematically searching first the
major cities and then all the port cities in France. If that
proved fruitless, she'd move along the coast to Spain.

Every place she went she concentrated on two areas – the
harbour and the section of town the oddballs frequented.
And everywhere she stopped, her main difficulty was language. Her French was not good. Still, she persisted and
managed to make herself understood. Eventually she became
better at understanding.

Very quickly she discovered it was silly to be discreet.
People didn't understand what she was getting at – because
she didn't know colloquialisms. It saved time to just ask
if there were any vampires in town. Occasionally someone
would admit to having seen one, and once, in Algeciras, she
got a lead on Gerlinde. But that lead and every other reached
a dead end and Carol always felt she finished precisely back
where she had begun. It inspired her to hire a detective from
London. Six months and several thousand dollars later she
had learned nothing useful.

All throughout that year Carol was in touch with Rene.
'Are you discouraged yet?'
'Yes and no. I'm not giving up.'
'How are you feeling. Physically.'
Carol sighed. 'I work out – I've got weights in the van now
– and jog every day. And I'm taking mega doses of vitamins
and herbal extracts to build my immune system.'
'You haven't answered me.'
'I've had a few colds this year.'
'Maybe you should see a doctor.'
'What's the point?'
Early on she had decided to work at maintaining her
health. She made sure she ate and slept properly. If she
was going to find her Michael – the name she'd given
to her son – she couldn't afford to get seriously ill, and

worries about the virus were always at the back of her mind.

But her life was exhausting and she often felt she just existed rather than lived. Other than to obtain information, she talked with few people. There didn't seem to be much to say. Besides, being single-minded – obsessed, really – unless someone could help her, she wasn't interested in them or their small-talk. She slept in the day and searched after dark; now that she had faced those memories, darkness no longer terrified her. In fact, she found the night comforting – it hid her more despondent face from the world.

She also read books and scanned the Internet, researching any subject that might be useful: lock picking, zen meditation, the psychological effects of meeting a birth child. She also read up on vampires.

Vampires had been sighted in every country throughout recorded history and mentioned as early as 2,500 BC in the Epic of Gilgamesh, lending credence to the idea that the myths are based on fact. And despite speculation about those prematurely buried, blood-drinking anaemics, and sado-masochistic sexual practitioners, some incidents just could not be explained away. The more she read, the more likely it seemed that there were other species walking the earth who are not strictly human but who can pass.

After France and Spain, Carol went to Germany. She tried bustling Berlin first and then the outskirts. When Berlin had been exhausted, or rather Carol became exhausted with Berlin, she searched Munich and after Munich, Bonn, and then smaller cities and towns.

Eventually she reached the Scandinavian countries followed in the fall by Italy and Greece. She felt certain they would avoid countries where there was a chance of war, or where they would stand out. For those reasons she did not move east just yet.

Before she left Philadelphia, with Rene, she had remembered the name 'de Villiers'. Everywhere she went she checked phone books, residents' directories, newspaper libraries, birth, death and marriage records. She looked up all the spellings she could think of, hoping that she might stumble on Jeanette or Julien. But there was nothing, not a trace. It was as though all of them had been apparitions, figments of her imagination. And in her gloomier moments that's exactly what she thought – I've dreamed this all up. I must be really crazy. There were times when only Rene's voice kept her cemented to reality.

'You didn't imagine this, Carol. You've got to hold on to what you remember. These people used and abused you. Now, whether or not you want to give up the search, that's a different matter.'

'I'm not giving up. I can't.'

A year elapsed. Carol's money had dwindled at a pace she could not have anticipated. Her spirits were often low. Physically she felt her energy dimming. She could wander through Europe aimlessly and never find them. They could be anywhere on the planet. Out of desperation she went back to Bordeaux.

Inspector LePage had retired. She obtained his home address and managed to stumble onto him 'by accident'. He was reluctant to talk with her but she persisted.

They sat together on a varnished wood-and-iron park bench just inside la Terrasse du Jardin public. It was December, the trees bare, the air crisp. The policeman blew streams of cigarette smoke through both nostrils. Seemingly uninterested in Carol's pleas, he stared across the grass at the half dozen children bundled in snow suits, playing.

'Please, I know you're under their control. They've hypnotized you as they have everyone else they come in contact with. But you've got to help me. They have my child.

If you feel any human decency, you'll try to remember.'

'Mademoiselle Robins, I should never have helped you in the first place and now you want my help again, which can only lead to catastrophe.' The white hairs on his head outnumbered the brown.

'Please. I don't have anyone else to turn to. If you know anything, if you can remember, tell me.'

'What I know I cannot tell you and what I do not know would fill *la bibliothèque*.' He inhaled deeply on his cigarette.

Carol looked at the children too. Her son, Michael, would be nine years old soon. A boy who could have been him, a slender child with dark hair and rosy cheeks, ran full out, blue jeans and a plump red jacket and matching hat. He bumped into and then hugged a woman, likely his mother. The woman laughed and kissed the boy. Carol sighed.

'I'm running on empty,' she said, more to herself than to the policeman. 'I've been empty for a long time. What's driving me, it won't let me stop until I find my son. It's taken on a life of its own.'

She looked at LePage. 'Do you have children?'

He crossed his legs and glanced at her, then away. 'I have two sons, and a daughter. They are grown. My sons are married, with sons of their own.'

Carol looked away from him too. She felt so completely sad, so hopeless. She knew she would never give up the search. She also knew that Michael could be anywhere in the world. Her money was disappearing. Her health would go soon; she felt that coming as much as she felt snow on the air. Where at first she had searched methodically, with a plan, full of energy and enthusiasm, now she was planless. She would look haphazardly, at random, because there wasn't anything else she could do. In an instant her future flashed before her eyes – a worn out person, destroyed at the roots, wandering the world alone, obsessed, until fate or God or some divine providence pitied her, drawing the last breath of life from her, bringing her the only peace she would know.

Inspector LePage must have seen something similar. 'Mademoiselle, I am not under their control.'

Carol looked at him. He would not meet her eyes. 'You're saying you've protected them by choice? All these years? Why?'

LePage stared across the park. He lit a fresh Gitane. 'My daughter, she is one of them.'

Carol couldn't speak.

'Our eldest. She was dying of leukemia. They saved her from death.'

'Are you the only one who knows?'

'My wife also.'

'Where is your daughter now?'

'I do not know. My wife and I, we see her several times a year; she tells us where to visit her. She looks the same, always, even as we and her brothers age.' The creases in his face deepened.

'Do you regret it?'

'Perhaps I should. Cheating death, it is not natural, at least as we understand nature. But I do not regret our decision and she does not blame us.' He turned to Carol. 'I love my daughter.'

'But they're killers!'

'Elisse, she has killed no one.'

'But the others have.'

'I do not know.'

'What about the old man by the docks?'

'I told you then Mademoiselle as I tell you now – the carpenter, he died of a heart attack. I do not begrudge André for taking blood from a dead man when he needs it to survive any more than I begrudge my daughter. One must have charity when dealing with them.'

Carol felt stunned. All this time he had known. And kept the truth from her. 'Inspector, please, I'm begging you . . .'

He held up a hand. 'All I can tell you, Mademoiselle, and of course I should not tell you even this, is that I once overheard my daughter mention Mürzzuschlag, which I know to be in Austria. The context was that an important visitor was coming from there to Bordeaux. Who that visitor was, whether one of us or one of them, I cannot say. I may even be leading you on a chase after a wild goose, as you say in English. It is all I know and if I were you I would dismiss it immediately. And if you cannot dismiss it, then may God help you, and may God protect them.'

That night Carol left for Vienna. She drove continuously and arrived two days later. The first thing she did was to obtain a map of Austria and then decided she might as well check out the name de Villiers before she left the city. She was stunned when she found it. 'de Villiers' was an old name dating back many generations to the middle of the sixteenth century. She was shocked again when she discovered Julien and Jeanette listed as living in Mürzzuschlag, just like ordinary citizens. And it was only when she had calmed down that Carol remembered clearly Jeanette saying, 'Julien's back in Austria with Claude and Susan.'

As soon as the call was put through, Carol said, 'Rene, I've found the de Villiers. They're in a town not far from Vienna. I'm in the city now.'

'Carol, wait! Don't do anything foolish. You don't know what they're capable of.'

Carol paused. 'I don't know if it's the connection or not, but Rene, somehow it's coming through in your voice that you believe me. Why do I have the feeling that this might be the first time?'

There was a pause from the other end. 'You're right. I think I went along with all this believing you'd never find them. Now . . .'

'You still don't believe they're vampires.'

'I . . . I don't know what to believe. They're definitely real and they're involved in the abduction of the child they forced you to bear, that I don't doubt. But vampires? Beings who enjoy eternal life, or at least eternal youth . . . What are you going to do?'

'Find my son.'

TWENTY-THREE

As the sun set, Carol drove up the steep mountain incline towards a medieval castle that looked Spanish in design. She wondered just what would happen here. Now that she was on the verge of finding them, she felt almost depressed, which surprised her. But she sensed fear underneath. She was getting near, very near, she could sense that too. But she had to remember that there were still major hurdles to overcome. The de Villiers might be travelling. They probably wouldn't help her. They could warn André and the others. And above everything she had to keep in mind that they were vampires, all of them – they too drank blood, and might drink hers; they had no reason not to.

She drove to the end of a dirt road; she'd have to travel the rest of the way on foot. It was cold out here, in the always snowy mountains, so far from a more populated area. She zipped her short wool jacket to the top and pulled the hood over her head, then closed the van door and made her way along the cinder path to the door. Firmly she brought down the large knocker shaped like the head of a wolf. Within seconds, the handsome young man she'd seen at the château opened the door. He looked hungry and he eyed her first with that intent. A split second later surprise washed over his face.

Immediately behind him the young girl appeared, then Jeanette, who did not look exactly startled to see her.

No one said anything for several seconds. Finally Jeanette said, 'Come in Carol. I've been expecting you.'

They entered a massive living room. Within half a minute Julien joined them, a large black Persian cat with green eyes the same shade as Jeanette's trotting on his heels. The five sat by the walk-in fireplace, which more than heated the room. Immediately the cat leaped onto Julien's lap and the harsh-looking vampire began to stroke it.

The room was enormous, very old, with high cavernous ceilings and stone walls. Bookcases crammed with anti-quarian volumes filled one entire wall and carried on into another room. Finely-knotted oriental carpets covered the floor, on top of which sat dozens of pieces of antique furniture, much of it in excellent condition. A beautiful veneered lowboy with exquisitely carved faces on the legs caught Carol's eye.

Seeing the de Villiers again made her realize just how much time had passed. Almost a decade ago she had thought of Jeanette and Julien as much older than her. Now she knew that she looked only slightly younger, and far older than Claude and Susan.

'How did you know I was coming?' Carol asked. She noticed the four of them were all pale, hungry-looking.

'The cards,' Jeanette answered.

Carol nodded. 'I need your help.'

No one said a word.

'I've got to find my baby. Please, tell me where he is.'

The boy, Claude, said something in French, but a dialect she couldn't make out. And then the young girl spoke quickly, animatedly, also in French, although it was obviously not her native tongue. Carol could only decipher a few words.

Finally Jeanette said, 'Carol, we can't help you. We can't betray one of our own.'

'And you are here,' Claude said. He turned to Julien. 'We cannot let her leave.'

Carol's heart jumped in her chest.

'She'll tell people about us,' Susan added. The girl looked frightened. She stared at Jeanette and then Julien, as if looking for reassurance.

'No one knows your address but me. I won't tell anyone,' Carol said.

'You shouldn't have come here,' Jeanette said. She too looked at Julien. 'What are we going to do with her?'

Julien's dark eyes had never left Carol's face. She could feel their intensity even when she wasn't looking at him. But now she did. She remembered his eyes; they had been there with her throughout Michael's birth. The two of them had shared that experience, but she knew it didn't mean they shared anything else.

More minutes of dead silence crept by. Suddenly Julien deposited the Persian onto the floor, got up, walked to the lowboy, and took a pen and paper from the drawer. He wrote something down. He came to Carol and held the paper out to her. She took it and glanced at what he had written. Immediately she looked back up at him. His eyes were the darkest black she'd ever seen, and Carol sensed that if she stared into them too long at such close range she would completely vanish.

'They're in Québec? Canada?' she managed to say.

He said nothing, just kept looking at her, studying her.

Behind Julien the girl, Susan, jumped to her feet. In a high voice she said, 'You're not giving her their address, are you?'

Claude said, 'You cannot do this!'

Jeanette was clearly troubled. 'Julien, in all your centuries of existence you've never betrayed anybody, let alone one of our kind. Why?'

'I betray no one.' His eyes still bore into Carol's. 'But I have no intention of hindering destiny.'

Part IV

'The world will change less in accordance
with man's determination than with woman's
divinations.'

– Claude Bragdon

TWENTY-FOUR

Carol landed in Montréal's Mirabel Airport at three in the afternoon. The weather made her wish she had a warmer coat. She decided not to buy one; she wouldn't be here that long.

It was all she could do to keep from heading right for the address that Julien had given her. But she forced herself to stay calm as she took the long taxi ride downtown. She booked into a hotel, arranged to rent a car for the following day, gathered the supplies she would need then ate a light dinner at a pleasant bistro. The minute she returned to her hotel room, she phoned Rene at home.

Carol felt jet-lagged; the call was strange, their conversation out of sync.

'Carol, call the police.'

'No. André and the others are too good at hypnotizing the police, and everybody else.'

'I'm going to fly up there. You shouldn't be alone.'

'Rene, don't be ridiculous. I need to do this quickly, get

in there in the daytime when they're vulnerable and get out with my son before they wake.'

'Are you forgetting they kidnapped you? And your son? There are four of them and you are one. You're completely outnumbered. What makes you think you can get away with this?'

'They could only do what they did because I didn't really understand what they are. Now I do and I know how to beat them at their own game. I'm going to get my son.'

'And then?'

'And then I'll fly back to Philadelphia.' It was a lie. She had no intention of flying to Philadelphia – it was the first place they would look for her. She didn't want to tell Rene everything right now.

A sound, like ice in a glass. 'Carol, give me their address. Someone has to know where you are.'

She hesitated. 'If you promise not to phone the police or come here.'

Now Rene hesitated. 'Unless I don't hear from you by tomorrow night.'

'No, Rene, not at all. I need to find out what the situation is. I don't know if Michael's still alive . . . I don't want this complicated.'

Another pause. 'All right. But give me the address. Just in case.'

'You have to promise not to interfere.'

'I'll give you a week. That's more than reasonable. You have my word. After that, though, I'm calling in the Marines.'

Carol gave over the information. Again, that sound of Rene drinking something. All these years Carol had assumed it was ice water, but now she wondered, especially because Rene was slurring a few of her words.

'You know, Carol, I never thought I'd say this, but I think you're onto something.'

'I'm not following you.'

'I mean, what if they *are* vampires? The undead.' She paused to sip from her drink. 'They don't grow old. Do you have any idea what that means? There are so many people who would think of that as a miracle.'

'That may be the only benefit of their condition.'

'Benefit? That's putting it mildly. They have what all of us are searching for – life without end.'

'I'm not searching for that, I'm searching for my child. And I have to get some sleep. Wish me luck? I'll need it.'

'Of course I wish you luck. When you get right down to it, between the cradle and the tomb luck's all we have going for us.'

At seven a.m. the next morning Carol arrived at the Hertz office. She picked up a Toyota and received directions to Westmount, the area on the west side of Mont Royal, where they lived. She drove along Sherbrooke, a wide street of classic French-style buildings with ornate façades painted in lively colours, then turned right, towards the mountain with the large lighted cross at the top that dominated this island.

Over dinner she'd read that the Ile de Montréal on which Montréal sits was explored by Jacques Cartier in 1535 and established as a city in 1663. The ambience was old, by North American standards.

Following the directions, she turned left onto Pine Avenue. When she found Redpath Crescent she drove slowly along the narrow curving street.

This area, wedged into the side of the mountain, was wealthy, that was clear. Mansions were sprinkled amidst homes of a more modest size, yet clearly each was special. She saw houses resembling chalets and one that could have been an English country home, ivy vines covering the entire exterior. Other designs were modern, architectural wonders

of unique style and interesting materials. All sat at the top
of steep driveways that ascended from pavement level.

Number 777 blended in well with the tasteful opulence.
The three-storey grey fieldstone house had tinted glass at
the windows, its style less French and more Tudor.

She parked around the corner and glanced at her watch:
a little before eight a.m. She pulled the gym bag from the
trunk then walked back to Redpath. As she moved along
the sidewalk, Carol noticed the entrance was at the side of
the house, not out front; lucky. As she ascended the many
steps from the sidewalk to the house, she saw a garage at
the back.

Carol decided she'd better knock, just to make sure there
wasn't a maid or driver around. When no one answered,
she walked completely around the house, checking for the
easiest access. What if this isn't where they live? she thought.
I could go to jail for breaking and entering.

But the windows were the same arrangement as in
Bordeaux – tinted glass outside, plexiglass, which she now
knew could not be tinted, inside. She could score the exterior
glass with a glass cutter. That wouldn't take too long, but
it increased the chances of being spotted by a neighbour
because she'd still have the plexiglass to deal with. It would
only pop out, not inward, so she'd have to score that too.
But Carol had acquired a lot of skills and knowledge over
the years. Besides picking locks, she also knew quite a bit
about security systems. The box just inside the main door
told her an infrared scanning system protected the place.
That would be no problem, once she got inside. Getting in
quickly was the difficulty. A small sticker on the window
informed her that the house was protected by one of the
international security companies.

She suspected that if she tried any of the doors or
windows an alarm would be set off some place else.
Security guards or the police would arrive within minutes.

Fast was the best way in, and that meant a door, not a window.

She tried the skeleton keys – basically a professional thief's lock-picking set – until one fitted the lock. An alarm would have already sounded, but she forced herself to stay patient as she manipulated the lock. Finally it snapped.

Carol opened the door just enough to slip inside, then closed it slowly. She walked very gradually across the hallway to keep the infrared from sensing her form. She hid in a hallway closet, waiting for the security company, or the police.

She heard them drive up the driveway. Two of them. They checked all the doors and windows, apparently satisfied that it was a false alarm; they would not enter.

Within the next hour, Carol set off the alarm two more times. She'd read that after three checks the police think the system is malfunctioning and stop checking. When they left the third, and she hoped final time, she was ready to begin her search.

She entered the kitchen, a bright room done in yellows, reds and white with a counter/work space and stools in the middle. The refrigerator and cupboard were virtually empty – a sign she was in the right place.

Carol moved soundlessly, her heart thunderous in her ears; anyone nearby could have heard it too.

There was a dining-room furnished in pine, the Canadian version of French Provincial, a living room crowded with couches and tables and lamps; she recognized a couple of pieces of Queen Anne furniture, and the sculpture of the mermaid and dolphin. Her heart beat harder and she had to be stern with herself. If she got too excited, she might do something stupid.

She went up the stairs as quietly and slowly as she could. The house was cool, the temperature low – they preferred cooler temperatures during the day. Upstairs she found five doors, all locked except for a bathroom. There was also a stairwell to the third floor with two doors at the top, both locked. She decided to check the basement. She felt relatively safe – they would be asleep until sunset and unable to hurt her. It was mortals she could not afford to encounter. So far there seemed to be none around.

Back on the main floor, Carol found a stairway leading off the kitchen. She turned on the large flashlight she'd brought along and headed down the wooden steps. The basement was a clean, unfinished, cavernous concrete room. Behind the stairs, the two small storage areas were empty except for a couple of trunks. In one corner of the main room stood a new and almost silent gas furnace. Near it was a door, the only one she could see. Carol knew she would have to check it out.

The door had two clasps with a chain and padlock. But the chain only went through the clasp on the doorframe so she didn't even have to pull it away. Below that was a combination lock, the kind usually found on a safe. Carol thanked her lucky stars she'd read an entire book on how to crack a bank vault and had practised on an old safe she'd found at a flea market. This would be a cinch compared to that one which had been so sophisticated.

She put the bag down on the floor. Patiently she played with the dial, listening through a stethoscope she'd brought along for just such an eventuality. Each click sounded like an explosion. After each she pushed on the door. After the fifth the door creaked inward.

Carol's heart worked overtime. She was terrified of what she might find. She picked up the bag and gingerly stepped into the darkness that waited like a mouth ready to devour her.

With the flashlight she quickly scanned the room, catching glimpses of furniture, of memories. Here a silver chevron met a black triangle. There the edge of a dresser. A chair. And then a black lacquered bed with a form lying on top.

This is not the time to panic, she told herself. Do what you came here to do. Michael is all that matters now.

She looked around the room once more, just to make certain there was no one else. The only other door led to a bathroom. When she was satisfied she was the only living being in the room, she headed for the bed.

He lay to one side, almost as if he expected her to join him. She moved to that side of the bed. Carol ran the light up André's naked body. He had not changed. But now that she was more the age he looked, she again had that uncanny sense of herself being different from what she had been.

Nervously she set down the light and the gym bag on the night table. She reached in the bag and pulled out two objects. The one in her left hand she positioned over his heart and the other, in her right hand, she raised above it.

The light captured André's face and chest. Carol stared at him, mesmerized by this memory actualized. He's like a corpse waiting for burial, she thought – still, lifeless, removed.

Nine years, she reminded herself bitterly. You've stolen nine years of my life. And my baby. I hate you more than I've ever hated anyone. And you're not even human. You deserve death. So why can't I do this? But she could not bring her right hand, the one holding the mallet, down and drive the stake into his empty heart to destroy him.

She tried to talk herself into it. She knew all the reasons; she had dwelled on them endlessly with Rene: how he had mistreated her, abused her, used her, torn her away from the one person in the world to whom she had ever really been connected. He deserves more than death, she told herself. What is he but an unnatural thing that should have died a long time ago? He's a bloodsucker, killer of living human beings, cruel, sadistic, perverse. He'd destroy me in a second, without thinking. And maybe that was why she knew she couldn't do it. She was not like him – she *had* to think about her actions.

There's got to be another way to get Michael, she thought. They'll be asleep all day. I can just check all the rooms. If he's alive, if he's here, I'll find him and take him away. This time I know how to make sure there's no trace of us.

She was just lowering her right arm when a hand clamped onto her wrist. Stunned, she couldn't move for a second.

But then, as if by instinct, she raised her left hand, ready to plunge the stake into his chest after all. His other hand locked onto her left wrist.

His arms bent at the elbows and fanned out, spreading her, forcing her down until she lay across his chest, her face inches from his. She expected his eyes to snap open and his lips to part maliciously. And then he would kill her. But nothing else happened.

Carol was forced to lie there, pressed against his cool body, unable to do anything more than squirm. The hands circling her wrists were like icy steel handcuffs, merciless.

It had to come to this, she thought bitterly, her fear temporarily suppressed by an overwhelming sense of the injustice of life.

She knew there was nothing she could do but lie still, conserve her strength, watch the flashlight battery dim by the hour and wait until nightfall. Wait for her death.

A couple of times during the long day she thought she heard his heart beat, but it could have been her own. It's like narcolepsy, she thought. He's asleep but he's not. He's dead but he's alive.

'Turned into a crazed vampire hunter, or should I take this personally?' he asked when the sun must have set.

Even his voice is the same, she thought. Cynical, bitter, at my expense.

In one smooth motion he flipped her over onto her back and himself on top, still holding her wrists. The flashlight beam was really dim now but she could see him clearly. He looked exactly as she remembered him when he was hungry – thin, hollow, angry.

'Your tenacity has always amazed me,' he said. 'If you weren't so stupid I'd admire this. How did you find us?'

'Julien. He gave me your address.'

'Still lying, Carol? Some things never change, do they?'

'It's true. I saw them in Austria. I don't care if you believe me.'

'More importantly, *how* did you remember?'

'You're not omnipotent, André. We mere mortals have a few abilities.'

'Such as?'

But she wasn't about to tell him anything. 'What are you going to do to me this time?'

André laughed sarcastically and shook his head. 'You're still so naive. You break in here, try to stake me in the heart then ask me what I'm going to do to you. What do you expect, an invitation for cappuccino? Get real!'

'I didn't try to kill you,' Carol said weakly, remembering the feeling of how impossible it had always been to try to talk to him.

'I see. The stake was for what, to start a fire? Pitch a tent?' He shook his head again in disbelief. 'You're pathological – you don't even know when you're lying.'

'I tried to kill you but I couldn't do it.'

He laughed sharply but then stopped and looked at her.

'You're like a virgin to me – your blood has always been just beyond my reach. But not any more, Carol.'

She panicked. 'Wait. If you're going to kill me, let me see by baby first. Just let me see him and know that he's all right before I die. Please?'

He shook his head. 'You know I can't do that.'

'You can. Just let me see him. I won't say a word to him, honest.'

'When did you acquire honesty?'

'Just let me see him. Just once.'

'No.'

Carol felt near tears. All these years, all this work, so much pain. And now I'll die without ever seeing Michael, she thought bitterly.

'Close your eyes. Think of something pleasant,' he told her. 'I'll be quick, for auld lang syne.'

She glared at him but she just couldn't hold onto the anger. She felt too distraught. 'Has he ever asked about me?'

André hesitated. 'Yes.'

'What did you tell him?'

'The truth. You tried to take him away. We found you, rescued him. You wanted to stay but we said no.'

The truth, so naked and sharp-edged, she thought. Her voice softened with the pain she felt. 'Did you tell him anything good about me?'

'I told him you took care of him for the short time you were together.'

'I named him Michael. What did you name him?'

André looked startled. 'Michel.'

Yes, she thought, we both knew he was an angel. 'Promise me something. Tell him that I loved him. Please. Just that. That I loved him more than anything, even more than my own life. Will you tell him that?'

He said nothing.

'Will you?'

'All right,' he finally said. 'I'll tell him.'

It wasn't what she wanted but it would have to do. And something resembling peace did come over her.

'Let's get this over with. Close your eyes.'

She looked at him. His eyes were large, even in the dim

light. Sparkling, like polished grey botswana. He looked ravenous.

I won't let him tell Michael I was a coward, she thought. 'Let me give myself to you.'

His face clouded with both impatience and confusion.

'You're my death, you always have been. Let me give you my blood the way I gave you my body and my soul and everything else I ever had. Here.' She tried to move one of her arms. At first he wouldn't release her, but finally he freed her wrist.

Carol brushed her long hair back behind her neck. She undid the top two buttons on her jacket and then her flannel shirt, turning the collars under, exposing her throat.

He looked at it, obviously attracted to the vein. Lust filled his face. But he also looked upset. 'I'll try not to hurt you,' he told her, his voice low, practically a whisper.

'It's too late,' she said. 'I've already been hurt. And it doesn't matter anymore.'

Carol's pulse raced. She slid a hand behind his head and ran her fingers through his hair, pulling him down to her as if he was a lover. His cool lips pressed onto the skin of her throat and she shivered. His tongue, flicking like a snake's, probed the area briefly. Two sharp teeth, like the points of razor blades, rested on her flesh, irritating it, causing it to itch. Carol's body shook with terror; tears overflowed her eyelids and coated her face.

'Remember to tell Michael I love him,' she whispered, her frightened breath coming in thin gasps. And then she waited, wondering what death would be like, how it would feel to have his teeth tear into her, how long it would take for him to drain the life blood from her body.

Time stood still. She couldn't tell how much time passed. It might have been a second or an hour, but he never penetrated her.

He pushed himself up and looked down at her. His face

was still thin, haggard, hungry. But there was something else, something she couldn't understand. And then, as she watched, he cocked his head like an animal, listening.

Suddenly he jumped off the bed and leaped towards the door, trying to close it, but he wasn't fast enough.

Carol sat up and in that second saw a short form in the opening, dimly outlined by the nearly faded light. 'Michael!' she cried.

'*Qui est-ce, André?*' a small but confident voice asked.

'*Arrête, Michel! Va en haut!*'

She heard André say something else and then the young voice again and then André sighed. Finally the door was pulled wide open.

The child came into the room, right up to the bed. Even in the poor light she saw that his hair was as black as André's, his face as handsome. Large blue eyes, much like her own, looked back at her with surprised curiosity. He's beautiful, she thought, just the way I imagined him.

And then he said, 'You're my mom, aren't you?'

TWENTY-FIVE

'Good Grief! The Return of Dracula's Son's Mother!' Gerlinde shouted as the three of them entered the living room.

'Find Chloe,' André told Michael, who ran back out the door.

André tossed the gym bag onto the coffee table.

'What's all this?' Karl asked, sorting through the contents, picking out stakes and crosses.

'You weren't going to use those on us?' Gerlinde sounded shocked.

'No. I couldn't,' Carol tried to explain. 'They were just in case.'

'In case she wanted to start a bonfire,' André said sarcastically. 'Sit over there,' he told her.

She sat down in a mauve winged chair by the window, away from the main body of furniture. Near the fireplace were two more chairs positioned across from a large five-sectioned couch, all surrounding an enormous circular walnut coffee table. There were also two loveseats, covered in light blue flowered fabric, which contrasted with the other upholstery.

Michael ran back into the room followed by Chloe. The boy approached Carol slowly but then perched on the edge of the footstool in front of her chair. He stared at her as though mesmerized, his face a blend of shock and curiosity. He's adorable, she thought. He's not shy or unconfident. She wanted to reach out and hold him but felt she might frighten him. And then she realized she would probably frighten herself.

'Listen,' Gerlinde announced on the way out of the room. 'I'm gonna defrost a couple pints of hemo. Looks like we'll be dining in tonight.'

'Carol, where did you get our address?' Chloe asked.

'She says Julien gave it to her,' André answered.

'I don't believe it,' Karl said.

'Neither do I.'

'Tell us, Carol,' Chloe said.

'Julien did give it to me.'

'How did you find Julien?'

She had no intention of betraying Inspector LePage. 'I remembered their last name is de Villiers and then I remembered that Jeanette once said Julien was back in Austria with their children so I went there and found them listed in a residents' directory.'

'And why did Julien give you the address?'

'I don't know.'

'This doesn't make any sense,' Karl said.

'That's what his family said,' Carol offered. 'But when they questioned him about betraying you, he said that he wasn't. That he just couldn't stand in the way of destiny.'

'I'll call Vienna. Make certain everything is all right,' Karl said.

'How did you remember?' Chloe asked.

'Therapy. Years of it. Hypnosis, mostly. I had someone who believed in me.'

'Someone knows about us!' Chloe said, looking at André.

'She won't interfere.'

'Does this therapist know our address?'

Carol hesitated. She didn't want Rene dragged into this. 'She only helped me get back my lost memories. She knows I'm in Montréal, that's all; you're not in danger.'

Michael was still staring at her and she looked at him. He's healthy, she thought. Intelligent, that's obvious, sweet too. He's inherited the best of both of us.

'Why did you come back?' Chloe asked.

Gerlinde came in just then with a tray of large goblets. She offered one each to everybody, Michael included. 'RH Positive,' she said. For Carol she had a small glass of red wine. 'Better drink this, kiddo. It's gonna be a long night.'

Carol watched her son down the contents of his glass as if it were milk. The red stained his mouth and created a moustache effect on his upper lip. He licked it off then wiped his lips with the back of his sleeve. She didn't find it repulsive. He's just a child, she thought. My child.

'Why?' Chloe asked again, bringing her back to the present.

'I came back for Michael,' she said, then decided to tell them everything. It didn't really matter now.

'I've been struggling for years, trying to reclaim the memories. The hypnosis undid what you did,' she told André. His face was a pallid mask she could not read.

One by one they sat down around her, listening to her story. She told them about the therapy. About Rob's death, her mother's death, about her loneliness, and how hard it all had been. She looked at Michael. 'I spent the last two years searching for you. I always believed I'd find you some day,' she told the boy. 'I looked everywhere: France, Spain, Germany, most of Europe.'

'We were in Germany,' Gerlinde said. 'Bonn – for five years – before moving here.'

'I was in Bonn,' Carol said. 'Eventually I remembered about Austria. When Julien gave me your address I came right here. I did all this to find you, Michael,' she told him.

'Carol, this is a difficult time for Michel,' Chloe said. 'He's at an age when he needs to make decisions which will affect him in a permanent way.'

'I gotta decide on my birthday if I wanna be mortal or immortal,' the boy confided, seeming not too weighed down by the decision.

His eyes are so like mine, she thought. He's so gentle but so solid. I love him.

'I don't want to interfere,' Carol told him. She looked at the others. 'Really. I just want to be with him.'

'Being with him is interfering,' Karl said as he came back into the room. 'It's not a good time for your influence.'

'There's never been a good time for my influence!' Carol snapped. 'But I'm his mother. I have a right to be with my son.'

'The only rights you have are the ones we allow you, and at the moment you have none!' André stood.

'I want her to stay.' It was Michael who said it. Everyone looked stunned.

After minutes of pregnant silence, Gerlinde said, 'Hey, maybe it's not such a bad idea.'

'Are you crazy?' André turned on her.

'I think it's the worst thing that can happen,' Karl said. Chloe was silent.

'I mean, what harm can it do, really,' Gerlinde continued. 'Michel should get to know his mom. And it's not going to affect his decision one way or the other.'

'I want her to stay,' Michael said again.

'I'm against it,' Karl said.

'It can't hurt,' Gerlinde smiled.

'André, I think you'll have to be the one to decide this.' Chloe told him. 'As you can see, we're split. And you are Michel's father. If you agree that she stays, Carol will have to be your responsibility. And if not, it's up to you to decide what to do with her.'

'*Papa, laisse-la rester!*' Michael said, running to André. 'Please let my mother stay!'

André looked down at the boy. Carol saw that the two of them not only had a special relationship but that Michael could melt André's heart with just a glance, just as she could already feel her son was able to melt her own heart.

André ruffled Michael's hair and the boy clung to his arm. Finally he said to his son, 'We'll take a walk and talk about it.'

After they had gone, Chloe left the room saying she was going to phone Julien again and that she would order Chinese food for Carol.

'You've had a hard time, kiddo,' Gerlinde said.

'Yes I have,' Carol admitted. 'But I had to see him. He's so beautiful. You've raised him really well and I'm grateful.'

'We all raised him, but thanks. You know, you're not looking so good. Of course, you're older. It always wigs me out to see mortals age.'

'I'm only thirty-four,' Carol laughed. 'But it's been painful, the last years. I've had to work hard to keep myself in as good shape as I'm in.'

'What about the virus?' Karl asked.

'Three years ago I tested positive. I don't know if that's changed. I've been sick a lot, colds, flu, that kind of thing. I haven't been to a doctor since that test. I guess I didn't want to find out anything worse.'

When André and Michael returned, Chloe joined them in the living room for the verdict.

Everyone sat but André. 'Michel's convinced me he does

need to get to know Carol. We'll try it for five nights, then I'll decide where to go from there.'

Carol and Gerlinde hugged each other.

'You can spend part of the night with Michel but one of us will always be in the same room with the two of you,' he told Carol. 'I'll be responsible for you most of the time; during the day you stay with me. I'll return the car. Where are your clothes?'

'Mostly just what I have on. I checked out of the hotel.'

Michael came over to Carol. This time she didn't restrain herself. She reached out and hugged him. He felt warm and soft as she pulled him to her heart. He hugged her back, wrapping his arms around her neck. She touched his hair, it was silky, childlike. She smelled him, remembering the scent. He's sturdy and fragile at the same time, she thought. Suddenly she realized that all her struggle had led to this moment and she broke down.

'Why are you crying?' Michael asked her, stroking her hair the way a child comforts an adult.

'Because I love you so very much it hurts.'

Later that first night he dragged out his pet iguana and his hamsters and showed them to her. He told her Chloe took him for walks in the woods and up through the mountain and they picked plants and he was memorizing the names of all the trees. He told her he liked to read adventure stories and play computer games and go to the movies with Gerlinde. About the baseball games André took him to and how they went swimming a couple of nights a week and worked out on the weight machines. He told her he had been skiing last winter for the first time and he wanted to learn to play hockey and that he was building, with Karl's help, a laboratory where he would be able to do chemical experiments. He said he liked rap and hip hop and Madonna and that when he got older he was going to dye his hair orange and get a mohawk. Carol laughed with delight.

Everything about him charmed her. She asked him questions about his likes and dislikes and all his interests. They played a dungeons and dragons-type game with Gerlinde. Michael was excited as they played and Carol had to keep herself from hugging him every five minutes. And when the night ended she couldn't believe how the hours had flown.

'Let's go,' André said to her. The others went upstairs but she went below ground with him.

'Why do you sleep down here?' Carol asked.

'It reminds me of a mausoleum,' he said sarcastically. He closed the door and snapped a newly-installed deadbolt into place. They were in darkness for a moment before he turned on a soft light above the bed.

While he took his shirt off he said, 'You can sleep here with me.'

Carol eased out of her shoes and lay down.

'You don't have to sleep in your clothes. I'm not going to fuck you,' André said. When he finished undressing, she saw him open the top drawer of the smaller of two dressers and remove something.

'It's cool here,' she said, feeling nervous about being alone with him. 'I don't want to catch a cold. I get them easily.'

He pulled a blanket out of the closet and tossed it at her.

While she spread it over her body, he got in beside her.

Suddenly André leaned over and she tensed. He snapped one half of a metal handcuff around her left wrist and the other half to a bar of the headboard.

She was shocked. 'You don't have to lock me to the bed. I'm not going to try to hurt you. And I'm not going anywhere. I'm here to be with Michael; I won't run away.'

He sneered. 'Carol I trust you about a tenth as much as you trust me.' He switched out the light.

They lay in silence. Carol had so much to think about, Michael being her dominant thought. But she also had

worries, one of which was her former therapist. She hoped
Rene wouldn't try to intervene, at least until a week had
elapsed. If she phoned the police, by morning this entire
house of creatures would be exposed for what they were.
That would be a disaster. They would be dragged out into
sunlight – all of them – Michael might be injured by sunlight.
At the very least he would be taken away until a court case
could determine that she was his mother. And he would
hate her for breaking up his home, for betraying them.
Carol wished she could call Rene and tell her that things
had worked out, at least temporarily. But she couldn't call
Rene without confessing that someone else *did* have their
address. And that would not be wise – at least tonight.

'André, I appreciate you letting me stay.'

'I did it for Michel, not for you.'

'I know. And I can see you love him very much, as much
as I do. I'm glad.'

TWENTY-SIX

No police showed up at the door the following night, nor the one after that. Carol felt relieved that Rene *had* respected her wishes, at least for now. But she'd have to find a way to contact her former therapist soon. She was never by herself so that ruled out using the phone, unless she told them, and she wasn't comfortable with that idea. She just crossed her fingers that Rene would do nothing, and kept her eyes and ears peeled for an opportunity to contact her.

The next four days Carol was in heaven. She spent hours each night with her son. Early in the evening, while she ate, someone took Michael out – that was the routine. She figured it was for blood but never felt brave enough to ask how he got it. When he returned, they talked in the living room or watched TV together, played games, built things, all under the watchful eyes of one of the vampires.

He was a creative child, full of imagination, never boring or repetitive. He asked a million questions about everything, from Bon Jovi's hair styles, to how Japanese Samurai warriors could sit down with such big swords, to the chemical components of various household cleaning agents. They painted pictures together and worked with clay. He had a guitar and played her songs he'd made up and did a very good imitation of Michael Jackson dancing. He's a genius, she thought. My child is a complete genius. And yet he's the most normal boy in the world.

On the fifth night, while Carol waited for André to bring Michael home, she said, 'Gerlinde, what exactly does it mean, Michael choosing to be mortal or immortal?'

'Well, on his ninth birthday – I don't know why, but that seems to be some crucial time – he has to make a decision. He'll be nine on New Year's Eve.'

'Yes, I know.'

'Ah, right. You were there. I forgot. Anyway, depending on what he decides – and it has to be his decision – that effects what he does from then on. Like food. If he wants to be mortal, he can never drink blood again, I mean as an entire meal.' Gerlinde was obviously uncomfortable talking about this. 'Hey, kiddo. Wanna see my paintings?'

'Love to.'

They went up to a white-walled studio on the third floor crammed with canvases.

'This is terrific,' Carol said, admiring a half-finished portrait of Michael still on the easel.

'Yeah, that one's pretty good. There's some others over here.'

Gerlinde had painted Michael alone and with André. There were also paintings of Chloe and Karl, Julien, Jeanette and their children and others who may have been vampires. One woman looked a little bit like Inspector LePage, but Carol didn't ask about her. Each oil was very realistic. Gerlinde's style favoured bright colours, definite lines and sharp contrasts, but there were also abstracts and a few paintings done in a photo-realism style.

'These are really good,' Carol said. 'You've got talent. You could be a world-class painter.'

'Thanks,' Gerlinde said shyly. 'But that's one thing about being supernatural; you gotta keep a low profile.'

'Hey! You painted me!' Carol said, surprised. Three canvases resting against a wall showed a younger Carol. In one she sat by the living room fireplace at the château in Bordeaux, a melancholy look on her face. In another her head rested against the back of the seat on the passenger side of the green sports car. She looked relaxed, laughing, her hair flying in the wind. In the last Carol and André stood face to face. Both had their hands on their hips and were glaring into each other's eyes.

'These are from memory, huh?'

Gerlinde laughed. 'I didn't get around to having you pose.'

'Has Michael seen these?'

'Uh huh.'

'So that's how he knew I was his mother.' Carol moved the canvases back against the wall. 'Did you ever talk about me?'

'All the time, kiddo. I told him you were a spectacular mom and a truly great person.'

'Thanks, Gerlinde. It's too bad the way things worked out.'

'Yeah. Maybe this time there'll be a happy ending.'

'Maybe,' Carol said, but she didn't feel convinced of that. Still, she didn't feel entirely hopeless either. As long as she could be with Michael, she didn't really care about all the rest of it.

'Gerlinde, I have a request and I really need you to keep a confidence here.'

Gerlinde shifted uncomfortably.

'I'm only asking you because you're my friend and I don't want to betray you the way I did the last time. I've got to make a phone call.'

'Somebody knows you're here!'

Carol sucked in her lips and nodded. 'My therapist. I just want to call and tell her I'm all right so she won't worry or do anything. If she hears from me it will be okay.'

'Oh man!' Gerlinde said, holding her head. 'I mean, how can I let you use the phone without telling the others?'

'Gerlinde, you'll be standing right next to me, you'll hear everything I say. With your hearing probably everything she says. Please. I don't want to put any of you in danger and if André finds out . . . You know how he is.'

Gerlinde shook her head but then said, 'Okay, but make it quick. We only have a phone in the living room. I must be cracked!'

Carol dialled Rene's home number. Fortunately Rene used a machine rather than a service at home. She wasn't in but Carol left a message.

'Rene, it's Carol. I'm just phoning to let you know everything's all right. Great, really. It's not like before. I'm staying here, getting to know Michael. Everyone's treating me really well. I just wanted to let you know so you don't worry. There's no need to do anything. I'll be in touch in a while. Take care and, Rene, thanks for all your help.'

When she put the phone down, Gerlinde's face was creased with anxiety. 'It's okay,' Carol said. 'You guys are safe. I've fixed it.'

'I hope so, kiddo, I really hope so.'

Late that night, Carol and Michael were in the living room with Gerlinde watching *The Wild Ones*. Suddenly Michael asked Carol, 'How'd you meet my dad?'

Gerlinde lowered the volume on the TV.

'It's a long story,' Carol said. 'Are you sure you want to hear it?'

'Yeah.' He squirmed back from the edge of the couch and shifted a little, closer to her.

Carol wondered where to begin and how to tell him. 'Well, it was in France, nine years ago. I was in a café and André wanted to share my table.'

'You're kidding?' Gerlinde shrieked. 'What a line! The guy's a hundred years old and he's so original.'

Michael laughed.

'Don't laugh,' she told the boy. 'I'm putting your papa down.'

'How come?'

'Because that's the oldest come-on in the book. Anyway, go on, Carol.' Gerlinde turned both the television and the VCR off.

Carol felt uncomfortable talking about it. She didn't know how to present what had happened in a way that Michael could understand. And she didn't want to hurt him or his relationship with André.

'Well, I wanted to be alone so I said no at first, and then yes, when he pointed out there weren't any other seats.'

'Did you like him?' Michael asked, grinning from ear to ear, seeming to enjoy the story already.

Carol crossed her arms over her chest. 'Not exactly.'

'But you did later, huh?'

Gerlinde's gaze shifted towards the door, as though she sensed someone about to open it.

'Well, there were times later when I liked André.'

Michael looked a little bewildered. 'But he liked you?'

'I'm not sure. You'll have to ask him.'

This obviously wasn't what the boy wanted to hear. He looked down at his fingers and began popping the joints.

'Michel, if you do that you'll get big knuckles,' Gerlinde said.

'What's wrong, Michael?' Carol asked him.

'Well, if you didn't like each other, how come you had me?'

Carol wondered how to alleviate his fears without lying to him. Finally she put her arm around his shoulder.

'Your father and I have had a strange relationship. You know your birth was very unusual. Special.'

'Yeah. Chloe told me all about it,' the boy said matter-of-factly, as though it didn't really interest him. He picked up a palm-top computer and began punching the buttons. 'Where'd you take me when you ran away?' Suddenly his mood brightened. He switched subjects in the same way he flipped channels on the TV.

'Well, I hitch-hiked on the highway for a long time, heading for England. You were only a baby, just born, only two days old. It was snowing a little and very cold but I kept you close to me. I don't think you were cold.'

'I didn't cry, did I?'

'No. You were a wonderful baby.'

'Then where'd we go?'

'Well, we stopped a couple of times in gas stations and I fed you milk and changed you, the things you do with babies.'

She hugged him. He blushed and shifted away a little.

'There was one place that was all burned out inside. I took you in there because it was so cold and there was no other place to go.'

'I 'member that!' Michael yelled, looking up. 'It smelled!'

'Maybe,' Carol said. 'I sang you songs too.'

'Sing one.'

She smiled and kissed the top of his head then sang the lullaby that she'd sung to him as he had nestled against her heart. 'Way down yonder, in the meadow, poor little baby crying mama. Birds and butterflies, flutter round his eyes, poor little baby crying mama. Dapples and greys, pintos and bays, all the pretty little horses.'

The computer rested quietly in Michael's lap. His eyes

were very round. Suddenly he said, 'How could I've been born if you didn't love each other?'

Carol took his chin in her hand and turned his face towards hers. She felt very serious and wanted him to understand that. His eyes widened as they stared into hers with an expectation she had to meet. 'Michael, listen to me. Both André and I love you very very much. We may not always have loved each other, but I know that the night you were conceived we did because I remember that night. André loved me and I loved him for those moments and that's how you came about, through that love. You're the child of that love. Don't ever forget what I'm telling you. No matter what happens, always remember that it was love that created you.'

The three were quiet. Michael snuggled in Carol's arms.

Gerlinde watched mother and son with a look of wonder on her face.

Suddenly the door opened and André came in. He crossed the room and sat opposite the couch on the chair closest to the fireplace.

'Hey, André. Did you see this movie with the guy on the motorcycle?' Michael jumped up. He switched on the TV and the VCR. A surly Marlon Brando appeared briefly on the screen before Gerlinde annihilated the image.

'Sorry, kiddo, it's bath time. Last one in's a rotten bratwurst.'

Michael groaned, but he kissed Carol and then went over and kissed André, who held him tightly. He ran towards the door with Gerlinde on his heels. Just before he went out Michael turned and yelled, 'I love ya both,' then disappeared.

Carol smiled and sighed. Everything about Michael almost brought tears to her eyes. He's an amazing child, she thought. So warm and human.

She glanced at André. His grey eyes were soft, like old

pewter, as he watched her. He didn't seem as distant as she remembered him.

He rested his head against the back of the chair and she brought her feet up under her. They sat that way for a good half hour, each watching the other, without speaking, contained in the silence of the room. Outside the wind moaned softly and a branch tapped persistently against the window.

The sky was lightening and eventually André stood and switched off each of the lamps. Then he walked into the hallway and set the alarm. Carol got up and followed him downstairs.

She stood on her side of the bed, slipping her running shoes and socks off and then her shirt. She unsnapped the clip that held her hair up. From the night table she picked up her brush and began brushing out the tangles.

Five nights are up, she thought. Will André let me stay? And if he won't, what's going to happen?

She drew the bristles through her thick hair many times, from the scalp to the ends, before finally pulling the hair over one shoulder.

Michael's such a darling, she thought. I want to be with him more than anything. Now that I've found him I can't live without him again.

She gathered the hair in one hand and brushed just the ends, and as she did so her head turned slightly. She caught André's eye and stopped brushing. He stood naked on the other side of the bed watching her. She looked away nervously, embarrassed, not wanting to encourage anything.

She ran the brush through her hair from the top of her scalp again but within seconds felt him up against her. His hands gripped her waist. He brought his lips to the exposed side of her throat and kissed her there. He smelled faintly of a spicy aftershave but his beard was a little rough against her skin.

His body was hot, even through her jeans she felt that. A sudden memory of familiarity erupted; he was hard and powerful. His pelvis rocked from side to side as he rubbed against her. He unsnapped her bra and caressed one of her breasts.

Carol felt trapped. Part of her locked into fear and another part clamped down on feelings that were startling. 'I haven't had anyone since you,' she blurted out, immediately wondering what had made her say that.

André kissed her hair. His lips slid along her ear, his breath tickling her skin, then down to her neck again.

His hand wandered across her waist. He unzipped her jeans.

'Don't,' she said softly, feeling torn, afraid.

He pulled the snap on her pants open and with one hand eased her pants down over her hips.

'No,' she moaned as his fingers went up into her. Her vagina contracted and the wetness broke inside. She moaned again.

His warm penis pressed insistently against her skin. Carol pushed herself back against him, responding. But she heard herself say, 'No,' once more.

He turned her face up and to the side so she would look at him, his eyes large silver-grey almonds. His fingers continued to massage her, spreading warmth into the wetness.

'Carol, should I listen to your words or your body?'

She felt her legs go weak, her heart race and her breath quicken. She couldn't answer him. More than anything she wanted him to make that decision so she wouldn't have to. And when she hesitated a strained look marred his face. He started to edge away.

'No!' she cried, locking onto him, forcing his fingers back into her, grabbing his hair, dragging him down until his lips joined hers in a passionate kiss.

He manoeuvred them onto the bed. She lay face down with him on top, his fingers still inside her, triggering sensations in her and sounds out of her. But soon he moved them both onto their sides, him behind.

Why? she tried to ask herself. Why is this happening again? And why am I doing this? I don't want to start anything. I don't want to get enmeshed.

He lifted her leg and entered her. The feel of him sliding in so deep left her breathless and interrupted the questions. Gently he bent her leg and pressed it down again, filling her.

'Kiss me,' she whispered, her throat dry, her voice low. He held a handful of her hair and gently pulled her back until her upper body lay flat against the bed. While his tongue and lips spoke to hers and his fingers answered the demands of her swollen clitoris, he moved inside her, his thrusts deep, responding to another need.

At first Carol saw herself as a starved animal that had waited too long; she was overhungry and couldn't take anything in. But then, suddenly, sensation flooded her and she felt ravenous, on the brink of receiving what she had forgotten she needed. He thrust harder and faster and within seconds both of them came together, moaning, interlocked, intertwined.

Afterwards Carol cried. Not because she was either happy or unhappy, just because she felt released.

André covered her with the blanket and snapped off the light. He nuzzled her hair and wrapped his arms around her as if he would never let her go. And she held onto him as though she wouldn't let him let her go.

She could still feel him inside her as they both drifted off to sleep.

TWENTY-SEVEN

As Carol awoke, cool lips kissed hers passionately in the darkness. 'Is it night?' she asked groggily, wrapping her arm around André's neck.

'Yes. Why don't you sleep a little longer? Karl and I are taking Michel to a science shop. We'll be gone for a couple of hours.'

'Okay.' She curled into a ball under the blanket he tucked around her. She'd been exhausted lately and needed a lot of sleep.

But as soon as André left, she felt his absence and couldn't go back to sleep, so she switched on the lights. She dressed quickly, realizing she'd been wearing the same clothes, jeans and a flannel shirt, for five days. Maybe Gerlinde's got something I can borrow so I can wash these, she thought.

Carol hugged herself and smiled. She felt warm and soft and wanting. This could be the beginning of something good, she thought. Maybe we can make it work this time, despite what he is.

After she showered and dressed, she decided to look

around before going upstairs for breakfast. She'd been in André's room many times in Bordeaux, and every night since she'd been in Montréal, but had never really seen what he kept hidden away. She knew so little about him.

She slid one of the closet's double doors open. Hangers holding stylish, new-looking clothing crammed the space that took up one entire wall. On the shelf above sat an array of hats plus a baseball bat, a lacrosse stick, a couple of mitts and softballs, a tennis racket and a soccer ball. On the floor below dozens of pairs of shoes and boots, casuals, sandals, dress, sports shoes filled a shoe rack. She closed the door.

Besides the bed, there were three other major pieces of bedroom furniture. The larger dresser and the armoire contained what she expected, more clothes, neatly folded or hung, orderly, precise. Another, smaller dresser, held a bunch of odd items in the top three drawers, including a *fleur de lis* pin, a banner and a program from the 1941 World Series, where the Yankees beat the Brooklyn Dodgers four to one, coins from different countries, ancient military medals, old grainy French newspaper photographs and clippings of a sports team – she tried to pick out André and thought she did in a couple of pictures – a faded grade school primer, in French, with the name André Francois Emil Moreau written in a precise but childlike hand. There were other things from his life too: a photograph of André, Karl and a blond-haired man who looked very sensitive, arms around each other's shoulders, all smiling for the camera. On the back was the inscription Victory Studios, Madison Avenue, New York, and the year 1949. There were ticket stubs for *La Soif*, by Henri Bernstein starring Jean Gabin in Paris, dated February 20, 1949. Also two playbills: *Cat On a Hot Tin Roof* starring Burl Ives and Ben Gazzara at the Morosco Theater in New York, March 15, 1955, and Shakespeare's *Coriolanus* at Stratford-on-Avon, July 7, 1959, starring Laurence Olivier and Edith Evans. Inside the last, a *New*

York Times review had been clipped out, the paper yellow with age. She read part of it:

> Coriolanus is the least likable of all Shakespeare's tragic heroes, because the sin by which he falls is a fierce, intolerant personal pride. He is that most difficult character – a man undeniably great who is yet not great enough to be humble. No modern audience in this age, which prefers its great men to be regular fellows when not on show, can readily take to such a man.

He's been all over. And he must have lived in the States, she realized. That's why his English is so good.

There were also tin-types of a young man and woman and a later sepia photograph of the two of them, now middle-aged, with a baby. She wondered if they were his parents. The woman was dark-haired and beautiful, soft-looking, shy. The man, tall, well-dressed, sporting a long moustache, had a humorous grin on his face. They both resembled André. The baby was in a long white dress of the day and it was impossible to tell if it was a male or female or even see its face clearly. There was also a family shot, the same man and woman, the same age, with the same baby and six boys ranging from fifteen or so to probably early forties. They all had dark hair and looked a bit like André.

The bottom drawer was locked, but she'd seen a key in the top and tried it. It worked.

Inside the drawer were only four items, two together, neatly aligned in a row. On the left sat a gold heart-shaped locket, the chain carefully arranged to make a larger heart around it. Carol lifted the locket out and opened the clasp. On the left was a portrait of a young woman with warm eyes, dark hair and a generous smile. She looked French. André's picture was on the right. He appeared exactly as he did now except the shirt and sweater he wore and his haircut were obviously from another era, maybe the twenties. On the back of the locket words had been inscribed: *Mon Amour, Mon Coeur*. She replaced the locket and carefully rearranged the chain around it. In the centre of the drawer was a beige ladies handkerchief, old-fashioned, with a delicate lace filigree border, the initials SV embroidered in pink at one corner. She lifted it out and smelled it – a faint trace of lavender. The most surprising things were on the right.

There was the Tarot card, *The Empress*, and the smoky quartz Jeanette had given Carol. The card was perfectly centred between the top, bottom and side of the drawer and the crystal stood upright in the middle of it. She picked both up. Memories pressed in on her, moments with Jeanette, with André, Michael's birth, alone with Michael in the burned-out garage, snippets of time when André had been kind and loving to her.

He's sentimental, she realized. I never knew that. She wondered who the woman in the locket was and whose initials were on the handkerchief. They must be old loves. But where are they now?

Carefully Carol replaced the items. She fussed with them until satisfied they were in exactly the place she had found them, then locked the drawer and replaced the key. She went upstairs, made breakfast and had just walked into the living room when there was a knock on the front door.

Chloe went to answer it and returned with Julien and Jeanette. Carol sat by the fireplace watching the vampires greet each other. They were all very affectionate, hugging, kissing, even nibbling at each other's ears like puppies, really glad to see one another. Nobody noticed her, but for the moment she didn't mind. They're all so respectful, caring of each other, she thought. Yes, caring, respect, those are the right words. More human than many human beings. It was fascinating to watch.

A few minutes later Karl came in, with André right behind

him. André looked at Carol; she had the sense he wanted to come to her first but Julien called him and he joined the others. She saw Michael peer into the room then duck back out again. Then she heard him thundering up the steps to the second floor.

If they had a problem with Julien giving her the address, they had obviously worked it out. She couldn't discern signs of hostility between any of them. It was strange to see, really. A group of vampires, and Carol wasn't even sure what that meant because she knew they weren't like in the movies. They seemed ordinary, like everybody else – except for the blood. But it was always in the back of her mind that, for them, the bottom line was she never ceased being food. Yet there was something enviable about them. They were connected somehow, connected yet separate. Carol felt a yearning to be part of something larger than herself, to have what they had.

The door bell rang and Julien answered it, just as though this were his home. He returned with an extraordinary-looking woman. Everyone stopped talking and turned towards her.

She was as tall as Julien who was, himself, about six feet. Her hair, mostly silver, shone in the incandescent lighting. She wore it in a loose chignon. One thin streak of jet black ran from a widow's peak all the way back. Her skin was clear and pale but strange; her features looked Eurasian, especially her eyes. They were slanted and possessed the quality of stars, flickering, like jewels when the facets are caught just so by the light. Intense, intimate geodes the deepest shade of violet Carol had seen outside the flower itself. Her eyes reminded Carol of Julien's and she wondered if the longer these vampires existed, the more they became like the deepest geological layers of the earth itself, closer to the source of life. And death.

The woman was dressed in very casual but stylish cotton

and silk clothing, layer on layer, calf-length pants over longer pants, and a skirt overall. Two or three shirts, a sweater and a loose open jacket, two scarves, a shawl, all in shades of black and grey with dabs of white. She wore large chunks of silver jewellery embedded with turquoise and another stone, brownish green, with what looked like streaks of blood running through it.

This startling woman walked towards the group, gliding almost, smiling, her bearing regal. She was ageless but not young.

Julien introduced Jeanette to her in English. Jeanette, tall herself, didn't quite reach this woman's stature. He then said simply, 'Jeanette, Morianna, of whom I have spoken.'

The woman smiled so warmly at Jeanette that the latter melted before Carol's eyes. Morianna took Jeanette's face in her hands and Jeanette touched the older woman's waist. 'Oh, yes!' Morianna exclaimed, her laughter shimmering through the air. 'You are a match for him.' She kissed Jeanette on both cheeks.

Next she was introduced to Karl and Gerlinde. She spoke in German to them, touching both lightly on the face. Gerlinde blushed a little.

With Chloe she spoke in French, smiling warmly, hugging her, calling her, 'Ma soeur.'

Then she was introduced to André, also in French. Her voice softened as she spoke to him. Her eyes held his. She extended a hand, which he took and clasped between his and kissed.

Suddenly Michael raced into the room. 'André! André! I got an idea. Listen!'

André caught the boy, turned him towards the visitor and introduced him in French. Michael looked at the woman and she smiled at him, her eyes sparkling, her face filled with delight.

'*Mon petit enfant naturel.* Come,' she said, bending from the waist, opening her arms to him.

Michael took two steps into her embrace. She held him as though he were delicate. Carol watched the look of complete bliss on her face as she pressed him to her.

But Michael disengaged himself quickly. 'Who're you?'

The woman smiled. 'I am Morianna, as your father told you. And you are Michel, André's son, yes?'

'And Carol's,' the boy said. Carol felt a lump in her throat. 'She's gonna be one of us soon.'

Everyone stared at Michael. André said, 'What made you say that, Michel?'

'Well, I want you to change her.'

'I told you this would happen.' Karl sounded irritated.

Chloe said, 'Michel, that may not be possible.'

The boy looked obstinate. 'It is. André can do it.'

He ran across the room and stood in front of Gerlinde. 'And I want him to!' Michael folded his arms over his chest in stubborn defiance.

'Because you want it doesn't mean it will be,' Karl said.

'André may not want to,' Gerlinde added. She put a hand on Michael's shoulder.

'He has to!' the boy announced.

'What's that supposed to mean?' André asked.

'If you don't change her I'll become mortal.'

'Like mother and father, like son,' Gerlinde mumbled. No one else said a word for several seconds.

Carol was startled. She loved Michael so much she tried to overlook his attitude. It was because he loved her that he wanted this. And she wasn't sure she wouldn't go along with it.

'Michel! Get over here! Now!' André said.

Carol looked at André and her heart raced. His body emitted waves of fury. She became frightened for her son. She stood up and started to move towards Michael, to shield him, but André turned on her, his eyes menacing. He pointed a finger at her. 'Stay out of this!'

She stopped but stood ready. If he tries to hurt Michael I'm going to protect my baby, she assured herself.

'I said come over here!'

Gerlinde took her hand away from Michael. The boy looked wide open, upset, frightened. His eyes had widened, his lips parted. Slowly he walked towards André.

Carol prepared to act.

When Michael was right in front of him, André squatted down and grabbed him by the shoulders, his face stern, his voice angry. 'Michel, don't try to blackmail me! I won't put up with it! It's all right for you to want what you want, but don't you ever threaten me again. Understand?' He gave the boy's shoulders a little shake for emphasis.

Michael's eyes became even wider than before. He stared at André as though terrified. Then suddenly he flung his arms around his father's neck and cried.

André held him tightly, cradling the boy in his arms, kissing his hair.

'I just want my mother here too,' Michael wailed. 'Please, Papa, make her like us so she can stay and not die and leave us.'

Carol felt her heart breaking. She wanted more than anything to hug them both but was afraid to move because what was happening was so precious.

The others in the room began to relax and eventually Michael's crying stopped.

But the moment André stood up, Morianna confronted him in English.

'Well?'

'Well what?'

'Would you do it? For the boy?'

André was quiet and Carol thought she could have heard a pin drop. Finally he said, 'I don't know. Possibly.'

'And do you think you could for his sake alone?'

'Probably not.'

'And yet together you formed *l'enfant de l'amour*,' she said, her voice was complex, rich, reminding Carol of a full orchestra.

André said nothing. Suddenly Morianna turned to Carol.

'Would you become one of us?'

Carol hesitated.

Morianna's eyes penetrated deeply into hers until Carol felt she would fall asleep from the intensity of the contact. But then she sensed Michael by her side. He took her hand and she looked down at him and smiled. 'If it's the only way I can be with Michael, yes.'

Morianna turned away from them and looked at the others in the room. 'Julien, what do you think?'

'I believe there is more here than words make apparent.'

'I agree,' she said, turning back to André.

'I know you,' she said simply. Carol saw André's jaw tighten, as though his teeth were being clamped together. 'It is not always so difficult.'

André turned away. He walked past Carol and Michael to the fireplace. He shoved the screen aside then threw in a couple of logs, poking them aggressively until they fell into place.

When he'd finished, he pulled the screen back across and straightened up, still holding the poker. 'What are you saying?'

'I'm saying help is available.'

'What help?'

'The benefit of our collective experience.'

André sneered. He slammed the poker back into its stand. The sound of metal angrily clanked against metal.

'And the ritual. It may be foreign to you but has worked in the past. Julien knows. And Chloe understands. We can aid you.'

André crossed his arms over his chest defensively. He looked angry but also upset.

'Can you accept this?' Morianna asked.

He thought about it for a few seconds. Finally he said, 'I'm not sure.' But then he looked at Michael and Carol. She had her arms around the boy's neck as he stood in front of her.

'*Oui*.' His voice was strained. Carol had never seen him this way and was fascinated to watch the conflict tumbling his emotions. He seems more real to me, she thought.

Morianna turned and said, 'And, Julien, we will work together?'

Julien nodded.

'And Chloe? Sister.' She held out her hands.

'I'm honoured,' Chloe said, taking them.

The three left the room immediately. As soon as they were gone André stormed out. Karl took Michael and left too, leaving Carol alone with Gerlinde and Jeanette.

'What's going on?' Carol asked, totally bewildered.

Jeanette sat down on the couch. 'There are ancient rites. They aren't used anymore, but sometimes, when there's ambivalence . . .'

'What do you mean?'

Gerlinde said, 'Because you're both so unsure – you and André.'

Jeanette continued. 'The three act as elders, I guess you'd call them. They'll figure out a ritual so that the transformation process can be contained. Otherwise it will be a disaster.'

'But why?'

'Because it takes a strong emotion to effect the change.'

'Kiddo, you don't know how hard it is,' Gerlinde told her. 'Giving up the blood, I mean. I've never been able to do it. I've never been motivated. That's why there aren't that many of us.'

'It can be done out of love, or hate,' Jeanette said. 'I once created another because I was extremely lonely. But to do it because Michel wants it, that wouldn't be a strong enough reason for André. He admitted it.'

Carol sat down too. 'You're saying he has to love me enough. But he doesn't love me. And I don't love him. At least I don't think so. I don't know anymore.' She held her head.

'It ain't just that,' Gerlinde said.

'What else?'

'Well, for André there's something more involved.'

'Are you going to tell me?' Carol asked, irritated. This is all getting to be too much, she thought. First they offer me immortality and then tell me how impossible it is. And they're vague besides.

'Well, even if André loves you, it still might not work.'

'But why?'

Gerlinde said nothing and Jeanette looked at the fire.

'Has he ever tried to do it before?' Carol asked.

Gerlinde's brown eyes met Carol's and her lips formed a kind of tortured grin. 'Twice.'

'And?'

'And what?'

'And what happened?' Carol asked impatiently.

'Kiddo, you don't want to know.'

'Tell me.'

'Tragedy. Both times.'

'How?'

Gerlinde turned away. 'He ripped their throats out.'

TWENTY-EIGHT

While Morianna, Julien and Chloe consulted together, a pensive silence hung over the house. Midnight came and went, then one, then two a.m. Carol spent an hour with Michael watching him and Karl organizing chemicals in jars and boxes, but they weren't paying much attention to her and she was too worried to participate. She wondered what she'd gotten herself into.

Obviously the locket and handkerchief were all that remained of André's two former lovers. But what she found even more disturbing was that by placing reminders of her along with them, André had already relegated her to the position of a memory.

The whole thing was getting confusing. Obviously vampires could make other vampires. She knew Gerlinde's story. And that Julien had changed Jeanette. And Chloe had changed André. She wondered why André couldn't do it. There were moments, like last night, when she felt he loved her a little and that the love could grow. But maybe that was just sex or romance and her need to be with Michael let her fool herself.

But more than all this, she wondered if she had just verbally signed her own death warrant.

At three in the morning the phone rang. Carol was still in the living room, now with Karl as well as Jeanette, Gerlinde and Michael. Gerlinde picked it up.

'It's for you,' she said, a strained look on her face, handing the receiver to Carol.

Carol took the phone reluctantly. 'Carol, are you really all right?' Rene's voice sounded odd, as if she'd been drinking heavily.

'Rene, yes, I told you I was. Why are you calling, and at this hour?' The others watched her and she felt nervous – now they all would know, including André.

'Oh, Carol, you've found them. You've found the vampires!'

'Yes. Look, this is not a good time to talk. I'll be in touch in a little while.'

'Do they really live forever and never grow old?'

'Rene, please, I've got to go. I'm fine, really. Everything is fine. Take care. I'll call you soon, I promise.'

When she hung up, Carol faced the others.

'Our number is unlisted. How did she get it?' Karl asked, his voice tight.

'I . . . I don't know. I didn't give it to her,' Carol said. 'Gerlinde, you know I didn't give it to her.'

Gerlinde looked uneasy.

'What else do you know?' Karl asked Gerlinde.

The redhead crossed her slim legs, and her arms over her chest. 'I kinda let Carol make a phone call. So this woman wouldn't bother us. I guess she knows somebody at the phone company. Maybe she got Carol's call traced back.'

Karl stood. His body was tense. '*Kommen sie mit mer!*'

He left the room and Gerlinde followed him looking guilty and nervous.

Carol sat down. She was worried. This wasn't like Rene.

The call was so odd. And such bad timing, too. Now Carol had gotten Gerlinde into trouble with the others. And herself. She didn't know what to do. Suddenly she looked up. Jeanette was staring at her. She felt she had to say something. 'Rene's harmless. I'll call again soon. Keep her reassured.'

'They'll have to change the number,' Jeanette said. 'And move. Maybe leave Montréal. This puts everyone in danger.'

Carol didn't know what to say.

About five in the morning Carol went into the kitchen to make herself something to eat. She had finished a meal of brown rice, brussels sprouts, carrots and a small T-bone, and was just pouring a cup of herbal tea when André appeared at the door coming up from the basement. He looked terrible, tight and restrained.

'André, can I talk with you?' He stopped and stared at her. Something in his face told her to be careful and now she regretted stopping him.

'I . . . just wanted you to know I loved the way you dealt with Michael. You're very caring towards him.'

He said nothing, just continued staring.

She sat down on a stool across the counter from him. She took a sip of tea. It was too hot and burned her upper lip, forcing awareness of how nervous he was making her feel.

'You gave out our address.'

'I . . . I'm sorry. She's my therapist. She was worried. Gerlinde let me use the phone so I could assure her I was okay and . . .'

'And you gave Michel the idea, didn't you?'

This took her totally by surprise, so much so that at first she couldn't answer him. She spilled a little tea putting the cup down. 'No. What makes you think that?'

'Where else?'

'But you or one of the others was always with us. How could I? I didn't. You've got to believe me.'

'Why should I believe you?' He looked angry and she was startled by this turn around of his feelings towards her.

'Why shouldn't you?' she said in a small voice.

'Are you joking? Do you want a list?' He took two steps towards the counter, gripping the edge so hard his knuckles went white. A warning bell went off in Carol's head. 'First you think you'll kill me with a virus and then you try to kill me with a stake through my heart.'

'I didn't. I told you . . .'

'And you ran away – twice! And kidnapped Michel. And now you've betrayed us, made us vulnerable to the outside world. And you fed Michel milk when he was born. Now he's having a hard time deciding . . .'

'You're putting things together. Surely you can understand why . . .'

'Yes, I understand! I see you clearly, what a liar you are!'

His voice was growing louder, his face paler. He seemed to be altering, becoming less human, more animal-like, and Carol felt frightened. 'André, calm down, you're getting . . .'

Suddenly his arm shot out and swept the teapot, cup and saucer across the counter and onto the floor where they smashed against the tiles. 'Don't patronize me, bitch!'

Carol stood, shaking with fear. She took several steps back. He picked up the stool she'd been sitting on and hurled it across the kitchen. It slammed into the wall and broke apart.

'André!' He spun around to the door where Jeanette stood. 'They're ready,' she told him.

He stormed past her and out of the kitchen.

Carol began to shake. She hugged herself and looked at Jeanette. 'He's crazy. He'll kill me.'

Jeanette walked over and put an arm around her shoulders. 'You've got to stand up to him, Carol.'

'Oh, sure!' Her eyes filled with tears. 'Easy for you to say. He's so much stronger than me. He can snap me in half like a pencil.'

Jeanette smiled a little. 'After you've changed you'll be more equal physically, and in other ways too.'

'I'll never get that far. I'll be dead, pulverized by an enraged madman.'

'You don't have to take him on physically. Try responding.'

'But it's always been like this. Whenever I start to say anything reasonable he tries to hurt me.'

'Well, he might hurt you anyway. That's no reason not to include yourself.'

'Right, either way I get a broken neck. But one way I die feeling like a doormat and the other I have the satisfaction of going out like a martyr.'

Carol started to pick up the pieces of the broken teapot but Jeanette stopped her. 'We'll clean it up later. Let's go into the living room.'

Morianna sat on the large couch between Julien and Chloe. André sat rigid in a chair across the table from them. Opposite the fireplace Gerlinde snuggled close to Karl in a loveseat. She held Michael on her other side. Jeanette and Carol took the other loveseat.

'I shall speak in English because all of us understand that language,' Morianna said. She looked at André. 'In five nights it will be the eve of a new year. Nine years ago on the day of the New Year, Michel was born. At that time he must make a decision that will alter the course of his existence. The moon will be full, which seems an auspicious time. And given recent developments – you may no longer be safe here – I believe we should proceed as quickly as possible. We three,' and here she looked at Julien and then Chloe, 'feel that the giving and taking of the blood can best be accomplished, in your case, from a position of reverence.'

Carol noticed André's jaw clench.

'We will detail the ritual as it proceeds. For now it is enough to know that on Friday you will go out and take sustenance, the last you will consume until completion. At midnight Friday the ritual begins. Throughout its duration you will give your blood to the woman until you are emptied. At midnight on Sunday, as the old year ends and the new begins, you may then reclaim the blood from her.'

André jumped to his feet. He looked totally startled. 'Three days? You want me to go without blood for three days?'

'It will not be as difficult as you imagine,' Morianna said.

Chloe added, 'It won't be like the other times, André. We've set it up for you.'

André looked at her, then at Morianna and finally at Julien. His face said it all – they had betrayed him. 'Forget it!'

He turned and strode towards the door, but Julien beat him to it. '*Va't'en!*,' André shouted.

But Julien didn't get out of his way, he just spoke softly in French. André argued, his voice loud, brimming with bitter fury, his fists clenched at his sides. But Julien persisted, despite the fact that André's anger was escalating. Finally, in a moment so brief Carol could hardly trace it, André slammed his fist all the way through the solid oak, right beside Julien's head. When he pulled it out of the shattered wood, his hand was bloody.

The anger had broken. André's shoulders slumped and his body shook a little. He ran his undamaged hand through his hair. Julien continued as if nothing had happened, talking softly, reasonably, like a father explaining something to a frustrated son. He placed his hands on the sides of André's face. André's blood-streaked fingers curled tentatively around Julien's wrist. Julien continued talking.

From where she sat, Carol could only see André's profile. His eyes seemed to glisten and she wondered if he was crying but she couldn't tell. But she was fascinated by what was happening.

André continued to say nothing, just nodded his head once in a while, while Julien talked. Finally Julien called to Karl and the three men left the room together.

Carol turned to her son. Michael sat perfectly still. He looked scared. Suddenly he bolted from Gerlinde's side and raced after them. Now the women were alone.

The four looked from one to the other. Gerlinde asked a question in German and Chloe responded in English. 'A male *must* be admired by an older male, or there is no movement.'

Carol felt dismal. 'I don't want to leave here or leave Michael,' she said to no one in particular.

'You don't have to leave,' Chloe told her.

'But André won't do it. He said so. He can't. He hates me.'

'He'll do it,' Gerlinde assured her.

'And he doesn't hate you,' Jeanette added.

Carol looked at her and shook her head. 'How can you say that? You saw what happened here. And what happened in the kitchen. That's not love.'

'Fairy tales are beautiful, yes?' Morianna said, her voice as smooth as spun silk. 'Unfortunately they reflect only parts of the puzzle of a relationship. There is more than kindness on the road to love.'

Carol shot her an angry look. 'I'm supposed to let him push me around? Whenever he's upset I just stand in front of his fist? You wouldn't do it, why should I?'

'No one's asking you to do that,' Jeanette said. 'But you're not going to get through to him by challenging him either.'

'But you just told me in the kitchen to stand up to him.'

'I told you to respond, from your soul. With compassion.'

Carol laughed bitterly. 'This is all bullshit. He doesn't need compassion, he needs a straitjacket. He's insane. One minute he's kind to me and the next ready to rip my head off. I can't predict it. And I can't defend myself.'

'Then stop trying,' Chloe suggested.

Carol stood. She felt agitated, angry, thoroughly confused. She paced the room shaking her head. 'This is ridiculous. I don't know what you're talking about, any of you. He doesn't want to do it, so why should he? And I don't want him to because the way he feels I'll just end up like the other two, and my son will be permanently traumatized by watching his father tear his mother limb from limb on his ninth birthday. Well, I don't care if André will do it or not, I won't.'

'Don't say that, kiddo,' Gerlinde said.

Carol turned on her. 'And why not?'

'Because you don't have a choice anymore.'

They talked with her longer, trying to persuade her to bypass her fear of André's volatile nature, but Carol was unconvinced. They suggested she stop reacting to him and try to see what hid behind his rage.

'Why should the woman do all the understanding?' Carol argued bitterly.

'You've got to start somewhere,' Jeanette said.

'Why doesn't he try to understand me?'

'He's too frightened,' Chloe told her.

'He's frightened? Well, he should be. He's psychotic!'

They talked for hours, until the sun began to rise and Gerlinde took her to the door of the basement.

'Kiddo, you gotta try to reach him. I know it ain't easy. If only there were vampire psychiatrists, or even a decent tranquillizer. Anyway, you're right, he's nutty as a fruit cake; doesn't know the word "sorry" in any language. I oughta know, sharing a house with him for over a quarter of a century. But believe me, startling as it might seem, the guy does have a warm side. You just have to defrost him, that's all. Besides, André's gonna do it whether you want it or not so you might as well make the best of things.'

'You know something, Gerlinde, I never seem to matter. Nine years ago I agreed to this and he refused. Now I don't want to change but I'm being forced to anyway.'

'Yeah, life can be a bitch,' Gerlinde said. Then she grinned. 'But dull it ain't.'

When Carol reached the basement room, she found André sitting before the fireplace. He did not turn when she came in. She switched on the light above the bed and sat down. His back was to her.

Don't try to talk to him tonight, she told herself. But you've got to talk to him. Tonight's Tuesday and Friday is only a few days away. It's now or never.

She walked over to him hesitantly. When she came around the side of his chair he didn't look up. His eyes were fixed on the fire but they held a dazed, far-away look and she knew he wasn't really seeing anything in the room.

She sat on the footstool in front of him. A minute went by, the only sounds the roaring of the flames and the popping of chunks of resin imbedded in the logs. Carol nervously rested a hand on his knee. His eyes travelled from the fire to her face.

She was conscious of her cool breath, her dry mouth, the fear. She rubbed his knee a little. 'I think we can work out our differences,' she said, trying to sound cheerful. His face was vacant. 'I know things haven't always been smooth between us, but I want to try. I want this to work. I think everything will be all right – the ritual, I mean. Everybody says it won't be so bad. You'll be able to do it.'

She had to keep control of herself so that her body wouldn't tremble. She touched his other knee. She smiled a little. His face showed no response.

Before she realized it, he had clamped his hands around her upper arms, pulling her towards him, his fingers digging painfully into her flesh. Suddenly his face was enraged. 'Don't you dare feel sorry for me! I won't tolerate your pity!'

Carol was stunned for a moment. But some inner voice took over and, despite the danger she knew could erupt, said, 'André I don't pity you. That's not what I'm feeling. I'm trying to care for you but you won't let me in.'

More emotions flickered across his face than she could identify. 'Don't!' he said. She didn't know if he meant don't try to love him or don't talk or what. But gradually he eased her away from him, as though afraid that too sudden a movement on his part might trigger the violence that rampaged just below his skin. He opened his hands slowly, releasing her, then leaned back in the chair. Suddenly he looked weary. His eyes retreated to the fire. 'Go to bed,' he said dully.

Later, when he joined her, she waited until she thought he was asleep. He was so still, so quiet. She started to slide a hand across his chest when his came up to block it. But after a couple of minutes she slid hers further along, stopping over his heart, and he didn't resist. At some point his hand covered hers and held tight.

TWENTY-NINE

The following night André told her, 'Get dressed. We're taking Michel out.'

They sat in the back of the limo with Michael between them until he wanted to sit by the window and Carol moved over.

Twenty minutes later they were at the waterfront where the large ships dock when they come through the St Lawrence Seaway. André got out alone.

As Michael turned on the mini TV, Carol asked, 'What happened last night, Michael? When you left the room with André, Julien and Karl?'

The boy flipped the channel a couple of times and stopped at a rerun of *Star Trek: The Next Generation* series.

'What happened last night?' Carol asked again.

'Huh?' He looked at her blankly until his brain cleared of TV reality and he said, 'Oh, they talked.' He turned back to the set.

'What about?'

'Stuff.'

'Like what?'

'Hey, Carol, look at this! These guys can disappear and come back again somewhere else.'

'Umm.' Carol watched Captain Picard and Lt Riker materialize on a rather barren-looking alien planet.

'Did they talk about the ritual?'

'Yeah. I guess.'

'What did Julien say?'

'He told my dad not to worry. He said he'd teach him what to do and everything'll be okay.'

Carol glanced at the screen. Picard and Riker were discussing what course of action to take.

'What did André say?' Carol asked. She felt a little guilty pumping Michael for information but she needed to know anything that might be helpful.

'Hey, Carol, can I have a phaser? Can I, huh?'

'I don't know if they sell them, Michael.'

'They do. We saw 'em in the science store. Can I?'

'I guess so.'

'When can we go?'

'Maybe next week.' If I'm still alive, she thought.

'Michael, what did André say? When Julien told him everything would be all right?'

A commercial was on and Michael flipped channels. 'Nothin'.'

'You mean he didn't say anything?'

'Yeah.'

The boy flipped the TV off and the radio on. 'Wow! Madonna! She's a sexy babe!' He snapped his fingers and swayed to the music and Carol laughed. Then he really got into it, closing his eyes, making wild faces, really hamming it up for her benefit. 'Oh, baaay beee, baaay beee!'

Carol was in stitches, her eyes watering.

The door opened and André got in. They both slid over to make room for him.

'Sounds like a wild party,' he said, smiling.

'Oh baaay beee!' Michael crooned. Carol was still laughing and André laughed too.

When the song was over, André called the driver and they sped away. He turned the radio off and Michael said, 'Aw, why can't I listen?'

'Later. First you eat.'

He handed the boy a jar. Michael sat back against the seat and took off the lid. Carol watched, fascinated.

'Don't spill it,' André said. He put an arm across the back of the seat behind Michael who was in the middle again.

Carol watched her son drink the red gore down slowly, as though he was enjoying it the way any boy would enjoy a milkshake or a coke. She noticed André watching her watching Michael.

As Michael finished they drove over a bridge onto Ile Sainte-Hélène, a small island, and after a while pulled into a parking lot. Ahead the sky was bright with the coloured lights of an amusement park. Michael showed no surprise and apparently knew they had been headed here.

The weather was extremely mild for December, but Carol was surprised the park was still open.

'I'm going on The Monster alone this time.'

'Be my guest,' André said.

'And I wanna go on the Salt and Pepper Shakers too.'

'That one you definitely go on alone.'

The three of them passed through the gates of La Ronde, the amusements left over from Expo, the 1967 Montréal World's Fair. The air was filled with laughter and music and chatter and shrieks and the smell of sweet and greasy food sizzling on grills. 'It's crowded for this time of year,' Carol said.

'They keep some of it open all year and the rest as long as the weather permits,' André explained.

André bought several strips of tickets and they headed for the roller coaster, Michael running ahead.

'Do you bring him here a lot?' Carol asked.

'Half a dozen times since we've been in Montréal. He likes movement. So did I when I was his age. I still do.'

He was trying to tell her about himself and Carol didn't miss that.

At the ride, André handed the boy the required number of tickets. They watched him going up the steep incline and then descend, screaming with fear and delight, just like all the other children.

'Does he ever play with other kids?' she asked.

'Sometimes. He had friends in Bonn and there are a couple of boys around the corner. But we have to be careful, obviously.'

She nodded.

André bought Michael cotton candy. She was surprised. 'So he eats real food.'

'Not often.'

'Hey, André, win me one of these mirrors.' Michael was standing at a carnival-type gallery pointing to a cheap framed mirror with a picture of L.L. Cool J etched on it. He had just tried the game himself, without success.

André paid the vendor and tossed three balls into a bushel basket designed to expel them. But he tossed them carefully, with the grace of an athlete, letting the balls roll easily up the sides, explaining the procedure to Michael, and all three stayed in the basket, much to the operator's chagrin.

After Michael got his mirror, both of them tried the game again. Michael's went all over but, as before, all three of André's stayed in.

'They should make you illegal,' the vendor joked.

André turned to Carol. 'Pick something.'

'I'll take that,' she said. The man inside the booth handed her a silly-looking stuffed vampire bat.

As soon as she got it in her hands, she pushed it into André's neck saying in a Transylvanian accent, 'I vant to suck your blllooooodd.'

André laughed and grabbed her around the waist with one arm, pulling her hips into his. 'Later,' he told her, his dynamic energy sending a thrill through her. 'She's kinky.' He winked at the vendor, making him laugh too.

The three rode the ferris wheel together, even though Michael complained half-heartedly, 'This ride's stupid. It's no fun,' until they got stuck at the top.

'Turn around and sit, Michel. You'll fall out,' André warned him.

Carol looked over the side. 'Gee, it's a long way down. I forgot how high these things are. It's nice up here, though. Look, Michael. There's the moon!'

To the left, the large blue-white globe hung in a clear sky, not quite full. It will be by the weekend, she thought. This may be one of the last moons I see.

She glanced at André. He must have been thinking something similar because the look on his face matched what she was feeling. They turned away from each other.

While Michael drove the bumper cars, she and André stood at the rail watching their son. André slid his arm around her shoulders. He's strong, she thought. If only I felt protected by him instead of threatened. Why can't it be different?

'À gauche! à gauche!' André called out, shaking his head.

But Michael turned right, trying to squeeze between two cars, colliding head on with both, trapped from behind by a third. 'By the time he figures it out the ride will be over. He'll want to do it again,' he laughed. And Michael did stay on for a second ride.

While they watched, Carol turned to André. 'Do you think you'll have any trouble on Friday?' She had worked out a different strategy – asking him his thoughts rather than telling him hers. He looked back at her. A darkness, like a solar eclipse, descended over him. He removed his arm.

When Michael got off the ride, André said, 'Let's go.'

'Aw, we just got here! And I wanna ride the Salt and Pepper Shakers.'

'Next time.' André seemed tense. 'Come on.'

They followed him to the gate and then to the car. Along the way he snatched the stuffed bat from Carol's hands and shoved it into a trash can.

'I'm gonna ride up front with Guy,' Michael announced.

In the back, when she and André were alone, Carol, feeling totally frustrated, threw her hands up in the air. 'What did I do? What did I say this time that got you mad?'

He looked out the window.

'I don't understand. Is the ritual a taboo subject? If it is, let me know.'

Still he said nothing.

'I'm just trying to find out what you're thinking and feeling about it. Maybe I can help.'

'It's going to be hard enough,' he said, still not looking at her. 'Why don't you worry about your part and let me take care of mine.'

'Maybe I can help you?'

'You can't.'

'But if you tell me about the other times, maybe we can figure out what went wrong.'

His head snapped around. He pointed a finger in front of her face. 'I'm warning you, Carol, get off my back. I mean it!'

'Okay! We don't have to talk about it,' she said, backing down. 'I was only trying to help.'

He lowered his hand and his voice. 'You're Michel's mother, not mine. Try to remember that.'

They were quiet for most of the ride back, but as they

neared the mountain, Carol said, 'Can I ask you something? It doesn't have to do with Friday.'

'What?'

'It's just that I'm confused. You don't want me to mother you but I don't know what you do want from me.'

He was silent for a few seconds. The car turned onto Redpath Crescent. 'I want you in my bed,' he finally said looking straight ahead.

'Is that all?'

'Maybe a friend.' He stared out the window.

'Friends confide in each other.'

The limo pulled up the steep cement driveway. Just as they came to a stop beside the house, André turned to her. His voice was low and flat. 'Stop wasting your time on semantics. It doesn't matter what either of us want because by Saturday morning you'll be dead.'

THIRTY

'Hey, kiddo, you look like *Night of the Living Dead* revisited. What's wrong?' Gerlinde asked when Carol walked into the living room. Jeanette, Julien and Chloe were also there.

Carol flopped heavily onto the chair by the window, away from the others, and said in a monotone, 'Wrong? What could possibly be wrong? André just told me that by Saturday morning I'll be dead, that's all. Nothing to get excited about.'

'Why did he say that?' Jeanette wanted to know.

'I guess he was just trying to be nice.' Carol stared out the window at the last of the dry shrivelled leaves covering the raw earth.

'So what happened,' Gerlinde pressed her.

Carol sighed. 'We were at La Ronde. Michael was on a ride. Everything seemed to be going okay then I asked André if he thought he'd have any trouble on Friday. He went berserk, as usual.'

'Boy, you sure go for the jugular,' Gerlinde said.

'What do you mean?'

'I mean tact ain't your speciality.'

'What was I supposed to say? "This weekend might be a fine time for imbibing, if one were so inclined. Would you care to venture an opinion on the subject?"'

'Tell us exactly what happened,' Chloe said.

'It won't do any good.' But Carol related the conversation, almost word for word.

When she finished, Julien stood. 'You are correct, Gerlinde.'

'About what?'

'Subtlety is not her forte.' He turned towards Jeanette.

'Perhaps instruction in one of your arts, my love, *l'art du plaisir*.' He kissed his wife and left the room.

'Julien's got a point,' Jeanette said to the others.

'What's that?' Carol asked, her voice saturated with apathy.

'Well, if André wants you for a lover, why don't you start with that.'

'Terrific idea!' Gerlinde yelled. She jumped to her feet and said, 'Come on,' pulling Carol up. The redhead waved for Jeanette and Chloe to follow.

'I have something to do,' Chloe told them.

Upstairs Gerlinde sat Carol in front of a vanity in a room furnished much like the one she'd stayed in when she'd been in Bordeaux. 'What a mess.' Gerlinde tugged at the ends of Carol's hair. 'You wash, I'll cut,' she told Jeanette.

'You're going to do my hair? My life's on the line and this is your solution? A haircut?' Carol felt disappointed.

'A new "do" works wonders for a gal,' Gerlinde laughed, dancing her way into the bathroom, dragging Carol behind.

While Gerlinde cut her hair, Jeanette gave her a manicure and pedicure, painting her finger and toe nails with a bright red polish.

'You two are crazy. This is the most ridiculous scheme I've ever heard.'

'It's not ridiculous at all,' Jeanette said. 'André's very physically oriented. He's like Julien in that way. In a couple of other ways too.'

'This is so typical. First you want me to "understand" him and now you want me to seduce him. Women have been doing this for thousands of years.'

'And it's worked,' Gerlinde said, pulling the sides of Carol's hair straight down to check that the cut was even.

'But it's so devious. And so unliberated.'

'Kiddo, if you wanna run for *Ms Magazine*'s "Woman of the Year", yeah, this probably won't get you any votes. If you want to keep André from decapitating you, vamping him just might do the trick.'

'And it's not devious,' Jeanette said. 'I think André trusts what comes through the body because he can understand it.'

'Talk to the neurotic in his own lingo, right?' Carol smirked.

When her hair was nicely shaped to frame her face and they'd made her up to accentuate her best features, they stripped Carol and Jeanette applied a drop of *Obsession* between her breasts saying, 'Just a touch.' She wiped most of it away with a tissue. 'Our sense of smell is finely tuned.'

Carol submitted to it all but secretly thought it was a complete waste of time.

'What's she gonna wear?' Gerlinde asked. 'My stuff's probably too small and too weird.'

'Be right back,' Jeanette said.

'Gerlinde, do you really think this will make any difference?' Carol asked.

'It might not help but it can't hurt, as any vampire granny will tell you.'

'How reassuring.' Carol sighed.

When Jeanette returned she was carrying a lime-green satin negligée. 'If it was blue it would bring out your eyes.

But I bought it for my eyes.' She slipped it over Carol's head. The nightgown was far too long and hung from her like a discard at the thrift store.

'I look like a little girl wearing my mother's clothes,' Carol giggled.

'We'll cut it,' Jeanette said. 'Hand me the scissors.'

'Don't do that, it's too nice,' Carol told her.

'I've got lots more. And this is an emergency.'

Jeanette snipped the spaghetti straps and tied them into big bows. The dress was still too long. The two vampiresses stepped back to look at their handiwork. 'Pretty close to perfect!' Gerlinde cried.

'Lovely,' Jeanette added.

'I don't look bad, do I?' Carol studied herself in a full-length mirror. She hadn't bothered about her appearance in years. 'Now what?'

'Go get him.' Gerlinde gnashed her teeth.

'Just like that? Anybody have a chair and a whip?'

Jeanette turned her towards the door and Gerlinde opened it.

Carol sucked in her lower lip. 'I don't know . . .' They gave her a shove out and then each took an arm and led her down the steps to the kitchen, stopping at the basement door.

'Some advice, strange coming from a chatterbox like me,' Gerlinde said. 'Don't talk about Friday, or the ritual. Better yet, don't talk at all.'

'And I have something to suggest too,' Jeanette said. 'I don't know what your sexual relationship has been like up until now, but this would be a good time to let your own passion lead the way, know what I mean?'

'Not at all.'

'It's called seduction,' Gerlinde said. 'You used to be an actress, you can figure it out.'

'But you can't fake it,' Jeanette warned. 'It's got to come from the heart.'

'Well, maybe a bit lower,' Gerlinde grinned.

Carol made her way nervously down to André's room. When she entered it was pitch dark. She turned on the little light over the bed. André sat in the same chair by the fireplace as he had the previous night, only this time there was no fire. The room was cold, dismal. He did not turn around.

Carol chewed on her lower lip, tasting lipstick. He's instigated all the sex we've ever had, she thought. This is so new to me. I'm not sure what to do.

She closed her eyes and took in long slow breaths, imagining air travelling down past her lungs, into her stomach and lower, swelling her genitals. She tried to relax and get some energy circulating there so she could find an erotic wellspring from which to draw. The theatre exercise made her think back to years ago, to the plays she'd been in back at college and then at the amateur theatre in Philadelphia. She had never been cast as a lead. The roles she'd usually auditioned for and gotten were bland, secondary parts like Cathleen in *Long Day's Journey into Night*. But once, in acting class, she'd played out the first scene in *Cat on a Hot Tin Roof*. The class had been amazed by her performance. She always thought she could have played out the sultry Maggie, all the way.

When she opened her eyes, she felt a little clearer and a little horny. Her nipples pressed against the smooth cool satin. An electric current zipped through her body, one she remembered from a few occasions on stage when things clicked and she and the character had melded.

Without looking at André, she went to the fireplace and knelt down. First she arranged sticks and paper and lit them. She watched until they caught fire, trying to keep her mind concentrated on what she was doing. As the fire got going, she added a couple of branches then two logs, propped against each other. Soon warmth and the sweet scent of red cedar enveloped her.

She turned slowly, sensuously. André was watching her. He looked haunted, his face torn by worry and doubt. His legs were stretched out on the footstool and one elbow resting on a chair arm propped up his head. Carol made her way to his chair and knelt by the side of it. She had never seen him so unconfident, so forlorn. In some ways she found it appealing.

'Where'd you get this?' he asked, flipping one of the bows with his finger.

'Jeanette.'

His hand went back to holding his head up and he sighed. 'They suggested you try to seduce me?'

Carol said nothing.

'It won't help. Nothing will help.'

She moved to the front of the chair, he watching her all the while. Don't get sucked into this negativity, she told herself. Rather than pay much attention to him, she focused on her breathing, taking the air in as deeply as she could, letting this wanton seductress energy fill her. A tingle spread through her labia.

Her hands moved of their own accord. She unzipped his pants and held his penis. It was flaccid, but she rubbed it from side to side then up and down and it firmed a little. Touching him aroused her.

'It's too late,' he said. 'Tomorrow night, then Friday and that's it.'

Don't get into it, she told herself – stay in character. She smiled. 'Well, since we've only got two nights, we'd better make the most of it.'

She untied one of the straps on her nightgown and the fabric fell away from her right breast. His eyes travelled there. Carol straddled his knees and rubbed herself against them, all the while breathing, undulating, working herself up. She let the other strap fall from her shoulder. Then she pulled his shoes, socks and pants off. He removed his own shirt.

When he was naked and firm enough, Carol sat on top of him, bringing him into her warmth. She moved up and down and at the same time rocked back and forth with her eyes closed, feeling him in her. André's hands began to caress her body and he brought his lips to one of her nipples. The direct link between her breast and vagina stunned her; she couldn't stop moaning. Her head snapped back, her body quivered and a deep throaty sound welled out as the sensations overwhelmed her.

Carol felt moist, dreamy, filled with passion. She pulled his lips to hers and kissed him hard and sloppily. And then she looked him in the eye. 'Take me to bed!'

The next night André whispered to her in the dark, 'Wait here for me. I won't be long.'

While he was gone, Carol made herself breakfast and chatted with Michael in the kitchen. Afterwards she showered, fixed her hair and applied make-up then got back into bed and waited. She had no idea if this would make any difference, but she felt wonderful. She had never experienced her body as so fully alive; she lived in each cell and each cell called out, wanting. And for once she didn't feel weak.

When André returned, he undressed quickly and joined her in bed, easing up her body, entering her slowing, making love to her passionately again and again, like a condemned man, desperate to savour his last meals.

Well after midnight he started to talk.

Completely out of the blue, without any prompting, he said, 'You're different from the others.' His head rested in her lap. She ran her fingers through his hair, remembering Gerlinde's advice. Carol let him talk.

'I knew Anne-Marie when we were children. We grew up

together. And then she became my paramour. She was so beautiful. Blue eyes, dark hair that curled around her face when we made love. She had the warmest smile. Sweet. Vulnerable. Shy. Alluring. After I changed I told her, of course. She begged me to change her. I wanted her, more than I'd ever wanted anyone. But she had become afraid of me, afraid of what I'd turned into, and I didn't see it in time. When I tried to take her blood she struggled. And then she begged me not to kill her. She looked at me as if I was a monster, something she not only feared but despised. I became angry. I've been over it and over it in my mind. I don't know what happened. I lost control.'

Carol massaged his face with her finger tips. The muscles were tense. She hung on every word, trying to understand.

'Sylvie I met in 1946. Karl, David – a friend of ours, like us – and I lived in New York then. Sylvie was visiting from France, visiting relatives. She was pretty, earthy, her feet more on the ground than Anne-Marie's. But she had the same dark hair and light eyes, eyes that I could see my soul in. Nearly twenty years had passed. I'd grieved over Anne-Marie. I wanted to love again. She said she understood what I was. But when it came to the blood the same thing happened. She pulled back, became hysterical. I was a monster and she tried to escape. It enraged me. And it wasn't just her words. I could feel her resisting me. I started seeing her as my prey instead of my lover. And when she begged for her life, just like before, I lost myself. I lost her. I swore I'd never try it again; I'd never let myself get that close. It's all so long ago but it's like yesterday to me.' He sighed.

'The blood's hard to give up. We resent giving it up. It's painful physically, but I can cope with that. But I should have been able to do it. Others have. I don't know. Maybe I'm kidding myself. Maybe it runs in the family.'

She wanted to ask him what he meant but was afraid he

might shut down. Instead, Carol bent and kissed him on the lips. He pulled her down until she was on top of him then he flipped them both over and penetrated her.

Later, before morning, he told her about his parents. 'I know I loved them, but I don't really remember them,' he said.

They had been face to face but he turned onto his back and lay an arm across his eyes. The corners of his mouth angled down and she had the feeling that each word was a struggle.

'They were middle-aged when I was born. By the time I was Michel's age I was used to being parentless. They were gone, and only three of my brothers were still living. Chloe took my father. She was his sister.'

Carol was shocked.

'The way it works with us is that it's a chain – we're linked, one to the next, so it's as if we're all related. Chloe was formed by someone she didn't know and hasn't seen since, a chance encounter one night. We think he's the same one who changed Karl and our friend, David. But it doesn't matter because we *feel* each other. When one of our kind dies, each of us experiences the death, even if we're not present.

'My father insisted Chloe change him. It was just after my fifth birthday. I remember the cake my mother baked for me. It was the last one. Anyway, my father talked Chloe into it – he was handsome, beguiling, and because he was the youngest, as I was, he had always been like a baby to her and she loved to indulge him. He had contracted tuberculosis and knew he was going to die soon.

'Chloe says women found him charming. But he loved only my mother and once he had altered, naturally he tried to change her. From what Chloe tells me, my mother reacted the same way as Anne-Marie and Sylvie. To make a long story short, he failed. After he destroyed my mother he destroyed himself.'

'How?' Carol managed to ask.

'My father chained himself outside in a field in such a way that he couldn't escape the sun and he couldn't get food. It must have been a very painful death. Chloe says it took six days of frying and starving to finish him off. But I think he wanted to suffer because of the guilt. If I'd had the guts, I would have done the same thing.

'Chloe brought me up. When I was thirty-seven I asked her to change me because I'd lived in her world and by then I could see the advantages. It probably blinded me; I've never been able to figure out why mortals can't see the possibilities. And she was the only real family I knew. She refused at first but I talked her into it. I guess I'm like my father. In a lot of ways.'

He looked at Carol and for the first time she saw what the angry defensiveness hid. His sadness and loneliness were the heartbreakingly vulnerable face beneath the mask.

'I don't know what to tell you,' he said. 'There's an old Indian legend – it's common, I'm sure you've run across it. About the scorpion that asks the frog to take him across the river on his back. The frog refuses, afraid the scorpion will sting him to death. But the scorpion argues very convincingly, "Don't be ridiculous. If I do that we'll both drown." Finally he persuades the frog. Halfway across, the scorpion suddenly stings the frog and they both start sinking. Naturally the frog feels betrayed and with his last dying breath wants to know why? Do you know what the scorpion tells him? 'Because it's my nature'.

'I don't want to kill you, but I don't know if I can do anything else. They're stretching this over three nights.' He laughed humourlessly. 'I can't even do it in one.'

He turned towards her. Gently he took her face in his hands and caressed her cheekbones with his thumbs. A look filled his face, a look she could finally understand because she had suffered too.

'Just don't plead with me, Carol,' he said. 'Whatever happens, don't beg for your life. Because the only thing I know for certain is that if you see me as a monster I won't be able to stop myself from turning into one. I'll tear you apart.'

THIRTY-ONE

On Friday evening, the first night of the ritual, just after sunset André left the house to find blood. Carol walked him to the car. They kissed but didn't speak. There really wasn't anything more to say.

She phoned Rene. No answer. She didn't leave a message. Either she'd be around to call again on Monday, or not.

Just as Carol hung up there was a knock at the door. She heard a voice she recognized and hurried to the entrance. 'My God! What are you doing here?'

'Let me in,' Rene said, shoving past Gerlinde. 'Carol, I'm so relieved you're all right. I've been worried about you.'

'Of course I'm all right,' Carol said as they hugged. 'I told you that.'

'I had to be sure they hadn't coerced you to phone me.'

'This, no doubt, is the therapist,' Karl said. He nodded for Gerlinde to close the door. She did, and Carol noticed her slide the deadbolt into place.

'I am. Rene Curtis, and you're Karl.' She extended a hand, which Karl ignored. A small crowd gathered in the hallway.

Besides Karl and Gerlinde, Jeanette and Chloe arrived to greet this unexpected visitor and, behind them, Julien.

Rene looked around, assessing them. 'So, these are the vampires.'

Carol sucked in air. 'Rene, you shouldn't be here. This is really bad timing . . .'

Rene turned to her. 'Carol, you're like a daughter to me, you know that. I couldn't just forget about you, not after all we've been through together. Besides, I've wanted to meet them.'

'Now that she's here, what should we do with her?' Gerlinde said.

'Do with me? Why you'll invite me in, of course. I want to know exactly what's going on with Carol, every step of the way. She needs an advocate.'

'Carol has never needed anyone to speak on her behalf,' Chloe said. Carol had never heard her voice so cold. 'She's perfectly capable of doing that herself.'

'I don't think that's the case at all. It seems to me she's been more than mistreated by you people. Is people the correct term? She's definitely vulnerable here and someone has to be on her side.'

Carol put her hands up and shook her head. 'Wait. Just wait a minute. Rene, I don't need help. I told you that.'

'Perhaps you are the one who requires aid,' Julien said, looking directly at Rene.

'And you must be Julien. The description fits.'

'God, she knows us all!' Gerlinde said.

Julien, however, just stared at Rene, who said, 'Your hypnotic expertise won't work with me. You see, not only am I familiar with the latest techniques, but I'm consciously unreceptive to your powers of suggestion.'

Julien smiled a little smile that Carol did not perceive as pleasant. 'I suggest we invite Ms Collins in, as one does when a vampire wishes to enter a private dwelling.'

Rene laughed, but Carol felt really uncomfortable.

They sat in the living room, all of them forming a semicircle around Rene, who was directed to a chair in the middle of the room facing them; the doorway was behind them. No means of escape, Carol thought. Rene has no idea what she'd gotten herself into. Carol suddenly worried about what would happen when André returned.

Morianna joined them and stood across the room from Julien. The two elders interrogated Rene.

'You have come here for another purpose, one not stated,' Morianna said.

Rene turned to her left. 'I don't believe I know you.'

Morianna didn't introduce herself. 'Please disclose your hidden agendas.'

'Hardly hidden. My main purpose is to ensure that Carol has a future.'

'And that you yourself have one,' Julien said.

Rene smiled. 'The future is important to all of us, isn't it Julien.'

'Why are you here?' Morianna demanded. Her face was composed, as if she already knew the answer to that question. Carol noticed the same look on Julien's face.

'To find out what's happening with Carol.' Rene turned to her. 'Well, what is happening?'

Carol glanced around the room, not knowing how much she was at liberty to say, afraid to tell her anything, afraid not to tell her. No one gave any indication as to what Carol should do. She decided it didn't matter at this point; they weren't about to let Rene leave, she was convinced of that.

'I'm taking part in a ritual this weekend. André is going to transform me. I'll be like them.' If I'm not dead, she thought.

'I see.' Rene paused. 'Is this something you've agreed to, Carol, or is it being foisted upon you?'

'I . . . I've agreed to it, yes.'

'Carol, you don't seem very sure of your decision.'

'I want to be with my son. And with André.'

'After all he's done to you? You sound like a typical battered wife fighting her rescuer to return to her batterer. Have they brain-washed you into thinking you're safe here?'

Carol felt confused. Having Rene here complicated things, reopened issues she'd made peace about, made her question things that had already been decided. 'Rene, I think you should go home. This is not a good time.'

'I won't leave you in the lurch, Carol. Someone has to protect you from falling into their clutches again. I'm staying.'

'Not if I can help it,' Gerlinde said.

'Unfortunately for you, you can't help it. I've left two audio cassettes with a friend. By now she's handed one over to a friend of hers, a person even I don't know the identity of. You see,' she turned back to Julien, 'even if your hypnosis had worked, there's no way you can forestall what will come to pass.'

Carol felt horrified. 'And just what will come to pass, Rene?'

'If I fail to phone my friend Monday morning, and every morning after that until I arrive home safely, that tape will be sent to the media. The second one as well.'

'Rene, for God's sake, why are you doing this?'

'To protect you, Carol.'

'To protect yourself,' Julien said. 'You do have an ulterior motive, do you not Ms Curtis?'

'A negative way of framing it.'

'Ms Curtis would like to join our ranks.'

'What?' Carol yelled.

'What is this, national Give-yourself-to-a-vampire-for-lunch week?' Gerlinde said.

Carol stared at Rene, dumbfounded. She watched her therapist open her purse, remove a silver flask and unscrew the top. She raised the flask, toast style, and drank long and deep from it, then returned it to her bag. 'Julien, you're better than I thought. With my training added to the powers acquired when I've changed . . .'

'Nobody here will change you,' Karl said flatly.

'Then you will all be hounded. There are sketches Carol did over the years, many very well executed, including a likeness of you, Karl. Close enough that each of you can be identified. Although I haven't met you,' she said to Morianna. 'And I dubbed Carol's more descriptive statements onto the tapes, as well as information on the residences in Bordeaux and Austria, the number of your corporation and so on. I'm highly respected in my field – my reputation should go a long way towards legitimizing the information although, of course, the media will run with it anyway.'

'Rene, this is a breech of trust,' Carol said. 'I told you those things in strict confidentiality.'

'And normally they would have been kept confidential, but the circumstances here are not normal. Tell me, Carol, if you change your mind, will they let you go?'

Carol hesitated. She looked around the room. 'I . . . I'm not sure.'

'I fail to see how this concerns you,' Chloe told Rene.

'Of course you don't. You're concerned only about what's best for you and your group. I doubt anyone here has Carol's interests at heart, except me.'

'You have your own interests at heart,' Julien said harshly.

'And Carol's. And surely Carol deserves someone to be present who cares about her. For that reason alone I will stay for the ritual.'

'Out of the question,' Karl said.

'Rene, please, it's not what you're thinking. Things have, I don't know, evolved. I'm ready to undergo this; I don't have much to lose. And I want to. I don't know what you hope to get out of thinking they'll change you, but . . .'

'Alone? You want to go through what amounts to having the blood drained from your body alone? With only these . . . beings present? Wouldn't you prefer that I be here with you? Someone you know and trust? A human being?'

Instantly Carol knew Rene had touched on some truth. 'She is like a mother to me,' she tried to tell the others. 'My own mother wasn't there, when I was going through all this, Rene was. I would like her to be here.'

Suddenly the door opened and André came into the room. His eyes narrowed. He glared first at Rene then Carol and when he looked at Carol she saw 'betrayal' scrawled across his face.

'You are, of course, the child's father,' Rene said coldly. 'You've been described to me in great detail. You and your violent acts.'

Carol jumped to her feet. This roller coaster ride, fighting to win André's trust, then seeing it crushed, over and over again, and now the complication of Rene and her multiple agendas, all of it was too much. 'I can't take this!' she shouted. To Rene, 'I'm going through with the ritual. It has nothing to do with you. It's my life, or my death. If you want to stay, fine, if you want to leave, fine. If you want to change that has nothing to do with me either. I just want to be left alone. All of you, leave me alone!'

She ran out of the room and upstairs to Gerlinde's studio where she sat on the floor and cried, unable to stop herself. Her head throbbed from the stress. The tears released some tension, but at the same time let her realize the extent of her terror. There was no way to know what would happen, no way to control any of it. Her life hung on a thin thread of trust between herself and André, a thread that kept breaking. Could she keep retying it endlessly? What if it snapped at a crucial moment? What if she snapped?

She was on overload, and the ritual hadn't even begun yet. And now André's distrust had returned, making everything harder than it already was. Maybe Rene was right. Maybe she had talked herself into wanting this because she knew she had no choice. She was petrified by the thought of being André's third failure.

Suddenly she felt a hand on her shoulder and jumped. Jeanette crouched in front of her. 'They're ready.'

'I'm not. I don't know if I ever will be.'

Jeanette sat on the floor next to Carol. Her pale skin was impossibly smooth, like cool, flawless alabaster. Her eyes, pale green oceans, glinted in the light. Her hair, so blonde it was almost white, glowed. Carol wondered what Jeanette had looked like before, and if she herself would appear as stunning to mortals. If she would be as mesmerizing. Mesmerizing enough that they would give her their blood!

'You know,' Jeanette said, 'I'm not as old as some of the others here – if I were still mortal I'd be close to seventy now. That's only one lifetime, but I think I've learned a few things, one of which is that no one's ever ready for life.'

'Or death,' Carol said.

'Mortal or immortal, most of us aren't truly prepared for the really big moments. They're like pearls on a necklace we string as time passes. No one knows how many pearls there will be, how long the chain will become with precious experiences. We resist them with as much energy as we crave them. I know you feel out of control. And in some ways you are. But Carol, like everyone else here who's gone through this, you just have to do the best you can. That's all you *can* do. At some point you just have to trust that it will be enough.'

Carol looked into Jeanette's eyes. There was a promise there, a prescription for the pain, something that would take it away forever. She felt a longing to just accept that palliative. But imbedded within those green pools lay a familiarity that held its own comfort. 'I don't know why, but I've always felt as if you, more than all the others, knew what I was experiencing.'

'I've been in a similar position, but I was alone. You have friends.' Jeanette took her hand.

Carol shook her head. 'Friends to bury me.'

'We have to go.'

The vampiress led her down to the second floor where they joined Gerlinde who was waiting in the hallway. The three entered the guest room. Chloe was in the adjoining bathroom preparing a bath. Morianna sat near the window watching the darkening sky. Rene perched on the bed – they were letting her stay.

'What can I do to help?' Rene asked.

'Nothing,' Jeanette said.

Gerlinde and Jeanette undressed Carol and led her to the tub. 'What's that?' Carol asked, wondering what Chloe was putting in the water.

'Rosewater and rose petals.' She sprinkled another handful of white petals across the surface. The bath was as cleverly disguised with roses as a pond in autumn is with layers of fallen leaves. She poured in the contents of a bottle of clear liquid.

'Why roses?'

'They're a sacred flower and have traditionally been the symbol of love, joy, elegance, pleasure and also of the seventh son.' Chloe looked up at Carol. The edges of the older woman's hair were damp from the heat of the water, sticking to her scalp. 'André is a seventh son, and so was his father,' she added.

Jeanette laughed from the doorway. 'Well, that's interesting. Finally, a seventh son of a seventh son who's a vampire. I guess the legends have to be right sometimes.'

The women helped Carol into the tub. The water was hot, but she managed finally to sit in it. Soon the steam made her skin pucker and left her drowsy.

'The bath is a symbolic cleansing,' Chloe said, pouring pitchers of water over Carol's head, shoulders and neck. 'It's a way of saying you're washing away the old life in order to embrace the new.'

Carol leaned her head back against the tiles and closed her eyes. She inhaled the rosy fragrance deeply. The lovely scent spoke of beauty and tenderness, reminding her of all the nicest moments of her life: A garden at her grandmother's when she was little, her high school prom, her wedding, a rose André had given her one night, Michael's birth. Suddenly worried thoughts cramped her peaceful, relaxed state. She opened her eyes and saw Rene through the doorway watching Morianna and, in the bathroom, Gerlinde sitting on the lid of the toilet seat.

'Gerlinde, you didn't do any of this, did you?'

'Nope. But with Karl and me it's different.'

'Yeah, I know. You both wanted it. Well, I'm not sure, but I think I might want this . . . change. I don't know.'

Gerlinde laughed, her chocolate eyes shining. 'Kiddo, that is the least definite thing I've ever heard you say.'

Carol sighed and closed her eyes again. 'Well, it's not easy, giving up my blood. Especially when André's not even sure he won't bite my entire head off.'

A voice that seemed to swirl through her soul spoke. 'It is never a male's weakness but a female's strength which determines the outcome in any liaison between the genders.'

Carol opened her eyes. Morianna stood in the doorway, wearing white, black and grey again, yet this was an entirely different outfit. Layered, the style looked like a medieval costume. Her eyes sparkled their violet colour and a soft smile played on her lips which Carol now realized were very full. She looked like someone caught in a time-warp. Like a Shakespearian actor. Or Eleanor of Aquitaine in *The Lion in Winter*.

'I'm not sure what that means,' Carol told the ancient vampiress.

Morianna studied her with those intense crystalline eyes

and Carol felt sleepy again. 'Then perhaps you should meditate. Gerlinde, you may attend from in here.'

Gerlinde followed Morianna out, closing the door, leaving Carol alone with her thoughts and the steamy rose-water bath.

She felt very, very unsure. If it wasn't for Michael, and also the fact that, she had to face it, her health was seriously declining, and too, because as Gerlinde had said, they weren't giving her a choice anymore, Carol knew she wouldn't go through with this.

Rene might be gung ho, but Carol found the idea of becoming a killer, dependent on human sacrifices, almost beyond her realm of understanding. Of course, most of them didn't kill. But André had. And close as she now felt to him, she also did not trust him to take her blood without destroying her. She cared for him. In a way she loved him. No, she had to admit it, she did love him now, despite what he was. She was at a complete loss to explain to herself how her feelings could have shifted so dramatically and so frequently. But she did love him. And she believed that he loved her. But she wasn't sure he could control himself. She wasn't convinced she would survive this.

André had told her details about the other times. Both women pleaded for their lives; that seemed to be the weak link. And André's father had killed his mother in the same way and apparently for the same reason; her pleas had triggered his rage. But could it be that simple? Carol knew she wouldn't beg for her life no matter what happened, at least she hoped she wouldn't. But there had to be more to it. What was Morianna trying to tell her? Or was she saying anything except that Carol had to be strong, persevere, all the things they were always telling her? How come all of this has to come from me? she suddenly thought, feeling petulant. Why can't André do more? Maybe he's already doing the lion's share by trying to master this urge that seems to send him so out of control. The worse thing for Carol was knowing that Michael was going to be present. And on his birthday. How would the outcome of this ritual affect his own decision? If André kills me, she thought, in front of our son . . . The image that flashed before her made the idea too gruesome to pursue.

Chloe, Gerlinde and Jeanette appeared in the doorway holding large towels. Carol laughed. 'You look like the Three Graces.'

She lifted herself out of the tub and was immediately surrounded with soft white terry cloth. They patted her skin, soaking up the sweet-scented drops until she was completely dry. Gerlinde led her, naked, to the vanity and towelled her hair dry. Sitting on the floor beside Morianna's feet, her sunny blonde hair being stroked by the older woman, was Jeanette's daughter. Rene watched everything, unusually quiet, concentrating intensely. Carol wondered if she'd been hypnotized.

'Susan and Claude were in Vancouver for a few days and just returned,' Jeanette explained. 'Julien and I thought they should be here. And they want to be.'

Like the other night, Jeanette fixed her nails and Gerlinde worked on her hair. But Gerlinde didn't cut this time. Instead she massaged a white cream into the dark strands, making them shine, then wove chains of rose petals in and out, letting them stick to the thick cream. They left her face free of make-up.

While they worked, Morianna spoke.

'Tonight the moon is waxing. Tomorrow Luna will be full, complete. Sunday she will wane. The moon represents the stages of a woman's life, the stages you will pass through as you transform. Tonight Kore, the young girl, open to the world, pure in body and spirit like Persephone in her innocence and beauty, blissfully picking flowers in a meadow. Or Artemis, the virgin huntress.'

Carol watched Morianna in the mirror stroking Susan's

hair. The young girl had a look of absolute trust on her face, a look of total innocence.

'Tomorrow you will become the Mother, Demeter, Hera, the pregnant one, full, bearing the seeds of life, your womb the container for the universe. By the third night you are the uncanny Crone, Hecate, the one who always precedes and follows Persephone. You will be Queen of the Shades, Goddess of the Underworld, a Funerary Princess. She who takes the soul through the dark spaces of non-being. The one who has experienced life, pain, sadness, joy, madness and death. The wise old woman. The witch. It is her wisdom you require in order to transform.'

Carol stared at Morianna in the mirror, enraptured by what was being said. Chloe, Gerlinde and Jeanette rubbed the same white oily cream into every pore. The cream smelled strongly of roses. The soft fingers of six hands moved in slow circles clockwise and Carol felt sensual and drowsy again as she listened to Morianna.

'You will fast, eating nothing tonight but for the six pomegranate seeds which symbolize the commitment to the dark that the virgin undertakes. That is all for three days, other than the blood.'

The mention of drinking blood woke Carol right up. Apparently it had a similar effect on Rene. 'Are you telling her she'll be drinking blood? Has it been sterilized? It's not human, is it?'

Morianna ignored her. 'There will be nine present, nine gifts, nine to transfer the life. From each you must receive what is offered. And to each you must return something of yourself. Nine is the number of completion, the final stage before the end, the one that decrees that change is now inevitable.'

Carol had little understanding of what Morianna's words meant but hung on each one, some occasionally making sense.

'There are four directions for balance. Fire, which will always be beside or behind you, representing the South and the warmth you provide André who must face you. He will be drawn to your fire throughout the ritual because fire is irresistible. It is the male principle, power, purification, intense desire, the ability to penetrate and, as well, destroy. The dross from all substances is burned away in the alchemist's blaze. In New Guinea it is believed an old woman is the keeper of flame, storing it in her vagina to be used when needed.'

Carol felt spellbound.

'To the West is water, compassion, healing, understanding. Here the river of life flows through you which you will offer to André in exchange for eternal life. This is the female principle, refreshment, sustenance, truth, wisdom, intuitive understanding. It is the direction of the moon, of emotion, and it is here you will sit as the virgin.

'Tomorrow night as you face André you will also face the North, the direction of Air. Here you may glimpse eternity, heaven, the soul. Dreams, inspiration, the love of freedom, the very sun itself will be revealed to you as your thoughts and André's merge.'

Jeanette had finished, but Gerlinde fussed with Carol's hair, shaping it with her hands, getting it to lie perfectly against her face.

'Sunday, when the ritual ends, you will be looking East, Earth, your body. Here is the lover of life, harmonizer, as well as darkness and death. It is in this place and at this time that the cyclic pattern of birth, maturity and decay come together and transformation is brought about through ravishment. It is here that you must seek the wisdom of Sophia.'

The women had finished with her. Carol turned and faced Morianna and the girl, Susan, still resting contentedly against the older woman's knees. Gerlinde crouched at Carol's feet, Jeanette sat at the foot of the bed, Rene towards the head, and Chloe in the armchair. There was silence. Finally

Morianna said, 'From this time, but for the kiss, no one will touch you until André takes you Sunday at midnight. It is especially important that you do not permit his touch, for the blood lust can drive him insane. The scent alone would be enough. The feel of it beneath skin becomes unbearable. You understand?'

Carol nodded.

'For two thousand years the major religion of the wise old Greeks revolved around the Eleusinian Mysteries. Over the next three evenings, through this ritual, you will experience what the ancient ones did – the process of birth, death and rebirth, the process which all but one here understands.' Morianna paused. 'It is time.'

She stood, as did each of the others. Chloe and Jeanette led Carol into the hallway with Susan, Gerlinde, Rene and finally Morianna walking behind. The women moved quietly up the steps to the third floor. They entered the room opposite Gerlinde's studio, a room Carol had never been in.

André sat cross-legged on a small oriental carpet which had been placed over the wall-to-wall broadloom. He too was naked. He glanced at Rene, a flash like lightning shooting through his grey eyes, then looked at Carol. His face relaxed, which relieved her mind. He seemed full, content. He even smiled a little and she smiled back. Julien, Karl, Claude and Michael stood in one corner together. Although she was naked, Carol didn't feel embarrassed.

Without touching her, Morianna took Carol to another small carpet in front of the fireplace, motioning that she should position herself so that her left side was to the fireplace and her right to André. Carol knelt. Immediately Morianna went about building a fire.

The room became hot quickly, especially for Carol who was right in front of the flames. Her left side pulsed with heat and the sweat ran down from her armpit and also from the small of her back, triggering the fragrance of the cream that covered her body. Once the fire blazed, Morianna stopped adding wood and, instead, added what looked like a braided rope. Immediately the room filled with a grassy scent impregnated with an undercurrent of sage.

'Can I have some water?' Carol asked Morianna.

The older woman glanced at her before moving away. 'Your thirst will be quenched,' she said. Then there was silence.

Carol noticed the room, or what she could see from the direction she was facing. The space had been cleared of furniture – she could tell it had been there from the impressions left in the black carpet.

There were large cushions in solid witchy colours – midnight black, deep purple, orange and forest green – strewn across the floor beside the fireplace and along the terracotta walls. The two corners within her vision had large vases filled with fresh flowers: orange gladioli, red and blue tulips, pale yellow tiger lilies, violet and yellow iris, white narcissus. The other three walls were glass, as was the ceiling. In front of her, the not-quite-full moon began to appear from the left, ready to wend its way across the clear sky behind the trees, passing in front of the glass wall before her. A window must have been open because she could hear leaves rustling and the sound of the wind, but it came from behind, from the other side of the room.

She heard church bells chime twelve times. Out of the corner of her eye she caught Morianna taking Michael up to André but she couldn't see what they were doing. Morianna then brought the boy to Carol.

Michael's lips were smeared with blood but he was grinning from ear to ear. Under Morianna's prompting, he kissed Carol's mouth. She realized that the blood must have come from André. It was cold, a little slimy, raw-tasting. She wanted to retch.

Her son held out a rectangular metal object for her to take.

'It's a phaser, Mom. Karl and me got it last night. You can zap Cardassians.'

This was the first time he had called her Mom, and Carol instinctively reached out to hug Michael.

'No!' Morianna shouted. 'You must touch no one. Accept his gift and find a space for it in the circle you must now form around yourself.'

Carol took the phaser and put it on the floor directly in front of her. As soon as she did, Morianna led Michael away. Then Claude went up to André, kissed him lightly on the mouth and touched his lips to a wound in André's neck. He knelt before Carol, kissing her with bloody lips. His large brown eyes seemed sensitive, caring. He offered her a small porcelain figurine, an exquisitely formed harlequin, caught in a dance, painted in iridescent reds, blues and yellows on white, holding a smiling golden mask on the end of a stick before its face. In its other hand the harlequin held the silver mask of tragedy.

'I made this for you,' Claude said simply.

Next the girl Susan approached, kissing Carol with crimson lips, staring at her with round innocent blue eyes. Shyly, she handed over a hand-bound book. 'Love poems. For you and André to read together. I wrote them.'

Carol had placed the sculpture to the left of the phaser and now put the book to the right.

Next to kneel before her was Jeanette. Carol was startled by the sight of the sticky red gore smeared across those sophisticated lips. After their kiss, Jeanette handed her three pieces of handmade paper, rolled and tied with a braided vermilion satin cord. 'They're astrological charts I cast, for you, André and Michel, based on Sunday midnight.' Carol took them and placed them behind her.

'It's a miniature.' Gerlinde handed her a small canvas. On it she had reproduced Bocklin's painting *The Island of the Dead*, depicting the loneliness of a soul being transported by

Charon across the silent river Styx. Gerlinde's eyes filled with pink-tinged tears and Carol almost started crying herself. 'Remember, kiddo, we've all been there,' the redhead said, kissing Carol's lips lightly, passing the ritual blood. Carol placed the little painting next to the horoscopes.

Karl approached. He handed her a vial of crushed rock he said was alum. 'Put this in water, in a dark place for five weeks or more. Be sure there's no movement.' His wet lips brushed hers. He hesitated and then quietly, tentatively, quoted lines from a T. S. Eliot poem, about a still point in time which allows a 'dance', a dance that is all that matters. When he finished, Karl looked a little embarrassed. He stood quickly. Carol placed the alum close to Gerlinde's gift.

Chloe gave Carol a ruby-coloured rosebud, tightly closed, its long thorny stem resting in a slender clear-glass vase. 'Because it will go from bud to bloom to fading, the virgin, the mother and crone.' She kissed Carol with scarlet lips. 'The rose has been called "The Flower of Venus". The old myths say the gods created the rose to celebrate Aphrodite's rising from the sea and that it became red when she pricked her feet on thorns as she sought her slain lover Adonis.' Carol placed the rose to her right, between her and André.

Morianna was next. By now Carol had figured that the order probably had to do with the length of time they had been vampires. The Eurasian woman pressed into Carol's palm a brownish-green stone of chalcedony streaked with carmine, a smaller version of the one she wore around her neck. 'Bloodstone. It endows courage, wisdom, vitality. The wearer is audacious, brilliant, courageous, generous, obedient,' she said, her eyes laughing. 'It was said by Pliny that heliotrope brings the owner success if a calm mind is maintained when engaged in hard combat,' she added, as their lips met. There was a mild but definite electric charge, a feeling that had intensified with each kiss. The stone was placed to the right of the rose.

Last was Julien. His dark eyes stared into Carol's, almost absorbing her. He said nothing and offered her nothing tangible, except for the kiss. But Carol felt a connection with him that seemed incomprehensible yet penetrated to the roots of her soul.

She suddenly realized that each of the gift givers was now seated in a circle about her and André, reflecting the exact position of their gifts around her. Chloe was behind André, so that Carol couldn't see her. Julian sat next to Susan, the only space left in her circle of gifts except for the fireplace.

Suddenly Rene, who had been seated against the glass wall watching, stood and walked towards André.

'No!' André said.

Rene must have felt the power of his furious rejection. She stopped as if she'd slammed into an invisible wall and turned away from him. 'Well at least let me offer Carol a gift,' she said, vaguely facing Morianna.

The vampiress considered a moment and Carol expected her to say no, but she said, 'The nine has altered. Proceed.'

Rene walked to Carol and knelt in front of her. There was a peculiar glow in her eyes and Carol smelled alcohol on her breath. She looked about to move forward, to kiss Carol, when Julien said, 'Do not kiss her,' in a tone that kept Rene back.

'Well, I didn't come prepared for a celebration,' she said lightly, and smiled. 'How about a set of earrings? Genuine rhinestone.' She pulled the triangular clips from her ears and pressed them into Carol's hand, making flesh to flesh contact.

Carol looked around her circle of gifts. She didn't know where to position them. Suddenly the earrings seemed oddly out of place. They felt hot from the heat of Rene's skin, and the points of the triangles sharp-edged in Carol's palms. That frightened her. Why? she asked herself. Rene's my friend. Has been my confidant for years. If it wasn't for Rene she would never have found Michael again. But something felt wrong, and she couldn't identify what. All she knew was that she had to battle an urge to toss the earrings into the fire. That would hurt Rene, and for no good reason. But at the same time Carol felt upset just holding them and upset that Rene had touched her.

She dropped them close to the hearth and suddenly realized she was sweating from more than the fire's heat. She looked up. Rene was not, of course, in the place corresponding with the earrings, as far away from André as possible. She could not have fitted into the space between Carol and the fireplace. But Carol wasn't prepared for the space Rene had chosen – on André's right, three feet from him.

Rene violated the pattern, which Carol felt was her fault. She should have paid more attention to where she put the earrings. She glanced at André. Clearly he felt his space invaded. She smiled, trying to reassure him, but his eyes reflected a murderous darkness that Carol couldn't stand seeing, so she looked away.

They stayed silent for hours except for the occasional music Claude played on a flute and the sound Morianna produced from a bell. She didn't ring the bell, but instead ran a thick baton of blonde wood around the rim creating an eerie reverberation that penetrated into Carol's bones.

Throughout the night the creamy moon ascended, crossing Carol's field of vision and then up and finally out of her sight as it edged behind the trees at the top of the mountain. She thought of many things. The gifts, the givers and what this ritual meant to her. She thought of Michael and of André and how her entire life had changed.

She could see that this was the passing of her lifetime and the passing of her solitude. Tonight she would come to André like the girl Kore, young, innocent, open. He was to be her lover, her eternal husband. He would give her his blood and then, on Sunday, he would take hers, the way a man takes a woman for the first time, fully, completely, 'a ravishment' as Morianna had put it. Carol had never viewed anything in this way before, but the symbolism made her feel the experience was larger than her existence and, at the same time, all her own. There *is* something sacred, even magical about what's happening, she thought.

Morianna placed a small unglazed clay bowl holding six pomegranate seeds before her. 'Take. Eat these.' Carol picked them out, one by one, placing the seeds onto her tongue. She bit into the bitter-sweet fruit, crunching the hard centres between her teeth. When she had swallowed all six, Morianna said, 'Now you must receive from André.'

Suddenly all her lofty thoughts plummeted to earth. Carol panicked. They had told her what she had to do and, until this moment, she had thought that she could do it.

'Receive,' Morianna said again.

Carol got to her feet. Her legs trembled, partly from fear and partly from kneeling in the same position for so long. She turned towards André. He was as he had been when she'd entered the room, what seemed like days before. Rene sat very close to him, too close.

As Carol walked towards André, his bright grey eyes fixed on hers, never veering even for a moment. When she was in front of him she knelt down. She tried to convince herself not to be frightened, afraid of showing him her fear. But she could already see he saw it in her eyes. And she was aware of a response – she felt the heat of his anger, intense as the flames that had nearly cooked her.

With Rene so close, Carol felt somehow pressured in a way she could not identify. It was as though her every move was being monitored. The others were watching as closely and yet she did not feel herself straining for them to do this 'right'. Rene scrutinized her movements, her gestures, and it shook Carol's confidence, but she didn't know why.

André's chest was covered with dried blood that had seeped from the wound in his neck which the others had touched their lips to. He reopened the wound with a fingernail. Rene gasped. Blood so dark it was almost black tracked fresh paths between the dark hairs on his chest. The rivulets ran down past his stomach into the hairs of his genitals. A macabre fascination overwhelmed Carol. It mixed with the terror coursing through her, and she felt unable to do what she knew she must.

'Carol,' Rene said, 'if you don't want to do this . . .'

'Silence!' Julien commanded. His voice rattled the air like a sonic boom, crushing all other sound. Rene fell silent. Carol trembled.

Time passed and more time. She was afraid to look at André's face, afraid of what she would see. His hand moved slowly up towards her head. He's going to force me to drink it! she thought. Suddenly she heard Morianna, the voice strong and clear as a bell, 'Avoid the touch!'

Immediately Carol remembered the consequences. Without another thought, she moved towards the red river flowing from him. She parted her lips and drank. Cool and thick. Salty. As it warmed a bit, the blood became coppery and sweet. Earthy. Familiar yet unfamiliar. She struggled to keep her mind blank. She held her breath and swallowed down several mouthfuls of the blood that streamed remarkably easily past her lips.

Suddenly the air coming in went to her stomach, the blood to her lungs and she was choking. She pulled back, coughing, gagging. Red sprayed from between her lips and splattered André's face and chest. She fought to get control of herself, to keep from vomiting. To keep from running screaming out the door.

Rene was on her feet. Before she could move, Gerlinde blocked her.

Finally, Carol's wheezy breath became more rhythmic,

her irritated throat not so raw. She heard Morianna say, 'Enough!'

Carol hurried back to her carpet, her mouth and face streaked with André's blood, her body quivering uncontrollably.

She was stunned by what she had done and also by the knowledge that her actions were irrevocable.

As she sat on the carpet, snatches of truths flashed through her mind. 'Blood of my blood, flesh my flesh.' 'For the blood is the life.' She had no idea whose blood flowed in André's veins, whose blood she had consumed. She began to grasp the outer edges of understanding, the seriousness of blood rituals and, consequently, the bond that was forming between her and André. The bond, too, seemed irrevocable.

As the sun rose, the group abandoned the room. Rene, chatting non-stop, was taken to the guest room where, presumably, she would be locked in until tomorrow night.

Carol and André went together to the basement. They lay in bed in silence, separate, not touching in the darkness.

The first night was over; aside from one brief trauma, everything seemed to be going well. André wasn't having any trouble controlling himself, as far as she could tell. And they both had the support of the group to help them through any difficult parts. She was starting to feel pretty good about the whole thing and half looked forward to tomorrow night.

Suddenly, a voice as cold as the grave cut through the black air. 'Don't hesitate like that again!'

THIRTY-TWO

Carol woke when André snapped on the light. Her eyes opened slowly. Above her face hovered a stark mask with stone grey eyes imbedded in it. His cold stare unnerved her for a moment, until she got a grip.

As different as he looked, that's how different she felt. Her flesh rippled with sensuality. She couldn't tell if this was the result of drinking blood or what – maybe she was imagining it – but the effect produced a confidence she wasn't used to feeling. And, being alone with André, the way he looked tonight, she needed all the confidence she could get.

Without a word they left the room together. On the second floor landing, Jeanette motioned her into the guest room again.

Rene sat on the bed, this time at the foot, propping herself up with one arm. Dark circles surrounded too bright eyes; she looked a little confused.

'Are you okay?' Carol asked.

'Nothing a drink wouldn't cure.'

The others said nothing.

'Why don't you give her something?'

'Uh uh, kiddo. She's at the outer limits already.'

'Look, I think she has a drinking problem . . .'

'No kidding! The alcohol's seeping through her pores like poison vapour.'

'She's used to drinking, it keeps her stable. Maybe if we . . .'

'I? Have a drinking problem?' Rene laughed. 'Tell me, Carol, where did you get your degree to practice therapy?' Her hand slipped from the bed and she fell over onto her side.

Carol had never seen Rene like this. And in truth, she felt as in control as Rene looked out of control.

'I came to meet your vampires, and have,' Rene said, righting herself. 'And they are a disappointment.'

Carol looked around. It was clear from the shared expressions that Rene was a major complication.

'Julien woke early,' Gerlinde said. 'When the sun dropped, he found her plastered.' She unscrewed the cap and turned the silver flask over. 'Empty.'

'He's wonderful,' Rene gushed. 'Just as you described him, Carol. Vibrant. Ancient. He knows me, deeply, I can feel it. His hypnotic powers are nothing short of miraculous.' Her hands trembled and even her head shook a little.

'Rene, you shouldn't be here . . .'

'We don't have time for this now,' Jeanette said. 'Julien's determined that she hasn't told anyone else about us. Yet. The rest is true, about the tapes.' She nodded to a chair and Carol sat. 'We'll have to deal with Rene after Sunday.'

Morianna said, 'Tonight the ritual lasts from sunset until sunrise. Many hours. You must take the blood from André three times. Chloe has offered to prepare a mixture you may wish to drink throughout the night, to aid your cause.'

'Cause and effect,' Rene said to no one.

'What's that mean?' Carol asked Morianna.

It was Chloe who answered. 'Tonight will be hard for André. I have a herbal potion that causes the body to produce a scent which may disguise the blood scent.'

'So he'll be distracted from my blood and won't attack me?'

'Hopefully.'

'Is there a money-back guarantee?' Carol joked.

No one laughed but Rene, who giggled, 'Blood-sense.'

'Okay,' Carol sighed. 'I'll drink it.'

There was silence for a moment until Jeanette said, 'I think you should tell her everything.'

Carol stared at each of the females in the room, all but Rene, whom she avoided looking at – Rene was added stress she didn't need right now. The others were tense, except for Susan, who was probably too young to understand what they were worried about. 'Well, will somebody tell me?'

'Kiddo, it's an aphrodisiac,' Gerlinde said.

'Sex and blood and death!' Rene clapped her hands together like a child. 'A party!'

'Aphrodisiac? You mean it will make me feel sexual?' Carol asked.

'Yeah,' Gerlinde said. 'Your body will emit . . . odours. Know what I mean?'

'You mean I'll have a sexual smell?'

'Yeah. Something like that.'

'Well, won't that arouse André? I mean, I'm not supposed to let him touch me, right? Isn't this dangerous?'

Morianna said, 'The scent of blood is more of a danger.'

'If André was like Karl you could just read him *The Sorcerer's Apprentice*,' Gerlinde said. 'But André's brain's in a different place, and we all know where.'

'Look,' Carol glanced around the room from left to right, 'if you think it will help, I'll do it.'

Finally Chloe said, 'We can't guarantee anything, but it will probably work. However, there are consequences.'

'Death is the consequence of sex,' Rene intoned solemnly.

Carol wished Rene would just shut up. 'Consequences? What?'

'It could become painful,' Jeanette told her. 'It's a blend of Saw Palm Etto, Damiana, Celandine leaves and a few other ingredients. It will cause you to sweat a lot and you'll probably feel highly aroused for a while. It stimulates hormonal secretions that produce vaginal fluids; that's the effect you want. The problem is, it's uncontrollable.'

'In what way?'

'It will be like being on the verge of an orgasm. After an hour or so you might orgasm spontaneously. Eventually the contractions could become unpleasant.'

'Sounds like giving birth,' Carol said.

'The birth of death,' Rene mumbled.

The hairs on the back of Carol's neck rose. She glanced at Rene. Something had happened to her. She was more than drunk, she'd lost her mind. Carol just couldn't deal with it now.

'Similar,' Chloe said, bringing Carol back to the moment. 'Of course, you don't have to take it. It's up to you. What I suggest is this: I'll mix the herbs and leave them with you. If you feel everything is going all right, don't use it. If you sense things are getting out of hand – with André – then you might consider it.'

'That sounds okay,' Carol said. But she was worried. 'Do you think things will get out of hand?'

No one answered her and for once Rene said nothing.

Gerlinde and Jeanette pulled Rene from the bed and moved her to a chair. She screamed and struggled as they tied her arms to the chair's arms.

'No! Don't do that,' Carol said. 'She's harmless.'

'That, kiddo, I don't buy.'

'She just has a few problems.'

'The problem is time,' Rene said.

'She is a problem and she'll screw things up,' Gerlinde said.

Carol shook her head. 'She was there for me. I owe her.'

'The soul must go where it needs to. Obligations should not mar the preordained path,' Morianna said.

Carol was not ready to hand over her humanity so easily. Her relationship with Rene went beyond therapy, even beyond friendship; they were the same species. Carol knew Rene was not being helpful, but she needed her present. It was like holding onto this world while reaching out to the next world. She feared a moment might come when she would lose her grasp on both and free fall through space alone.

Morianna must have seen that need in her. 'As she wishes,' the old one said, and Gerlinde and Jeanette immediately let Rene go.

As they left the room, Rene babbling incoherently, terror clutched at Carol's spine. She had to put Rene out of her thoughts. There was too much going on and she couldn't afford to lose it for even a second.

When the women entered the third floor, Morianna built another fire. Everyone but Carol and Chloe sat as they had on the previous night. Tonight Carol faced André directly. Now she could see him clearly and her earlier observations in the basement were confirmed. He looked painfully thin, skin taut over bone, pallid face a little wild. His lips too were tight-looking and his eyes feverish. He stared directly at her and she had the mental image of a hungry dog, gaze riveted to a slab of meat. Rene's shifting distracted him from time to time. Eyes closed, her inebriated body, so close to his, weaved. Carol knew André found Rene's blood tempting. As tempting as he found her own.

Behind André, the longest glass wall exposed swaying pines and cedars covering the mountainside. Through the glass ceiling Carol could see over the tree tops. The moon swelled tonight and she wondered about the old myths connecting madness with the full moon.

In the right corner of the room, Chloe sat crushing herbs with a white stone pestle into a marble mortar. When she finished, she deposited them into a heavy cast-iron teapot, poured in boiling water from the electric kettle and let the herbs steep. Minutes later she filtered the tea into a large black wooden bowl. She placed the bowl on the carpet in front of Carol, in front of the red rose between her and André, now in full bloom.

After Chloe took her place behind André, Morianna said, 'You must take from André.'

Not so soon! Carol thought. But she was determined not to hesitate tonight. She stood right away and went to him, kneeling in front. She had to look away from his frozen steel eyes. He raised a trembling hand; his nails had grown overnight into yellow, dagger-sharp claws. The blue veins in his arms strained against the skin. The smell coming from him reminded her of wet earth.

She watched him slice open the vein in his neck. Immediately she pressed her lips to the flowing wound and drank the blood, only stopping when she heard Morianna say, 'Enough.'

Shaking, she returned to her carpet and faced him again, wiping the moisture from her lips with the back of a hand, aware that it did not taste as repugnant tonight and she did not feel nauseous. The blood seemed almost refreshing, filling, like a sweet wine. She might be filled, but André was still hungry.

The early part of the night went fairly smoothly, although clearly he was suffering. Rene drifted off and lay on the floor. Now she was even closer to André. Just after the church bells rang twelve times and Carol followed the descent of the perfect pearl of a moon behind the mountain top, then watched it reappear, Morianna again told her, 'Receive.'

This time, as Carol approached André, she felt more hesitant. Over the hours she'd watched the changes in him and they weren't pretty. Agitated, he shifted every few seconds. Intense pain blended with the hostility on his face. He was kinetically as aware of Rene as he was of Carol, the only beings in this room with their own blood pumping through their veins.

She knelt before him. His cold, predatory energy startled her. She tried to drink the blood as quickly as she could, all the while aware of his quick breathing and the thin sheen of sweat covering his flesh. The barrier between them was rapidly dissolving. She found this both exciting and terrifying.

When the clock struck three, Rene awoke. Immediately she began babbling nonsense, edging closer to André, catching his attention. Carol knew she would have to do something. He watched both women with hawk eyes, alternating his attention. Rene moved very close. André focused all of his attention on her, and as he did so she became frenetic. André looked tense enough to snap. Carol felt afraid to make a sudden move.

She glanced to her left. Michael dozed, his head on Susan's lap, his feet on Claude's. The others sat still as statues; apparently they would not interfere. It was all up to her. She picked up the black bowl, swirled the greenish-yellow contents then took a sip. The foul, bitter peppery taste made her gag. André's head snapped in her direction. She forced down another sip, hoping it would work twice as fast. Every few minutes she drank a little more.

The room was becoming extremely warm. Sweat dripped from under her arms and breasts, down her back and the backs of her knees. Her nipples hardened. Carol realized she felt sensual, erotic. Her body swayed a little, the same pace as the tree tops. She looked across the room. André's attention had shifted away from Rene. His features were ghastly – flesh white and thin as rice paper, eyes hard, cold steel points, laced with obsession. Sweat glistened on his body and matted his hair to his head. His beard had grown and his chest hair lengthened. His stomach expanded and contracted rapidly as he panted. She watched him fidget, his hands twitching and brushing his body as if insects crawled all over him.

Within an hour Carol was writhing. Sweat poured off her. Her hair was so wet that large drops of moisture dripped from the ends onto her shoulders. She worried she would dehydrate. Within, her hot vagina rippled at an alarming rate, slicking the insides of her thighs with fluids. Her nipples had become achingly hard and she found it almost impossible not to touch herself. She, like André, panted. She ended up on her hands and knees, crying, moaning, trying to dig herself into the floor like a dog digging earth. At the height of this orgasmic state she heard the clock chime six times and Morianna say, 'Receive.'

Carol glanced around the room quickly. Everyone looked so vital, so alive, so sexual. All the men seemed especially handsome and virile. She even found herself attracted to the women. Rene reached out a hand and mumbled something that sounded like, 'My baby.' Carol tilted her head up and stared at André, who stared back. A powerful, invisible vibration like ultra violet waves of light connected them, seducing her forward.

She couldn't stand and had to slither across the carpet to him on her belly, like a snake. Her vision blurred, her hearing distorted; was that her breathing or his or Rene's or the collective breath of this group of carnal beings? Only when she knelt in front of him, her body weaving, was she certain of the direction she faced.

A scent came off her that even she could smell. Animal,

sexual, female, magnetic. She felt in heat, wet and open, throbbing, her genitals pulsating fire, a fire he could extinguish. She thought about thrusting her desire under his nose so he'd get the point.

But André's body more than responded to that scent. He looked purely male to her, an energy that could satisfy her excruciating need, that could dampen the flames of painful longing. The space between them crackled with an electrical charge that could have lit the city. In a lucid moment she thought, at least it's working. And then, I'll never be able to keep him from touching me. Or me from touching him.

He cut the vein. She could barely keep her hands at her sides while she drank what tasted like good wine. When it was over and light began to enter the sky, they all departed for their rooms.

Gerlinde stopped on the second floor to get Rene settled for the day. As Carol passed that room, Rene called out to her, 'They're real, Carol, very real,' her voice close to hysteria.

'She'll be okay,' Gerlinde assured her. 'Things are going great. Just don't let him jump your bones.'

André had gone ahead. Carol made her way alone into the basement, half walking, half crawling. She wondered if the contractions would go on all day and if she could relieve some of the tension herself.

Finally she lay beside him, knowing she was tantalizing; instinct told her he desired her as much as she wanted him. She could not suppress moans nor could she keep from twisting and turning, although she was careful not to touch André's body.

Carol knew that the scent was still having the desired effect on him, but her need was so great that it no longer mattered. In fact, she had reached such a state that she really could not have cared less about his passions. She directed all her efforts towards quenching her own.

THIRTY-THREE

Carol awoke to blackness. A growl rolled through the darkness, from her left.

After a deliciously torturous day, she had finally collapsed into an exhausted sleep. Now she snapped awake. Something was really wrong. Instinctively she lay still, barely breathing.

The growling intensified. She heard heavy panting. A pungent scent reminded her of wild animals caged in a zoo.

In the darkness her heart banged against her chest wall and her body broke out into a cold sweat. She was trapped; at any moment he would attack her. She stayed immobile, listening to his guttural sounds until the tone deepened and she realized staying here was more dangerous; she had to get out.

With slow but deliberate movements, she swung her legs over the side of the bed and stood. Carefully she walked towards the door, feeling her way along the wall. She slid the deadbolt slowly. She had just turned the knob when he sprang.

He slammed into the wood beside her. Hot breath seared her cheek. He snarled in her ear. Carol had an instantaneous flash, the snap of a psychic shutter locking onto the future, a realization that if she didn't get out now she would not leave this room alive or in any shape to come back from the dead.

'André? Carol?' Susan's voice came from the other side of the door. 'Morianna wants you to come upstairs now.' Carol couldn't speak. Her hand clutched the turned knob. She pulled the door inward. His weight kept it closed. Suddenly he moved back a little. She got the door open wide enough to slip through.

Susan was already at the top of the stairs and Carol wanted to call out to her to wait, but making unnecessary sounds felt risky.

She walked through the basement as calmly as she could, willing herself not to run away in fear, aware that he would be at her throat in a second if she did.

Patiently she climbed each step to the kitchen, turned, walked to the hallway, then ascended the stairs to the second floor. All the while André hovered close behind, stalking her, a cold wind chilling her body and soul.

She entered the bedroom; the women were waiting. Rene sat on the bed, tied and gagged. Her skin without make-up was lined and sallow, her eyes prominent with a demented glint.

Suddenly Carol's nerves snapped. The released tension culminated in a furious outburst. She turned on Morianna and Chloe. 'Why the hell did you make this three days? He'd have a hard enough time with one. I think you're trying to sabotage this!'

'Sit down Carol,' Chloe said. 'You're upset. What's wrong?'

'What's wrong? I'll tell you what's wrong!' Carol continued standing, her limbs trembling. 'André's turned into something else. He almost attacked me downstairs. He'll rip my throat out before the night's over and the two of you are to blame!'

'An explanation is probably needed,' Morianna said in a gentle but firm tone. Carol glared at her. 'André is unlike the rest of us in this regard: his faith in his own power is weak. If we were to have permitted the transformation during the first night and, in the event he had been able to carry it through, he would have regarded it as a fluke. It would not have altered him. Two nights may have had the desired effect, but they may not have. But three is a magical number; the seers of old explained it as the number of change itself. More than one transformation can occur.'

'I don't know what you're talking about!' Carol screamed, holding her head. 'I can't understand all this mumbo jumbo. This could have been over by now. I could have been like all of you, and with my son.'

'And with André, whose feelings about you are unresolved,' Jeanette said. 'Morianna's trying to tell you that she, Chloe and Julien came up with this ritual as much for you as for him.'

'Well, thanks a lot!' Carol said bitterly. 'Don't do me any more favours because I don't think I can survive them.'

'Listen, kiddo.' Gerlinde's voice was serious and angry, the first time Carol had heard those tones directed at her. It caused her to listen to the red-headed vampiress. 'You want André to treat you better, right? Well, for him to do that he's got to respect you. And he won't respect you until you teach him how. That's why everybody's gone to so much trouble; to give you both a chance to figure it out. You can change just the body but I don't think you'd exactly have a ball with a guy who's on your case every other night for eternity. Unless you dig being the battered Bride of Dracula.'

Carol sat at the vanity. She put her hands over her face

and cried. 'I don't know what I'm doing. I don't know what he's doing. I can't understand this.'

'You love André and he loves you,' Jeanette said in a soft voice. 'It's important to remember that. You just need to put that love in a context where it can ripen and mature into something meaningful for you both. That's what this ritual is about.'

Carol just cried harder, frightened to the core.

'You know,' Jeanette continued, 'when a caterpillar crawls into a cocoon, it looks dark for a while and she probably feels nothing's happening or maybe that the worst will happen. But eventually, if she doesn't give in to despair, something mysterious occurs. And when she emerges she's no longer a caterpillar but an exquisite creature. That's the magic of it, the magic for both of you.'

'I'm afraid!' Carol said. She looked around the room, suddenly realizing that all but Rene had been right where she was now. 'I don't know if he'll be able to control himself.'

'André's ability to control himself is no longer in question,' Morianna said cryptically. 'But it grows late. And now we must finish. Gerlinde, see to Rene, please.'

'I want her there,' Carol said. 'I . . . I need her there.' She knew this was fear talking. Rene was beyond helping her, beyond even helping herself.

Morianna nodded. Rene was brought upstairs still tied and gagged. Carol didn't have the strength to argue for more.

In the room everyone took their place. Carol faced the wall opposite the one she had faced on Friday night; tonight she would not see the waning moon.

Morianna did not build a fire; the air felt clotted with finality. Carol did not look at André, afraid of the horror she would find.

'This evening,' Morianna began, 'just before midnight,

you will receive the last drops of blood from André. As the clock strikes he will then claim you.'

Her words sent a shiver through Carol. A sudden recognition of the inevitability of events descended, leaving her gasping for air and with a strong urge to flee. Tonight I'm going to die! she thought, battling down the hysteria that threatened to overwhelm her. I may come back or I may not. But I'll definitely have to embrace Death.

During the night Carol avoided looking at André, but she didn't have to. She heard and sensed him. He was manic, standing, sitting, pacing, his breathing laced with grating sounds. She was in the same room with a wild beast with only one thing on its mind – food.

Unlike the second night, the hours passed quickly, all too quickly, Carol thought. Some time after the church bells struck eleven o'clock, Julien approached her. He carried a small wide knife, the blade gold, the handle ornate silver.

She gasped at the sight of it and looked into his obsidian eyes, ancient as stones, the truth of existence coded within them. She felt a sharp pain as he cut into her neck. Her body trembled, far beyond her control now. Warm blood cooled almost immediately as it trickled over her collarbone. Julien kissed her lips then wet his on her wound. He walked across the room and pressed his lips to André's. An extended low hiss came out of André.

Morianna followed. She kissed Carol, took the blood onto her lips and passed it to André's. Then Chloe, Karl, Gerlinde, Jeanette, Susan, Claude and finally Michael, who looked a little frightened. Carol smiled at him reassuringly. She wondered if André would, or could.

What seemed only a few minutes passed and then Morianna said the fateful word, 'Receive.'

Carol stood on legs shaking so badly she could hardly keep her balance. This movement evoked a growl from André. He looked feral, fired up with a lust for blood. She walked slowly, not even daring to glance at him again, and knelt down. Out of the corner of her eye she saw Rene, still tied and gagged, kneeling so close.

The odour coming from André's body reminded her of walks in the woods in the fall, of wet animal fur, of newborn puppies and the birth of her son. She watched his skin quiver as the muscles beneath it spasmed; she felt certain she could feel the vibrations coming through the floor, infiltrating her from the knees up.

His hot breath on her face was liquid and intense. His breathing, so close to her ear, low and raspy, could have been a tidal wave rushing to crush her.

André's hand went to his neck; she saw the nails, impossibly long, dangerously ragged, yellow and bone hard. His body was thinner, the skin taped around the bone. That flesh stank of dark sweat – the little blood still in him. Pale blue veins bulged against startlingly white flesh, contrasting with the dark hairs. It was as though the blue veins would burst open any second and yet at the same time seemed curiously flat and lifeless.

When he cut into his vein, she reeled. A sickly trickle of blood came out, pale in colour. There was so little of it she braced herself to take all there was quickly, before it dried up.

Carol sucked on his throat. Being so close to his sounds and scents rattled her. Her heart hammered; he couldn't help being aware of that too. She heard thunder but couldn't tell if it had come from the sky or André. Eventually there was nothing more to take and she abandoned his wound.

As she leaned back, Carol was aware that Rene had crept forward on her knees. Despite the gag, she moaned; her eyes glittered unnaturally.

'Go back!' Carol heard Morianna say.

Before Carol could move, André pounced. She fell onto her back, the wind knocked out of her. He straddling her on his hands and knees, a wolf about to devour its prey. His face hovering over hers was so terrifying Carol couldn't even scream. Saliva dripped from gaping, panting jaws. Hair stood on end. His eyes were savage. He's starving, she thought, and there's nothing between him and my blood.

'André!' It was Morianna's voice carrying the weight of centuries. 'Wait! Midnight is soon!'

Julien said, '*Tu ne te souviens pas d'elle? Rappelle-toi!*'

Crucial seconds passed. No one moved. Out of the corner of her eye she saw Michael watching. André hesitated.

In the stillness church bells chimed the quarter before the hour. The sounds disturbed André. He threw his head back and howled like a wolf. Frenetic energy emanated from him.

Carol tensed and held her breath.

'If she doesn't want eternal life, I do. Take my blood!' Rene had managed to work the gag from her mouth. She struggled to get to her feet.

Julien stood to intercept her.

Lightning flashed.

André snatched Carol and threw her over his shoulder. At the same moment he grabbed Rene around the waist. Before the others could act, he crashed through the plate glass and leaped down the fire escape, taking the steps three at a time.

He bolted up through the trees and bushes behind the house, up the side of Mont Royal, streaking through the darkness and lightly falling snow, the dark night lit only by a dying moon. Cedars and pines whipped and scratched Carol's naked body. He ran so fast everything was a blur. She felt like Persephone being abducted by Hades. But this time Demetre, Persephone's mother, was along for the ride.

When he reached the large cross lit with dozens of light bulbs at the top of the mountain, André stopped. He dropped both women on to the packed dirt glittering with white crystals. He paused for only a second, then turned on Carol, his teeth aimed at her throat.

THIRTY-FOUR

Carol stared into the face of Death. André seemed to be no more and what drove him looked unalterable. The last vestiges of anything human had departed from his features. No kindness remained, nothing from which to evoke empathy or sympathy, just base survival instinct. And at the other end of his desperate need lay her fate.

'Take me. Me!' Rene whined.

André snatched Rene's shirt and yanked her to his side. He ripped the collar open. Every muscle in his body stood out, tensed for action. His mouth opened wide. Carol had never seen his teeth so large. Rene screamed as he plunged them into her neck.

Rene twisted and buckled, shrieking, 'No! No, stay away from me! Help me! Please, don't kill me!'

André threw his head back. Blood bubbled from his gaping jaws and overflowed down his chin. His pupils contracted to dots. He resembled a wolf, about to tear away Rene's throat and guzzle her life blood. His face distorted further and became less animal and more alien.

Rene's neck oozed red. The wound was not two clean little holes but a sickening chunk of severed flesh.

Despite her own terror, a knowledge welled within Carol, as old as the earth she lay upon, an instinct based on an ancient connection. It overwhelmed her; she felt fearless. 'André!'

His head jerked in her direction. She stared into eyes that no longer saw her, and said the most honest thing she could. 'I love you.'

His only response was the lack of further aggression.

As Rene sobbed, Carol found her fear reduced to ashes by an unfamiliar clarity of emotion. She held his eyes, the eyes of a madman, a starving animal, a monster, and her strength contained him.

With small movements, she slid back and away, out from under him, holding him with her gaze, and he let her go.

Julien appeared behind André, framed by the glowing cross. In the blackness of the night he resembled a marble sculpture. He seemed to float, a dark mist easing along the air, until he reached Rene.

André released her. Rene huddled in the snow, sobbing, looking worn, alone. Carol could only pity her as Julien slowly pulled her back to safety.

Carol sat up and turned away from André. Each of the others took the same positions they had before. All but Rene, who was with Julien, and Morianna, who now stood behind Carol, where the fire had been, her eyes glowing blue-red embers. Embers that had glimpsed another world. 'It is appropriate to be at the crossroads,' she said, 'where life and death meet, where transformation is possible. The wisdom of Sophia is what we know but have forgotten. To remember in time is the miracle.'

Off to the side, Carol noticed Michael in Karl's arms. His eyes so much like hers shone, his hair as dark as André's but sprinkled with white. Her son, whose birth had occurred over many hours nine years ago tonight. He waved and Carol realized again just how precious he was to her. Gerlinde stood beside them. And the others, Chloe, Jeanette with her arms around Susan and Claude, Julien holding the sobbing Rene in his arms.

In the distance, cathedral bells began chiming out midnight, filling the air. Through that melodious sound came Morianna's voice.

'And now, André must take.'

The snow fell harder, chilling Carol. Fear resurrected and she trembled. But despite the fear, she pulled her hair behind and over her left shoulder. She turned her head and looked into André's eyes again.

He moved on her immediately. Dry ice lips. Ice pick teeth. He stabbed her flesh, sharp and quick. Although her body shook, she was keenly aware of him pressing up against her, and he was shaking more.

When his incisors had cut deep enough, she felt his long razor teeth pulling out of her neck. His lips covered the painful wounds, numbing them. Sounds of lapping, sucking, swallowing. She felt him pulling back all he had given her, and more. Her heart beat erratically. Cold sweat chilled her.

'Hold me,' she whispered.

He gripped her shoulders and turned her body until she faced him, his lips never leaving her throat. He sucked firmly and continuously, the pressure on her skin and muscle intense. All the while his flesh changed as colour returned to it. His body grew warm, and she pressed against that heat because her own flesh had grown frigid and weak. Her heart skipped beats. She had trouble breathing and couldn't focus. A small moan escaped from her lips, a sob.

He held her close, stroking her hair, cradling her in his arms, wrapping his legs around her. 'I'm so afraid,' she cried, tears freezing to her face. He pulled her closer.

As she weakened, her breathing became laboured. Her heart skipped wildly; she was aware of sensation dimming.

She didn't know when he'd picked her up, but now he was carrying her back down the side of the mountain, through the darkness and the whitened trees. The scent of the pines, the sound of his lips, the heat from his body and the strength of his arms were the last sensations Carol experienced as the door closed and she entered the valley of death.

THIRTY-FIVE

Absence of light. Absence of sound. Scentless. Floating.
Drifting.

Passage. Traces of sound, nearly sensation. Feathery
movements through time. Another.

No rhythm. No sense. Nonsense. But again.

'Carol?'

Instinctive movement. Corridors of thin air, haunting
black light. A theatre of the void.

'Welcome.' She saw a face. Rob. Gentle and good, the best
he had been. Beside him Phillip, her friend. And her mother.
So sad. They smiled. Her mother opened her arms and she
floated towards them.

'Carol!'

She turned. A whoosh of energy. A vortex of light
sucking at her.

'Don't leave us!' her mother said. 'Carol.' Rob reached
out a hand. Phillip waved goodbye.

'Follow my voice!' The sound echoed and vibrated as it
expanded. She floated, around curves, drifting towards that

voice, suddenly aware of intense light.

'Open your eyes!'

Those words held no meaning, but suddenly she saw André. He smiled. His skin glowed. His grey eyes warmed her burning gaze. His face came towards her. Lips brushed hers. She felt nothing.

'Breathe!' he said, and she didn't understand what that meant until she heard the air move through her nose and felt it expand her lungs.

She wanted to know something but couldn't figure out how to get that knowledge.

'You're back. With us. With me,' he said, and then she realized she too had once known how to form sentences, to speak.

André caressed her face, her hair. His features were soft-edged, his body luminous. His eyes shimmered, like grey opals, as they glided over her face. She had never seen such a look before and wondered what it meant.

'You'll begin feeling your body soon. And then you'll be able to speak again. Just keep breathing.'

She concentrated on the air flowing like liquid through her and became aware of sounds. Her hand shifted and sensation spread through her fingers. 'I . . . live,' she gasped, amazed. Inside she felt a presence.

'Yes,' he laughed. 'You live. You'll be here soon. And then you'll feel sick. Your body's got to get rid of the poisons. But I'll be with you. Don't be afraid.'

The presence inside Carol assumed form as sensation returned. She experienced herself lying on a bed that she now knew belonged to André. Her mouth felt strange; her tongue found two upper teeth longer than the rest.

'Michael,' she said.

'Upstairs. They're all upstairs. We'll go up later.'

The dark presence inside crushed the light that had filled her just moments ago. It took on the shape of a man, then a woman, floating back and forth, the faces of Rob, her mother, Phillip, Rene. In all its manifestations, the figure sobbed.

'Is Rene . . . dead?'

'Julien absorbed her memories. She'll be all right.'

She felt sick to her stomach. Her brain cells hurt.

'You'll throw up. It'll come out of you from all directions. But afterwards you'll feel better. I love you, Carol.' He sounded relieved, as though the words released him.

She looked at his eyes. They sparkled and glowed, two grey beaches with innumerable plankton glittering under a star-filled sky. Her stomach lurched. The being inside cried out.

'You'll be sick soon,' he said, kissing her forehead, her nose, her lips. She moved to touch him, but pain streaked through her skull. Her body convulsed. She screamed.

'Once it's all out, the pain will stop. I'll give you blood and you'll feel strong again. I want to make love to you. Now. Forever.'

The being inside became too sharply defined, so stark and knife-edged she had to look away. Cramps shot down Carol's arms and legs and speared through her chest and deep into her stomach. She panted, terrified. She and the being inside spoke in unison, 'Am I dying?'

André helped her to the bathroom. He lifted her into the tub and held her as her body forcibly ejected what had once been necessary to existence but was no longer useful. She staggered from the pain. The being cringed, caught in the grip of agony and despair. 'He doesn't love you,' a voice echoed. Both of them cried.

'Are you disappointed?' she sobbed. Another spasm hit.

'Disappointed? About what?'

She noticed for the first time that he looked different. His hair was no longer just streaked with grey at the temples but shot through with silver, and his face devoid of the anger that had lived in his features.

'That it's me.'

He looked confused.

'And not Anne-Marie. Or Sylvie.'

One final wave rocked her, leaving her too weak to move, to even cry out, only to tremble before this awesome power that had passed through her.

He cleaned her up and carried her limp body back to the bed, then lay down beside her.

The pain was gone but emptiness lingered. The being inside seemed listless, lost in a stupor of hopelessness.

André took Carol's face in his hands. He cut his neck with a finely manicured nail and guided her lips to the gleaming crimson stream. The pungent scent of sweet copper reached her first, then the taste, warm, delicious, textured, a complicated beverage of finely blended ingredients. Liquid energy, like quicksilver, spread out through her body. It coursed down her limbs, out to her extremities, expanding her as it went, filling in all the empty spaces so that she began to feel less flat and static.

As Carol grew stronger, the being inside shrank and finally receded, absorbing the darkness as it went. The being looked at her with sad eyes then disappeared, leaving Carol alone in the glow emanating from André's body.

It's just my despair, she thought. The old me.

'Michael? Has he decided?'

He paused. 'He says he'll tell us together, when you come up. I think we both know his answer.'

He looked sad. 'Carol, I'm not disappointed with you. I never have been. I disappointed myself. But not now.'

He pulled her close. His fingers sliding over her skin felt like velvet and touched the deepest layers. His lips awakened hers. She wondered if she had always been dead and only now was alive for the first time.

'Disappointed!' he laughed, his voice amazed, anguished. He said tenderly, 'Carol, I've always wanted you. Always.

My lover. The mother of my son. My friend. I just hope you're not disappointed with me.'

She pulled him close. As if she had done it a thousand times, her teeth reopened the vein in his neck. She pierced him deeply, as she would a thousand times in the future. He arched his body and cried out her name, riding a wave of agony and ecstasy, as she took his essence into her heart.